PRAISE FOR
THE AMISH QUILT SHOP MYSTERIES

Murder, Served Simply

"The Amish community and their traditions are nicely portrayed, adding great warmth and authenticity to the novel. . . . Angie's fearless sleuthing keeps the action moving. [Her] relationship and family drama further enhance the plot."   —*RT Book Reviews* (4 stars)

"*Murder, Served Simply* is . . . everything and more that I anticipate with her novels. . . . It is an adventure for which the pages seem to turn themselves."

—Open Book Society

Murder, Simply Stitched

"At turns playful and engaging as the well-intentioned *Englischer* strives to rescue her Ohioan Amish friends from a bad fate . . . a satisfyingly complex cozy."

—*Library Journal*

"In the Amish Quilt Shop Mysteries, Isabella Alan captures the spirit of the Amish perfectly. . . . Throw in the *Englischers* living in Rolling Brook and the tourists visiting and you have a great host of colorful characters."   —Cozy Mystery Book Reviews

continued . . .

Murder, Plain and Simple

"Who can best run a quilt shop in Holmes County's Amish country—an *Englisch* outsider or only the Amish themselves? With its vast cast of English and Amish characters in fictional Rolling Brook, Ohio, Isabella Alan's *Murder, Plain and Simple* will be a dead-certain hit with devotees of cozy mysteries."
—P. L. Gaus, author of the Amish-Country Mysteries

"Isabella Alan captures Holmes County and the Amish life in a mystery that is nothing close to plain and simple, all stitched together with heart."
—Avery Aames, Agatha Award–winning author of the Cheese Shop Mysteries

"This series' starter set in Amish country will delight readers with its details of the community's culture and lifestyle. The contrast between the simple life and a grisly murder plays out nicely in this well-done cozy.... [The] author does a good job of introducing several key players in the community, which develops a strong sense of place and provides plenty of material for future mysteries." —*RT Book Reviews* (4 stars)

"This is a community you'd like to visit, a shop where you'd find welcome . . . and people you'd want for friends. . . . There's a lot of interesting information about Amish life, but it's interwoven into the story line so the reader learns details as Angie does."
—Kings River Life Magazine

Also by Isabella Alan

Plainly Murder (a Penguin Special novella)
Murder, Plain and Simple
Murder, Simply Stitched
Murder, Served Simply

Murder, Plainly Read

AN AMISH QUILT SHOP MYSTERY

Isabella Alan

AN OBSIDIAN MYSTERY

OBSIDIAN
Published by New American Library,
an imprint of Penguin Random House LLC
375 Hudson Street, New York, New York 10014

This book is an original publication of New American Library.

First Printing, October 2015

For more information about Penguin Random House, visit penguin.com.

ISBN 978-0-451-47502-2

Printed in the United States of America
10 9 8 7 6 5 4 3 2 1

Penguin
Random
House

For librarians everywhere.
I'm honored to be counted in your numbers.

ACKNOWLEDGMENTS

Danki to my readers who eagerly await that next mystery starring Angie and Oliver. The Amish Quilt Shop Mysteries go on because of your support.

A very special thank-you to the Holmes County District Public Library and library director Bill Martino for allowing me to tour their library services to the Amish communities in the county and visit the district's bookmobile, which visits those communities. That visit inspired this mystery. I told you that I would kill off a character on a bookmobile that day, and now I have.

Special thanks to my agent, Nicole Resciniti, who helps me to dream bigger than I could alone, and to my editor, Laura Fazio, who makes me a better writer with every single book.

Hugs to my beta reader, Molly Carroll, who makes sure I never turn in an unfinished book or sentence to my editor, and to my friends Mariellyn Grace, who listens to me ramble for hours about who the killer should be, and Delia Haidautu, for letting me borrow her name.

Finally, gratitude to my Heavenly Father. I'm humbled that you called me to be a storyteller. I don't take the privilege lightly.

Chapter One

"Whoa!" Rachel Miller called to her buggy horse. The buggy shuddered to a stop behind a yellow school bus. Three Amish children climbed in. The youngest boy's Spider-Man backpack bounced as he disappeared through the door. I smiled. Clearly, he was a member of one of the more liberal Amish districts in Holmes County. A year ago, who'd have ever known that I would be able to know the difference? When I first moved to Millersburg, I had thought, like so many outsiders, that all Amish were the same.

Next to me on the buggy's bench seat, Rachel's bonnet cast a shadow over her delicate features. "It shouldn't be too long now," Rachel said. "Austina telephoned the bakery to tell me the bookmobile would be parked in front of Hock Trail School."

Austina, a county librarian, had commissioned a quilt from my quilting circle for her ailing mother. The ladies finished the quilt during our meeting last night. It was a breathtaking purple, rose, and periwinkle blue Ohio Star. The colors weren't traditionally Amish, but Austina had chosen them because they were her mother's favorites. The quilt was so lovely, I almost wished I could keep it in the shop for display, but I thought that about every quilt my circle created. Each one seemed to be more beautiful than the last.

I scratched my faithful French bulldog, Oliver, between his ears. He leaned into my caress like a cat. I sighed. "I hate for the ride to end. This reminds me of leisurely buggy rides I would take with my aunt and uncle on Sunday afternoons. It's nice to take a breath every so often and think about that time." My throat tightened as I thought about my Amish aunt. She had been gone for over a year now, but every so often the pain of losing her was like a baseball bat to the chest.

The crease in Rachel's brow smoothed. "Angie, you need to move at a slower pace. You are so busy with Running Stitch and being a township trustee. You need to take a breath. When was the last time you had a quiet evening with the sheriff?"

I found myself blushing like a sixteen-year-old girl. "It's been a while. He has Zander, who needs his attention. I don't begrudge Z at all. He's a great kid. And now that my parents have moved to town, they're taking up much of my time."

After my father's retirement, my parents had moved to Holmes County from Dallas to be closer to me, and my mother was in the middle of a colossal house renovation, the likes of which my Amish friends had never seen.

I zipped my jacket against the cool autumn wind whipping in through the buggy's open windows. "The latest debacle has been over throw pillows for their living room couch. Please don't ever ask me to help you choose a throw pillow. According to my mother, I'm not up for the task."

Rachel chuckled. "Jonah told me your mother bought two chandeliers for the house."

I rolled my eyes. "Jo-Jo exaggerated. There's only one."

Rachel's horse turned the next corner. Half a mile down the road, I saw the silver-and-green library bookmobile parked in front of a one-room schoolhouse. A small swing set, slide, and metal teeter-totter were next to the bookmobile, but there weren't any children in the playground. In fact, I didn't see any children at all. I frowned. It was autumn and school was in session. I was about to ask Rachel about it when my friend whispered, "Oh dear."

"What—" I started to ask, but soon my question was answered. Austina Shaker stood in front of her bookmobile with her arms folded across her chest. Her right foot jutted out, and she leaned back into her stance as if waiting for the perfect moment to throw a punch. Despite her bright pink cardigan and eyeglasses perched on the end of her nose, she looked more like a street fighter ready to go ten rounds with her opponent than a rural county librarian. The Amish man standing across from her appeared just as fierce, but I would categorize his look as more of an angry pilgrim than a street fighter. It was as if the crossing on the *Mayflower* hadn't agreed with him.

Rachel's horse came to a stop, and I hopped out. Oliver joined me, although he checked the area for incoming birds first. Oliver hated birds.

Behind me, Rachel said, "Angie, I don't think you should—"

I glanced over her shoulder. "I won't get involved. Don't worry."

My best friend sighed. She knew I was lying to her, and to myself, if I thought that was true.

From the doorway to the schoolhouse, children stared openmouthed at the arguing pair. Their wide-eyed teacher, a young redheaded girl who didn't look a day over sixteen, watched with them.

The Amish man pointed a bony finger at Austina. "You have no right to be here. I strictly forbade you from coming. You have to leave the schoolyard immediately."

Austina snorted. "You can't tell me what to do. I'm not a member of your church."

Rachel joined Oliver and me. We stood at the edge of the playground about four yards from where Austina and the Amish man argued. Austina was facing us, and I could see every expression that crossed her face. I saw only the back of the man's head. He stood erect, as if there was a board hidden under his navy coat, and his black felt hat sat perfectly straight on his head.

"Do you know who the man is?" I whispered to Rachel.

My friend nodded. "That's Bartholomew Beiler. He's the bishop of the strictest Old Order district in the county."

I frowned. "Do I know anyone in that district?"

"Joseph Walker was a member." She watched me out of the corner of her eye.

I grimaced. Joseph Walker was an extremely conservative Old Order Amish man I'd met when I'd first moved to Holmes County and who I later found dead in the stockroom of my quilt shop. I didn't have a lot of good memories where Joseph Walker was concerned.

The bishop glowered at Austina. "You're interfering with the members of my church, and you have no right to do it. I, with *Gotte*'s guidance, am the one who should be telling them how to live, not the books you insist on giving them."

"You act like I'm peddling vacuums door-to-door. Your church members come to me. *They* ask for them. All I'm doing is providing books to patrons to read. It's my job."

"It's disrespectful to our culture."

The librarian arched her left eyebrow. "I will not censor. Now, I think it's time for you to leave."

The bishop shook with anger. His hands balled into fists. He wouldn't hit her. It was not the Amish way. At least, I hoped he wouldn't.

Austina stuck out her chin as if inviting a blow from Bartholomew.

Slowly he relaxed his hands, and his arms fell loosely at his sides. His voice was low. "You will be sorry you ever drove that *monster*"—he pointed at the bookmobile— "into my district. You think you have the *Englisch* law on your side, but I have *Gott* on mine. We will see who has the last word when this comes to an end." He stomped away, straight for Rachel and me.

We jumped to the side, and Oliver dove under the teeter-totter. Bartholomew didn't even acknowledge us. His pockmarked face was molten red. I suspected he saw red too. The young schoolteacher and children in the doorway jumped back into the schoolhouse and closed the door.

Austina smiled as if his threat meant nothing to her and she hadn't single-handedly run him out of the schoolyard herself. After a moment, she noticed Rachel and me hovering nearby. Her round face broke into a smile. If I hadn't witnessed it myself, I would have never known she'd been yelling at someone just a moment ago. "Angie, Rachel, I'm so glad you're here. Did you bring the quilt?"

"Of course, the quilt." Rachel slapped her head with her hand. "I left it in the buggy. I will go collect it now."

"That looked intense," I said after Rachel left.

Austina waved my concern away. "If you're referring to Bartholomew Beiler, he is nothing to worry about."

He sure looked like something to worry about to me. You wouldn't see me going toe-to-toe with an enraged Pilgrim, especially this close to Thanksgiving.

The librarian started back toward the bookmobile. "Don't wrinkle that cute little nose of yours at me, Angie. Bartholomew is a blowhard. He isn't the first Amish bishop I've argued with about my books, and I doubt he will be the last."

Rachel returned with the quilt, and she and I unfolded it, holding it up for Austina's inspection. Tears sprang to the librarian's dark eyes. "Oh, it's more gorgeous than I imagined it would be. Mother will love it." She ran her tapered fingers over a rose triangle in the design.

"I'm glad," I said as Rachel and I refolded the quilt.

Rachel took the quilt from my hands. "Where would you like me to put it?"

"Put it on my desk inside the bookmobile."

Rachel disappeared inside the mammoth vehicle.

I cocked my head. "So what was the bishop so upset about?"

"I didn't think you would let me drop the subject that quickly," Austina said. "He's mad about the books I provide and believes I'm corrupting his followers with new and scandalous ideas. Small men always fear new ideas."

Rachel tripped down the bookmobile steps. Her lips were set in a thin line. She was open-minded, but she was still Amish and believed in that way of life.

"He wants to take away your books?" I asked.

Austina shook her head. "He wants to keep them out of his district. I guess he caught some of the teenage girls reading romances and flipped out." She snorted. "They weren't exactly steamy. I mean, maybe the characters shared a smooch at the end of the book. Nothing more."

"What are you going to do?"

Oliver wriggled out from under the teeter-totter and was now inspecting the bookmobile's tires.

"I don't censor. If a teenager from his district comes to me looking for a novel, I will give it to her. It's not my position to tell people what to read. In my business, any reading is good."

Rachel looked as if she wanted to argue, but my Amish friend was far too polite to do it. Instead she said, "I think we should be on our way, Angie. Aaron will be wondering what's taking me so long."

"Before you leave," Austina said, "I have another job for you, Angie."

That sounded ominous. "Oh?" I squeaked. By her tone, I doubted it was another quilt.

"Yes. Stella Parsons, the chair of our Friends of the Library board, had the nerve to break her hip and now she can't manage our library book sale this month."

"She broke her hip?!" Rachel exclaimed. "Is she all right?"

"She'll be fine," Austina said. "As soon as she gets out of traction." Her dark eyes zeroed in on me. "Angie, I want you to take over for her."

I pointed at myself. "Me? Why me?"

"Because you are the best person for the job, according to head township trustee Caroline Cramer," she said matter-of-factly. "When I spoke to her about needing someone to take on the job, she suggested you right away."

I bet she did.

"Isn't there someone else in the Friends who can take this on?" I asked. "I've never run an event like this before. Your Friends are the ones with the experience."

She shook her head. "Most of them are pushing eighty, and the ones that aren't, I wouldn't trust with a kid's lemonade stand, let alone a library book sale."

"B-but—" I stammered.

She jabbed her fists into her sides and looked as fierce as she did when she was staring down the irate bishop. "Don't tell me you won't do it. You'd be letting the entire county down."

I rolled my eyes. "That seems like a gross exaggeration."

She picked a piece of lint off of her cardigan. "It could be great publicity for your quilt shop."

She had me. I was always trying to grow my business. "When and where will it be?" I asked in a whimper.

Austina's lips curled into a small smile. She knew she was the victor. She'd had the same triumphant expression on her face when she'd shooed the bishop away. I wondered how long that smile would remain.

Chapter Two

Austina folded her arms. "It's this weekend. The bookmobile will be parked outside the main library in Millersburg."

Rachel made a small sound.

Both Austina and I looked at her.

She gave us a small smile, but I noticed the tightening around my soft-spoken friend's mouth.

"Rachel, what's wrong?" I asked.

"Nothing."

I put my hands on my hips and waited.

She sighed. "This weekend is the grand opening of the factory, and I wanted you to be—"

I smacked myself in the forehead. That's right. The Miller's Amish Pie Factory grand opening was that Friday and Saturday. I couldn't miss it. Not only was Rachel my best friend, but I had been tricked into being a township trustee to save the factory. It didn't seem fair that I would miss the main event or the pie. I deserved a piece of pie or two after what I had been through to see the factory up and running. "Austina, if the book sale is the same weekend as the Millers' pie factory grand opening, I can't do it. I need to be there to support my friends."

Rachel's brow cleared, and I knew that I'd made the right decision. Caroline Cramer would have to suggest someone else to take over for the lame Mrs. Parsons.

Austina wasn't giving up that easily. "What if the book sale came to you?"

Rachel cocked her head, unknowingly tilting it at the same angle as Oliver at our feet. "What do you mean?"

"What if we have the book sale at the pie factory? The book sale can be anywhere. The bookmobile is mobile after all." She tapped a finger to her cheek. "I like it. Rolling Brook Township is too small for a library branch of its own. What better place to have the bookmobile book sale than in one of the communities that we serve?"

I knew that Rachel's private husband, Aaron, would hate this idea. "I don't—" I started to interrupt her.

She kept talking as if she never heard me say a word. "There's plenty of parking there. The parking lot that your husband had built is huge. We could set up a tent as well. I'm really liking this idea."

"Won't the library have a problem with a change of venue?" I asked.

"The bookmobile is mine to do with what I please. My director has no interest in it whatsoever. If I told her I wanted to park the bookmobile on Mars, she'd shrug."

I looked to Rachel. "How would Aaron feel about this?"

Rachel pursed her lips together. "He won't like it at first, but I will talk to him. I think it might be a great way to bring some extra attention to the pie factory.

That's what Aaron ultimately wants. I'm sure he will see that after we talk."

I wasn't as sure, but Rachel knew her husband. Maybe she was right.

I twisted my mouth. "If you can move the book sale to the pie factory, we have a deal."

She adjusted her glasses on her nose. "Consider it done. In fact, I will park the bookmobile there tonight, so it's all ready to begin setup tomorrow. Why don't you meet me there at eight thirty tomorrow morning, Angie? Then we can talk details."

I winced. I was not a morning person, but since Austina had so readily agreed to change location, I didn't think I could fuss over the meeting time. "All right—"

My response was interrupted by the sound of screeching tires as a hearse-sized mustard yellow sedan came to an abrupt stop on Hock Trail in front of the bookmobile. Our mouths fell open as dust settled around the car and a large and disheveled woman got out. She didn't even pause to close her door before stomping straight at us.

Oliver whimpered and dashed back under the teetertotter.

The woman pointed a crooked finger at Austina. "You! You ruined me! You had no right."

Rachel and I gaped at each other.

Austina held up her hands. "You aren't allowed near library property."

"Because of you!" the woman yelled.

I glanced over my shoulder at the school. If those kids thought the bishop had been frightening, they must be hiding under their desks listening to this.

"I'm going to ask you to leave," Austina said in her best don't-mess-with-me-I'm-a-librarian voice.

The woman licked her lips. "You are so smug, but I'm going to wipe that smirk off your face. Just you wait." She dropped her arm and stomped back to her car.

After she sped away, Rachel and I turned back to Austina for an explanation, but none came.

Finally, I was forced to ask, "What was that all about?"

Austina brushed off her sleeves as if casting the Amish bishop and the mystery woman aside. "Not my problem anymore. She used to be my problem, but she's not anymore." She smiled. "Angie, I will see you at eight thirty tomorrow." With that, she walked into the bookmobile and closed the door.

As we walked back to Rachel's buggy, she said, "*Englischers,*" and shook her head.

I laughed, just as she expected I would, and I tried to put the thoughts of Bartholomew Beiler and the unknown crazy woman out of my mind. Austina claimed they weren't her problems, and they certainly weren't mine. I had bigger ones at the moment.

On the ride back to Rolling Brook, I chewed on my lip. What was I doing organizing a library book sale? How do I get myself into these things? Oh, I know. I can never say no. At least not convincingly. I would have thought that, by age thirty-five, I would have grown a backbone. Not so much.

The hooves of the Millers' horse clomped onto Sugartree Street, the main road and center of business in tiny Rolling Brook. Oliver wriggled out from under the seat as if he knew we were almost back to the shop.

I knew by his frantic movements that he was anxious to see my one-year-old cat, Dodger. Even though Dodger was full grown and as solid as a mountain lion, Oliver still believed him to be his baby brother who needed constant supervision and guidance. He was probably right, since Dodger still thought he was a kitten despite weighing a hardy twelve pounds.

I reached down to pat his head. "I'm sure Mattie has taken great care of Dodger, Oliver."

Oliver tilted his chin at me as if to say, *Yeah, right.*

I couldn't blame him. At best, my assistant, Mattie, and Dodger ignore each other. At worst, it's a chase scene out of a cop movie, Mattie being the irate cop and Dodger the jubilant thief.

At the end of the road, the two-story redbrick pie factory was the largest building on the street. Over the last few days, the scent of the fresh pie permanently perfumed the air as the Millers prepared for the grand opening, making me instantly hungry. I was happy for Rachel and Aaron. Their dream pie factory would finally be a reality, but it wasn't doing anything good for my waistline.

"Whoa," Rachel murmured and pulled back on the reins to stop her horse as a minivan backed out of one of the diagonal spots in front of my beloved Amish quilt shop, Running Stitch. As the minivan pulled away, I groaned, because it revealed my mother's small white sports car. My mother was the only person in Holmes County who would have such a low-riding car. It worked fine for her in Dallas but was totally impractical in rural Ohio with its harsh winters. Mom and Dad planned to stay in Holmes County through

Thanksgiving, and then snowbird it to Dallas for the winter.

Rachel didn't even bother to hide her smile as she directed her horse into the spot that the minivan had just left. "Did you know your mother was stopping by the shop?"

"No," I grumbled.

It was late in the day, approaching four, when most of the businesses on Sugartree Street closed. Rachel pulled on the reins, stopping her mare and buggy at the hitching post in front of my shop. I made no move to exit the buggy. Both Rachel and Oliver stared at me.

"Is something wrong, Angie?" my sweet friend asked.

"I'm afraid it's about throw pillows again. The last time I was with my mother we talked about throw pillows for a solid hour. The size, color, fabric. To get fiber filled or down. I couldn't take it if I had to go through that again. I nearly suffocated in literal pillow talk."

Rachel chuckled. "Angie, you are so silly."

If she only knew. She hadn't been there. With a dramatic sigh, I hopped out of the buggy. My prized cowboy boots made a satisfying clicking sound when their soles hit the pavement. Then I helped Oliver down. The Frenchie headed straight for Running Stitch. He wanted to check on Dodger, and wanted to check on Dodger right *now*.

Rachel secured her horse to the post, and I joined Oliver at the front door. Before I could open it, it swung inward. "Angie," Anna Graber, a sixtysomething Amish woman whom I had known my entire life and who was a member of my quilting circle, greeted me at the door.

"What are you doing standing there? Come on in." She yanked me into the shop and would've slammed the door in Oliver's face if Rachel hadn't been right behind me to stop it.

"Anna, what on earth—" I stopped midsentence when I saw the state of the shop. On the cutting table there were three bolts of fabric in various states of unwrap. Dozens more bolts were on the floor in haphazard piles. Of the two hundred bolts of fabric that we have in the shop, nearly two thirds were pulled from their shelves.

My gray-and-white cat Dodger sat on one of the piles with a mischievous glint in his eye. Dodger relished in disorder of any kind. Oliver ran over to check on his feline charge. The adopted brothers touched noses. I would have awwed at the cuteness, if the state of my shop hadn't stolen my ability to speak.

Rachel gasped. "What happened in here?"

My mother held up a scrap of damask fabric to Mattie. "No, this won't do. Can I see a sample of the mauve?"

"Mom?" I squeaked. "What are you doing here?"

My mother turned to me. "Angie, there you are. What does it look like I'm doing? I'm shopping."

"You're going to buy all of this?" I waved my hand at the fabric on the cutting table and on the floor.

My mother sniffed. "Of course not."

"Then why did you have Mattie pull nearly every bolt from the shelves? Look at this mess."

"How else was I going to pick the fabric for the quilt in the guest bedroom?" Mom asked. "I had to know what the fabric felt like and how the colors looked up against each other."

I sighed. "You could have walked up to them to feel them."

"Angie." My mother frowned. "In a shop such as yours, you need to make the customers a priority and go that extra mile in service. If this is how a customer like myself prefers to shop, you should allow it. If you don't provide stellar service, how else do you compete with the other Amish quilt shops in the county, including Martha Yoder's place next door?"

I bit down on the inside of my lip hard to avoid saying anything I might regret. Instead, I said, "Are you sure every fabric needed to be brought to you?"

"It's okay," Mattie said, coming back with the mauve damask. "I don't mind, and I will clean it up, Angie. Don't worry. Have you made your selections, Mrs. Braddock?"

My mother frowned. "I think the yellow muslin. Yes, that will be perfect for the roman shades I'm having made for that room."

"That's the fabric she wanted in the first place," Anna muttered behind me.

Mom looked at me. "Don't you think the muslin is nice? Also, I always liked yellow as a color for babies and children. It's supposed to stimulate their thinking."

"Children?" Anna asked. "What children?"

I wondered the same thing too, but was too afraid to ask.

"My grandchildren, of course."

All three Amish women looked at me.

My face turned bright red. "There won't be grand-children anytime soon from me. I'm not pregnant."

My mother sighed. "A mother can dream, can't she? I have waited a very long time for a grandchild. All my friends back in Dallas have oodles of them."

Who knew anything could be worse than the epic throw pillow conversation? I looked at the ceiling and allowed my eye to follow the faint crack in the plaster. I would have to ask Jonah to look at that and see if it needed to be patched. When I regained my composure, I said, "Mom, by the time I have kids, you will proba-bly want a completely different color scheme for the baby's room. I know you. And why would my fictitious kid have a room in your house anyway?"

"You never know what will happen. I want to be prepared. I'll use the space as my reading room until the baby is born," Mom said as she examined a piece of fabric.

My shoulders sagged. There was no point in argu-ing. Mom was just being Mom. She took interior design as seriously as I took keeping my shop afloat, which was why I found myself in another mess like organiz-ing a book sale. I inwardly groaned.

My mother folded the samples Mattie had cut for her and tucked them in her fine-grain leather purse. "Angie, I'd expected you would've been here to help me with the selection. Since it wasn't throw pillows, I thought I might depend on your advice."

Throw pillows would be the death of me.

"Rachel and I went to deliver a quilt the circle fin-ished last night," I explained.

Mom hung her purse's strap on her shoulder. "Yes, Mattie told me. She said that you went out to the bookmobile."

Anna settled into my aunt Eleanor's rocking chair. "Anything interesting happen?"

Rachel removed her large black bonnet, which she had worn during the buggy ride. "Angie is heading up the Rolling Brook library book sale, and it's going to be in the pie factory parking lot to go along with the grand opening this weekend. Isn't that wonderful?"

I squinted at her.

Rachel gave me a sheepish grin in return.

My mother spun around from the table where she was examining more fabric. "*You* are organizing a book sale?" she asked, as if Rachel had just revealed that I planned to give up the quilt shop and become an astronaut.

I frowned. "Sure. The person who was going to do it broke her hip, so I was the logical choice—at least as far as Caroline Cramer, the head township trustee, was concerned."

"I can help," Mom said, standing up straight and holding the fabric samples to her chest.

I froze, holding a bolt of fabric that I was about to return to its high shelf over my head. "Help?"

"Yes, I would love to help. I can already think of ways that we can get the community involved."

I slid the bolt into place. "Umm, I don't know. I know you're busy remodeling the house."

"That's all well in hand, and I want to be useful."

"What about the kids' room?" I asked after adamantly denying that I was having children in the near future. I was that desperate to talk her out of working on the book sale with me.

She frowned and didn't look at me.

I chewed on my lip. I knew my mother could do the work. In fact, the book sale would go much better with her. She was a drill sergeant when it came to organizing events, but she would drive me crazy in the process.

For the first time, I realized that my mother really did need to feel useful. When she was in Texas, she was involved in society life and organized a frightening number of children's beauty pageants, a society event that sparked her interest when I was a little girl. And one that she stuck with long after it was clear I wasn't going anywhere. I couldn't sing, dance, twirl a baton, or fake a smile.

Mom left all of her friends and pageants behind for at least six months of the year for me. She wanted to be closer to me, even when I made it clear that I had no interest in moving back to Dallas because I had inherited my Amish aunt's quilt shop.

I felt my quilting circle watching me. Talk about peer pressure. Of course a group of upstanding Amish ladies would make me feel guilty. "I'm sorry, Mom. I would love to have your help. In fact, I have a meeting with Austina—that's the bookmobile librarian—tomorrow morning." Restraining a sigh, I asked, "Would you like to come with me?"

Across the room, I felt Anna's smile on me, and I knew I was doing the right thing, however painful it would end up being.

"Wonderful," my mother said. "We'll go to the meeting in the morning, and I think we could have a dinner to discuss it. I have been wanting to host a little dinner for you and the sheriff since the dining room has been done. What about tomorrow night?"

"I'll check with Mitchell," I said.

Mom pursed her lips. "And why do you call him Mitchell? He's your boyfriend, not some drill sergeant."

I frowned. "I've always called him that."

Mom tsked. "Don't you think it's high time you started calling him by his Christian name?"

My Amish friends busied themselves with tidying up the shop. There was no way they wanted to join in this conversation.

Rather than fight with her, I said, "Mom, I will pick you up at eight tomorrow for the meeting."

She didn't even hear me. She was too busy mumbling a task list to herself.

Chapter Three

The next morning, Oliver and I were up bright and early. Dodger was not a morning cat and yawned from his post at the end of my bed. Oliver barked at him.

"Let him sleep," I told the Frenchie. "He'll get in less trouble that way. Besides, we have to go to Grandma and Grandpa's this morning. You know we can't take Dodger there after he went jungle cat on Grandma's new settee."

Oliver wagged his stubby tail as if he understood every word, which of course I believed he did. My dog was *that* smart.

Dodger watched me with one eye before curling into an even tighter ball. Maybe he could understand English too. I wouldn't be surprised if Oliver taught it to him.

An hour later, Oliver stood with his white forepaws on the dash of my little SUV as we made our way up the hill to my parents' house. The home was a stone two-story affair and was larger than most of the Amish businesses in Rolling Brook. Below it, the hillside, peppered with sheep from a neighboring Amish farm, rolled into the valley below. Mums and autumn sedum decorated the walk from the driveway to the double front door.

Oliver wiggled his tail as he hopped out of the passenger side. He loved visiting my parents. I suspected that most of his excitement came from anticipating the tasty treats my father would sneak to him. Neither one of them could ever say no to a treat.

The front door opened even before we were out of the car. Dad filled the doorway. His round tummy hung over his belt, and he grinned from ear to ear.

My Frenchie galloped to my father and placed his paws on Dad's leg.

Dad leaned over and gave him a good scratch between his one black and one white batlike ear. "I bought some new beef jerky. Don't tell your mom."

"I heard that," I said as I came up the cobblestone walk.

Oliver put all four paws on the ground.

Dad wrinkled his nose. "Heard what? I didn't say anything." He pointed at Oliver. "Did you?"

I jabbed my hands into my hips. "I heard something about the beef jerky." I looked from one to the other. "Which neither of you should have."

Dad winked at Oliver.

I sighed. They were both hopeless.

Dad stepped through the front door and led us into the foyer. The chandelier that Jonah had mentioned sat in a huge crate in the middle of the floor waiting to be hung. Mom insisted that every formal foyer must have a chandelier, and she had spent months picking this one for their Holmes County home. It was smaller than the chandelier in my parents' home back in Texas, but everything was bigger in Texas and rightfully so.

Oliver wagged his stubby tail as Dad slipped him a piece of the promised beef jerky from his pocket. I pretended not to notice and tried not to be alarmed that he carried it around in the breast pocket of his oxford shirt like a stick of gum.

Mom came down the main staircase in a royal blue business suit and black pumps that probably cost more than my monthly rent. She had a matching black briefcase tucked under her arm. "Angie, good—you're right on time." She checked the gold watch on her wrist as if to make sure that was true.

"Umm, Mom," I said. "You look really nice, but you do know we're just meeting with Austina to talk about the library book sale at her bookmobile. Don't you at least want to change your shoes? It rained last night. Didn't I tell you yesterday to wear comfortable shoes?"

"These are comfortable," she said.

Sure they were.

My mother sniffed and touched the sleek chignon at the back of her head. "You have to look like you mean business when you go into a meeting like this, even if it's volunteer work. A good outfit garners respect in negotiations."

Negotiations? What negotiations? Where should the Westerns go?

I looked down at my cords and denim jacket, which I wore over my favorite French bulldog sweater. I had found the sweater online at seventy percent off. "If you say so."

She sighed as if she had given up on trying to talk me into a proper wardrobe long ago.

Actually, a year before, when I had worked as a graphic designer for a high-powered advertising firm in Dallas, I had my share of power suits and fancy shoes. But, unlike Mom, I had always felt like I was wearing a costume. The casual look suited me better, and since I owned my own business, I could wear whatever I wanted. My one compromise to fashion were my beloved cowboy boots. I was even wearing them now. When I got up that morning, I knew I was going to need them since I was going to be stuck between Austina and my mother during the planning of the book sale.

After a lifetime as an executive with ironed pleats, Dad wore jeans and an untucked button-down shirt. His clothing choices made my mother's right eye twitch.

"You look beautiful," my dad told my mother.

She beamed, and I couldn't help but smile. It was nice to know that love could last forty-plus years. My parents were the proof of that. I hoped I'd find the same thing someday. With one broken engagement under my belt, I wasn't having much luck. My thoughts turned to Sheriff James Mitchell, but I pushed them away because I didn't want to jinx anything. I could fret over the status of our relationship later with a vat of Ben and Jerry's Cherry Garcia.

My dad wrapped me in hug. "What's wrong, Angie-Bear?"

I squeezed him back. "Nothing is wrong. I mean, other than the fact that I got roped into organizing another township function."

He squinted at me suspiciously. "Well, I'm glad that you've involved your mother in it. It was all she talked about last night."

Mom tugged on the bottom of her jacket, as if making sure it was perfectly straight, and arched her brow at my father. "You want to lend a hand?"

He waved her question away. "Oh no—you girls go and enjoy yourself. I will putter in my workshop before the day is out. Jonah was over here last night and taught me how to use the lathe."

Mom looked as if she wanted to say something more but thought better of it. She was the one who'd told my dad to find a hobby. She'd just never expected power tools would be involved.

Dad patted my shoulder. "Your chair is almost done. Jonah gave me some tips about reinforcing the legs."

"Thanks, Dad," I said, trying to sound upbeat. The last chair my father had tried to make me had fallen apart the moment I sat on it. I had the bruises to prove it.

"I'm glad James will be joining us for dinner tonight. I haven't seen him in a while," he said. "I hope you and your mother will have a story to entertain us both during the meal."

What I didn't know then was we would have a very thrilling story to tell.

As Mom climbed into my car, I shot a quick text to Mitchell telling him about dinner at my parents' house that night. I mentally smacked myself on the head. I'd forgotten to tell him about the dinner when my mom first invited us the day before.

Almost immediately, my phone beeped. "I'll be there," the return text read.

I opened the door and Oliver hopped into the back of the car. He circled twice on the backseat before settling on the flannel blanket I kept back there for him.

Mom straightened her knee-length skirt as she settled into her seat. "You know, the bookmobile used to visit school when I was a little girl. We didn't have a library in the building back then."

I put my keys in the ignition. "I didn't know that."

"Your father would always carry my stack of books home for me after library day." She smiled.

Sometimes I forgot that my mother and father were high school sweethearts and knew each other since they were schoolchildren. I wondered what that would be like. Mom and Dad knew everything about each other's history. I knew so little about Mitchell. There were so many blank spots in my knowledge of his personal history. I hadn't even met his parents yet. They'd retired to Florida. Although at least I knew his son, Zander, well, and his ex-wife, Hillary, was sort of my friend—okay, maybe "friend" was pushing it—but we didn't want to claw each other's eyes out on sight.

The drive from my parents' house to the pie factory took less than twenty minutes. I was grateful for the short drive. The entire time, my mother shared her "great" ideas for the book sale, and I grew more anxious by the second.

I powered down my window as we rolled along Sugartree Street. The township was just waking up. The only business with its lights on was Miller's Amish Bakery right across the street from Running Stitch. Rachel and her husband would have been at the bakery for hours preparing fresh breads, pies, and other baked goods for the day. My car slowed. I could really use a blueberry muffin to survive this meeting.

Mom noticed. "There's no time for snacks, Angie. We don't want to be late."

Oliver and I sighed in tandem. Sometimes I thought we shared the same spirit, at least when it came to muffins.

Beyond Running Stitch and the bakery were yarn and woodworkers' shops. Finally the sidewalk ended, and we turned into the huge parking lot for the pie factory. The factory itself was a one-level L-shaped brick building. The parking lot was as large as the sprawling building itself. The silver-and-green bookmobile and a small compact car, which I assumed was Austina's, were parked in the farthest corner from the factory entrance under a large oak tree. Over a year before, an old abandoned barn had occupied this property. It had burned to the ground, but I was glad to see the majestic tree had survived the fire and the new construction.

Other than the bookmobile and Austina's car, the parking lot was empty, since Rachel and Aaron were at the bakery and the factory hadn't opened yet. In less than a week, the pie factory would surely be one of the busiest businesses on the street. Rachel said they were already processing orders for restaurants and shops all over Holmes County and beyond. I was happy for my friends. It took a lot of convincing to have the township trustees concede to the factory. Some of them were still unhappy with the final decision.

I stepped out of the car and wrapped my scarf a third time around my neck. There was definitely a cold bite in the wind, reminding me that winter would arrive sooner than any of us liked. Maybe it was the cold wind, but a chill ran down my spine as I opened the back door to my car and let Oliver out. Noting the chilly temperature, I wondered whether I should have made him wear one of his winter sweaters.

"Where is Austina?" Mom asked.

"She's probably inside the bookmobile, where it's warm."

My mother wrapped her thin arms around her waist and shivered. "The least she could do is come out to meet us."

I silently agreed. My apprehension rose since Austina didn't appear in the doorway to the bookmobile. It was too quiet. She must have heard my car drive up in the stillness. I swallowed and walked toward the bookmobile. Mom and Oliver were on my heels. "Austina!" I called.

A sound between a grunt and a whimper came from the bookmobile.

I frowned. "Mom, stay here."

"Why?" she asked.

I couldn't think of a good answer other than, "I want to make sure Austina is ready for us, that's all."

She frowned at her watch. "It's eight thirty. She should be ready for us."

"Mom. Please?"

She sniffed and pulled the wool sleeve of her peacoat over her watch. "All right, but I hope I don't have to wait out here in the cold too long."

I managed to stop myself from rolling my eyes. It was a habit I was trying to break. "Oliver can stay with you."

My Frenchie plopped down next to my mother's feet on the pavement as if on guard. He wasn't very intimidating security, but I appreciated the effort.

I climbed the steps to the bookmobile and knocked on the metal door. There was no answer.

I tried the door handle, and the door swung inward. The inside of the vehicle was bright. All the lights were on. Spotlights focused on the dark corners, so that the book titles and call numbers could be easily read by the library staff and patrons.

"Austina?" I called out as I scanned the area.

The small circulation desk at the back of the bookmobile was clear, and the small worktable behind the passenger seat was stacked high with books in the middle of being priced for sale. The bookmobile was ready for a day of literary business—except for the dead body in the middle of the aisle, lying on its side in front of the cookbooks.

Bartholomew Beiler had not been an attractive man alive, and he looked even worse dead. There was a deep gash on his forehead. His right arm was outstretched as if he'd been reaching for something. I turned away before I could see how much blood had pooled and soaked into the carpet.

Trembling from head to foot, Austina loomed over the body. "This—it's not what it looks like."

What did it look like? my addled brain wondered. It looked like Austina was standing over the dead body of a man who I had witnessed her in a heated argument with less than twenty-four hours before. What was it supposed to look like? That she'd murdered her adversary? Because it just might. I opened and closed my mouth, but no words came out.

Austina stammered words I couldn't understand. "I got here five minutes before you and found him this way—I swear it." Her dark eyes pleaded me with. "Angie, you have to believe me that I had nothing—absolutely nothing—to do with this."

Then my mother stepped into the bookmobile and screamed.

Chapter Four

I always thought my mom was meant to be an actress. Her bloodcurdling scream à la Fay Wray in *King Kong* proved me right. I would probably need my eardrum replaced when the ringing stopped.

I rubbed my ear. "Mom, geez, calm down."

"Calm down?" she screeched. "That's a dead body! Not everyone is used to seeing dead bodies, Angie." She gave me a pointed look.

True. I had seen my share of dead bodies since moving to Ohio. I didn't find them. They seemed to find me. Or maybe I just had really bad luck.

"We need to leave the bookmobile and call the police." I turned to my left. "Austina, have you called the police?"

She shook her head dumbly.

Mom crept a few feet farther into the bookmobile and peered down at Bartholomew, showing me that she was made of sterner stuff than I'd thought. "Are you sure he's dead? Shouldn't we check?"

He sure appeared dead when I first entered the bookmobile, but Mom was right. We needed to be certain. If there was any chance we could save the bishop, we had to try.

I dared to take another look at Bartholomew. His face was drained of all color. I averted my eyes from the gash. "I think he's dead." But just to be safe, I squatted beside him and touched his neck, looking for a pulse, careful to touch a place free of blood. His skin was stone cold. "He's dead. Let's go." I jumped up like a coiled spring.

Once the three of us had exited the bookmobile, I called 911 on my cell. The dispatcher recognized my voice immediately. She doubled as the sheriff's secretary. I had spoken to her many times since Mitchell and I'd started dating. "Angie, did you find a dead guy or something?"

I didn't answer right away.

When I didn't say anything, the dispatcher exclaimed, "Oh my! You found one, didn't you?"

I told her the details, happy to see Oliver was safe and standing at my feet.

The dispatcher sucked in a breath, and I heard the rapid clicking of her keyboard through my phone. "The sheriff isn't going to be happy about this."

No, I supposed he wouldn't.

"Do you want me to call him?" she asked.

"Yes," I said quickly. That was good. At least I could postpone hearing Mitchell's freak-out over my involvement in another murder. The freak-out would come, but I was happy to wait.

Austina leaned on the hood of my car. She was shaking. I pocketed my cell phone, pulled a blanket out of my car, and wrapped it around Austina's shoulders. I hoped that she didn't have a problem with the thick layer of dog fur. "Are you all right?"

Oliver walked over and lay on the top of her shoes as if trying to keep her feet warm.

She gripped the blanket across her chest. "I didn't do that. I would never do that. You believe me, don't you, Angie?"

"Of course," I said, but I wasn't positive it was the truth. I didn't know what I believed when it came to Bartholomew Beiler's death.

She jerked her right hand from the blanket and grabbed my arm. "Angie, you have to help me. Everyone in the county will think I killed Bartholomew. He died in my bookmobile, and I've been arguing with him for months. You have to find the real killer."

"Maybe he wasn't murdered." I wriggled out of her grasp.

"He was murdered. Did you see that gash on his head?"

I had. "Austina, I don't think I should get involved. Mitchell will sort it out. He's a good cop." I glanced at my mother, who was wringing her hands over and over again on the handle of her briefcase. She looked ready to sell high-end real estate in the big city, not be questioned by the police about a murder in Amish Country.

"This is a bishop, Angie. He's a very influential bishop. Whether the other Amish in Holmes County agree with him or not, they will put pressure on the sheriff to find out who did this."

"Mitchell won't let anyone influence him." I said this from experience. When I was a murder suspect,

Mitchell hadn't let the fact that he had a crush on me influence his decision to make me the number one suspect in that case. Would Austina face the same nonpreferential treatment? I had to admit it looked bad for her.

She either was the killer or had been framed by someone who'd spent a good amount of time planning it. I shivered. Could Austina be a killer?

She grabbed my forearm and squeezed so tightly I would be surprised if I didn't find a bruise in the spot later. "You have to help me, Angie. Please."

The wail of sirens coming up Sugartree Street saved me from giving her my answer. An ambulance pulled into the parking lot first, followed by a police cruiser and Mitchell's department SUV. Mitchell climbed out of his car, and I wiggled my fingers in greeting. Sheriff Mitchell's startling blue-green eyes zeroed in on me, and it wasn't with a cheerful expression.

Mom reached the sheriff first. "James, there is a dead Amish man in there." She pointed at the bookmobile.

"I heard," Mitchell said, not taking his eyes off me. Usually, when Mitchell stared at me like that, I felt a thrill. This time, a chill ran down my spine. I was toast.

The EMTs ran into the bookmobile, and Mitchell's bumbling deputy, Anderson, went in after them carrying a camera. I hoped he didn't knock any books off the shelves and onto the crime scene.

I straightened my shoulders. "Mitchell, thanks for coming so quickly. I'm sure this isn't how you wanted your day to start."

"No, it wasn't," he said, barely moving his lips.

I ignored his cold shoulder and pressed on. "Like Mom said, there is a body in the bookmobile. I'm not an expert, but by the gash on his forehead, I would guess the wound is what killed him."

"Dispatch told me." His voice was clipped.

I scowled in return. "Is that a problem?"

"I would have preferred to hear it from you directly, so I knew you were okay. Instead I had to drive here, afraid a killer might still be there with you. Did you ever think of that? I swear you give me more gray hairs than Zander does."

"Oh," was all I could say in return.

"How did you find him?" Mitchell went on, all business.

I picked up Oliver and held him close to my chest. With so many men stomping about, I was afraid he might get trampled. "Mom's helping me organize the library book sale, and we agreed to meet Austina here this morning to talk more about it."

Mitchell quirked his eyebrows, and I felt myself relax with that small movement of his face. He wasn't angry with me. At least he wasn't *as* angry with me as he had been when he'd arrived. He'd been scared then. Now he was in cop mode. "Book sale?"

"The person who was originally going to head it up fell and broke her hip," I said. "Caroline Cramer thought I would be the perfect substitute for the job."

"I bet." The quirk morphed into a full smile, but it quickly faded. "Dispatch said that the victim was Bishop Bartholomew Beiler. Is that right?"

I rocked back on my heels. "Yep."

"I was hoping you could tell me that was a mistake." He patted Oliver on the head.

"I can't. I wish I could. It's definitely Bartholomew

Beiler. I met him yesterday, and he's the dead guy," I said.

"How did you happen to meet him yesterday?"

I went on to explain how Rachel and I had been delivering a quilt and ended up having Austina rope me into heading up the book sale.

Mitchell looked around. "Why is the bookmobile parked outside of the Millers' factory?"

"The factory's grand opening is this weekend. The book sale is the same weekend. I told Austina that I couldn't organize the book sale if it meant I'd miss the factory opening. I need to be there for Rachel. Austina suggested we have the book sale here. It's something we were planning to talk about more this morning."

"Do you know anything about Austina's relationship with the bishop?"

I chewed on my lip.

"Angie," he began.

I sighed, knowing it would come out eventually. I hadn't been the only one to witness Austina's argument with Bartholomew. Rachel had seen it, and it was impossible for her to even tell an innocent fib. And the teacher from the one-room schoolhouse had seen it too, plus all the children. "I don't really know," I said honestly. "When Rachel and I met the bishop yesterday, he wasn't visiting the bookmobile on a social call." I went on to describe the argument. "But surely Austina wouldn't kill anyone over books."

He frowned. "She's a librarian—who knows what she is capable of?"

I frowned in return.

His quirky smile was back. "Kidding. I agree—a

book motive is far-fetched." He sighed. "But I have seen people kill over much less."

Unfortunately, so had I. I snapped my fingers. "One more thing," I said, and went on to tell him about the crazy woman who had driven up to the bookmobile as Rachel and I were about to leave. "I don't know her name or anything, but you should probably ask Austina about her."

"I will." He gave Oliver one last pat on the head. "Wait here. I need to check out the scene. I will need to talk to you, Austina, and your mom."

I nodded. "Understood."

He squeezed my arm, then walked toward the bookmobile. I blew out a breath. I was certain this wasn't the end of his frustration at me for not calling him directly about the murder, but at least he wasn't angry anymore.

Chapter Five

Mom joined me after Mitchell went inside the book-mobile. "What did James have to say to you during all that time?"

I was saved from answering because Deputy Anderson came out of the bookmobile and stood a few feet from Austina. He didn't question her, but just stood there like a Roman centurion making sure she wouldn't run away. Things didn't look good for my librarian friend.

Mom held her briefcase to her chest. "Can we go home now?"

I shook my head. "Mitchell wants to talk to us."

She frowned. "Maybe he can talk to us at dinner. I need to call your father to tell him what happened, but I'm afraid he'll rush over here to make sure we are all right."

Yeah, that wouldn't be good. "Mom, Mitchell will have to cancel on dinner," I said, speaking from experience. Many times, I contended with canceled dates with the sheriff because of police work, and a murder was the biggest case of all. I did my best not to let it bother me because I knew Mitchell's absence was one of the key factors that broke up his marriage to Zander's mom, and I refused to resent a job that was so important to not only him but also to the entire county.

Mom patted her hair. The cold wind was still going strong and blowing her hair in her face. I was relieved that I tied my crazy curls back in a knot that morning, mostly because it was way too early for me to fuss with my coif. I refused to pick up a hairbrush before nine.

Mom sniffed. "But what about our dinner? The caterer is already booked."

I fluffed my scarf around my neck, trying to thwart any draft. "You hired a caterer?"

She pursed her lips. "I wanted it to be nice, and the kitchen is such a mess with the remodel, you can't expect me to cook a gourmet meal, can you?"

"I'm sure it will be. Oliver and I will still come, won't we, boy?"

The Frenchie cocked his head as if in a nod. He was getting heavy in my arms, but I was reluctant to put him down, with so much activity going on in the parking lot.

"I don't like this, Angie," Mom huffed.

"It's just one dinner. It's not the end of the world."

"It's not about the dinner." She sighed as if I were too dense to understand. "Are you sure you want your life to be so indefinite? What if you make plans? Do you want everything in your life to hang on whether or not the sheriff has to leave for a callout?"

"A callout? Have you been watching *Cops* again?"

She adjusted her grip on her briefcase handle. "I'm serious."

A knot tightened my stomach. "It's not like that. Mitchell has to do his job and keep the community safe. I understand that. He's a cop—the top cop in the county. It's the way it is."

But Mom wasn't finished yet. "What about your wedding? What if you have to cancel your honeymoon?"

I nearly choked. "Wedding? Who said anything about a wedding?"

My mother squinted at me. "Angie, you've been dating the sheriff for nearly a year. Are you telling me the two of you haven't discussed marriage? You will be thirty-six on your next birthday, and he has to be over forty. What are you waiting for?"

First, talk about babies in the quilt shop and now this? I wasn't in a rush. I had been with my former fiancé, Ryan, for nearly six years before he popped the question, and see how that worked out. My mother seemed to conveniently forget that part of my life history. "No—" I choked. "No, we haven't spoken about marriage."

She pulled at her coat sleeves. "It's the boy, isn't it? I was worried about you becoming involved with a man who has a child."

I clenched my jaw. "It's not about Zander. Zander is fine with our relationship, and he's a great kid."

My mother must have sensed the change in my mood. "I know that, dear. I think Zander is a very nice boy too, but you can't expect me not to worry about you. You're my only child." Her voice rose with every word.

"I know you worry, Mom," I murmured as I caught

Deputy Anderson staring at us with his mouth hanging open. Great. Just what I needed: Barney Fife to spread around the sheriff's station that my mother and I were talking about my marrying Mitchell.

"Let's not talk about it here," I said. "A man was murdered a few feet away from us."

That shut her up.

"Angie!" Rachel called. She and Aaron ran into the parking lot from the street.

I hurried over to them after handing Oliver to my mother. She juggled him with her briefcase.

Rachel held her bonnet in her hands. I suspected that she'd grabbed it from the bakery before running out but hadn't had enough time to put it on. I noticed that she had left the bakery without her cloak. She would freeze in only her dress and apron.

Rachel's eyes were huge. "What's going on? Why are the police here?"

Aaron, Rachel's stoic blond husband, stood beside her. "We saw the flashing lights and heard the sirens. It took a moment to realize that they were headed to the pie factory. What has happened?" Aaron, who was characteristically calm, gripped a rolling pin in his hand.

So Rachel had grabbed her bonnet, and Aaron a rolling pin. Despite the circumstances, that made me smile.

"The pie factory is fine," I said. "The problem is with the bookmobile." I went on to explain what had happened.

Rachel's hand flew to her mouth.

Aaron looked to his wife. "You said that the bookmobile wouldn't be a concern. You said it would bring more customers to the grand opening."

Rachel blinked back tears. "That poor man."

Aaron scowled.

I came to Rachel's defense. "There's no way we could have known this would happen."

Mitchell came out of the bookmobile and joined us. "Is something wrong?"

"Wrong?" I squeaked. "Nothing is wrong."

His mouth twisted in a way that told me he knew I was lying.

"Sheriff, will what has happened impact my factory opening this weekend?" Aaron asked, holding up his rolling pin.

Mitchell frowned at the rolling pin in Aaron's fist.

Rachel placed a hand on Aaron's arm, and he lowered the pin. I let out a breath I didn't even realize I'd been holding.

"I don't see why this would impact the opening," Mitchell said. "The murder occurred in the bookmobile, which we are impounding to gather more evidence. We'll have to check the grounds, but one of my deputies checked all the doors."

"Is the book sale off then?" I asked.

"Looks that way. Unless the library can think of another way to hold it," Mitchell said.

"Is it all right to go into the factory and make sure nothing was disturbed?" Aaron asked.

Mitchell nodded. "Anderson." He waved his hand at his officer. "Please go in the factory with the Millers."

Before Rachel and Aaron walked away to inspect the condition of the pie factory, Rachel squeezed my arm. That was so like my best friend to offer me comfort when something had more of an impact on her.

After Anderson led my Amish friends to the main factory entrance, Mitchell dragged a hand down the side of his face. "We haven't had a murder here in months. I was hoping we'd at least last out the year without a homicide."

"I'm sorry," I said as if I was somehow responsible.

He gave me a half smile. "Not your fault."

"Was there any sign of forced entry into the bookmobile?"

Mitchell dropped his hand from the side of his face and stared at me blankly.

"I'm asking as a concerned citizen. If this was a break-in, all the businesses on Sugartree Street need to be on guard, including Running Stitch," I said, wondering whether he would buy that.

"There was no forced entry," he said in a resigned tone, as if he knew that I would keep asking until he relented. He was a smart man that way.

I winced, and my eyes immediately fell on Austina. She stood with a different deputy now that Deputy Anderson had been called away to help the Millers. Her hair was disheveled and the buttons on her coat were askew. "This is bad news for Austina, isn't it?"

His smile faltered. "Yes. Yes, it is."

Chapter Six

After Mom and I were questioned, I took her home. As much as I wanted to, I didn't have a chance to speak to Austina again. That was Mitchell's doing. He wanted me to stay out of this case and had surrounded Austina by police. There was no opportunity for me to speak to her alone or otherwise.

When we reached my parents' house, I didn't get out of the car and told her I needed to return to the shop to relieve Mattie. Mattie would have opened it by now, and I knew she would want all the details of what had happened, especially since the murder had occurred on her family's land. I sighed. I hated the idea of the Millers being associated with a murder again. They'd been working hard for the pie factory opening. They should be able to enjoy it. Instead, it would be clouded by Bartholomew's murder.

Mom stood in the middle of her driveway and held my car door open. "What about the book sale?"

I sighed. "I'll find out if it's still going to happen. Mitchell doesn't think it will, unless the library finds another way to hold it."

"There has to be a way," she said. "I will make some phone calls to the library."

"Knock yourself out," I said without enthusiasm.

Mom sniffed. "Clearly, whoever did this targeted the library. We can't let them win."

"I would say they targeted Bartholomew Beiler."

She shook her head. "The library is involved somehow. Bartholomew could have been killed in a whole host of places in the county. Killing him in the bookmobile was a message."

I stared at my mother openmouthed.

She lifted her chin. "You're not the only one who can decipher a murder in this county."

The idea of my primly dressed mother as a sleuth shook me to my very core.

She smiled. "We will see you at seven for dinner."

I sighed. "Okay." I hoped it wouldn't be a grill-Angie-about-a-fictitious-wedding dinner. Maybe we *should* talk about murder instead. That would make much more pleasant dinner conversation.

As I expected, Mattie had already heard the news about the murder when I arrived. She held the shop's cordless phone in her hand when Oliver and I stepped inside. She set the phone on the counter. "There you are. I was just about to call your cell phone. Where have you been? I expected you over an hour ago."

"I found a dead body," I said as I unbuttoned my coat.

The bell jangled behind me, and Anna stepped in. "Did I hear something about a dead body?"

I grimaced. "I'm afraid you did."

"How on earth did you find another dead body?"

Anna asked as she removed her shawl and hung it on the peg on the wall. "I thought you were meeting with Austina this morning."

I wondered whether I should be concerned that my Amish friends were more curious than alarmed. Clearly finding dead people was a far too common occurrence in my life.

"Austina was with the dead guy." I removed my coat.

Anna blinked at me, and I started at the beginning. Mattie jumped in when she could with what she had heard from Rachel and Aaron, both of whom were back in the bakery by now. I was happy to hear that everything in the pie factory had been left untouched. It appeared that my mother could be right, and Bartholomew's murder might have a connection to the library.

Anna settled into my aunt's rocking chair with her quilting basket. "What are you going to do about it?"

"Me?" I squeaked as I stepped around the counter. I opened the cash drawer, preparing to count out the money for the day.

Anna arched an eyebrow at me over her wire-rimmed glasses. Her gray hair was pulled back into a perfect bun. Her prayer cap was in the exact position. She rested her wrinkled and callused hands from a lifetime of farm work on her dark-skirted lap. She looked like an Amish Whistler's Mother about to bring down a judgment. "*Ya*, you."

"Nothing. Why would I do anything about it?" I straightened a stack of one-dollar bills on the counter.

"I think that's a good idea, Angie." Mattie swept dirt tracked into the shop the day before into a plastic dustpan. "You shouldn't get involved. It's been quiet these last few months. Don't let what happened ruin that."

Anna clicked her tongue as if she didn't agree. "Austina has a mouth on her. There is no doubt about that, but I can't believe she could kill anyone any more than Rachel Miller could have."

Mattie grimaced. The year before, her sister-in-law, sweet Rachel, had indeed been a murder suspect.

My cell phone rang, and I slipped it out of the back pocket of my cords. Austina's name was on the screen. "It's Austina."

"Answer it," Anna ordered, using the same commanding voice that told me when I was child that Jonah and I were in big trouble.

Just like then, I obeyed. "Hi, Austina. How are you?"

"Terrible. I'm terrible, Angie. I need your help." I could hear the tears in her voice. "I know the sheriff thinks I did it. I could tell by the questions he asked me and how he made the boy cop follow me home to make sure I didn't leave the area. The boy cop is parked outside my house right now."

"Officer Anderson?" I asked.

"Yes. Who else looks like he should be getting his braces off?"

She had a point.

"I need to talk to you. Can you come to my house?" Her voice was pleading.

I turned around so that my friends couldn't watch my expression. "Austina, I don't know if that's such a great idea. I—"

Anna plucked the phone from my hand. She could move pretty fast for an older woman. Her troublemaking twin grandsons, Ethan and Ezra, Jonah's boys, kept her on her toes. "Hello, Austina, this is Anna Graber. Angie has told us what has happened. I'm so sorry you're going through this." She stopped until Austina's sobs subsided. "Certainly, Angie and I will be there within the hour." Anna handed the phone back to me.

"Hello, Austina?" I said into the phone, but the librarian had already hung up. "Anna," I said, stretching her name out into three syllables.

She wagged her finger at me. "Don't give me that look, Angela Braddock. Austina is in trouble, and we have to help her if we can. It's the Christian thing to do."

I propped my elbows on the counter. "I don't think Mitchell would approve."

She smoothed the sleeve of her plain navy dress over her arm. "When have you ever been concerned about what the sheriff thinks?"

"I care what Mitchell thinks," I said a tad defensively.

She adjusted her glasses. "I know you do. You haven't been involved in a murder in nearly a year. The sheriff should appreciate that."

Mattie leaned her broom against the wall. "I agree with Angie. I think this is a very bad idea. We should leave it to the police to sort out."

Anna ignored her and focused all her attention on me. "I can't sit by when an innocent woman is accused of murder."

"No one has been accused of anything," Mattie argued.

"You heard what the librarian said. The sheriff's deputy is parked outside her house. Sheriff Mitchell wouldn't do that unless he had a pretty *gut* idea she was guilty," Anna said."

My shoulders sagged. I don't know why I even bothered to argue. Maybe because when Mitchell found out later, I could tell him I tried and that it was all Anna's fault. But in my heart of hearts, I knew I would become involved. I had known it the moment I found Austina standing over Bartholomew Beiler's dead body.

"All right, we can hear what she has to say," I finally conceded. Turning to Mattie, I said, "Can you watch the shop while I'm gone?"

Mattie picked up the broom again. I didn't know what she planned to sweep. The floor was spotless. She ran the broom's bristles over the wide maple planks. "I don't like it, but *ya*, I will watch the shop, and I will start cutting the pieces for the quilted pumpkin class."

I slapped my forehead. "I totally forgot about the class."

Anna patted my hand. "Finding a dead body will do that to a person."

How well I knew.

"Thanks, Mattie," I said. "What would I do without you?"

She smiled for the first time that morning. "Honestly, I have no idea."

I removed Anna's shawl and Oliver's leash from the pegs on the wall, handing her the shawl and clipping the leash on Oliver's collar. "Let's go."

Chapter Seven

Austina Shaker's house was in Millersburg, just a mile from the house I shared with Dodger and Oliver. The home was a light blue two-story colonial. The large garden was turned over for the coming winter, but orange and yellow mums spilled over hanging baskets dangling from the wide front porch.

Deputy Anderson jumped out of his cruiser as soon as I turned my car into Austina's driveway.

He waited for Anna and me to exit the car before he spoke.

"Angie, what are you doing here?" He rested his hand on the hilt of his gun.

I pointedly glared at his hand. "Stand down, Anderson. Anna and I are here to visit Austina and make sure she's okay after this morning." I opened the back door of the SUV, and Oliver hopped out onto the pavement. He immediately waddled into Austina's front yard and began inspecting her flowerbeds. With his nose to the ground, he resembled a canine Watson on the trail of a clue. All he needed was a magnifying glass.

Deputy Anderson dropped his hand from his duty

belt. "Angie, the sheriff isn't going to like this." There was a whine in his voice. The last thing in the world the deputy wanted was to disappoint his supervisor, even though he did it on a regular basis. Mitchell was too kindhearted to fire him.

"Then don't tell him." I reached into the car for my ever-present hobo bag and slammed the door shut.

He gasped. "I can't keep a secret from the sheriff."

I rolled my eyes. "Then give me a chance to tell him. That's not really keeping a secret, is it?"

He frowned. "When are you going to do that?"

I smiled. "I'll call him right after I leave here."

His eyes narrowed. "I don't believe you. You've lied to me before."

"That hurts." I placed a hand to my chest as if wounded. "Deputy, it really hurts that you don't trust me."

Deputy Anderson opened his mouth as if to argue, but Anna beat him to it. "Young man," Anna said in that commanding voice again. "We're here to visit our friend, who is distraught by this morning's events. Were you given instructions not to let any of Austina's friends visit and console her?" She glared at him over her wire-rimmed glasses and gripped her quilting basket, which she took everywhere she went, in her hands.

"N-no," he stammered.

She loosened the grip on the basket's handle. "Then you may return to your car, and we will walk ourselves to Austina's door." With chin high, Anna marched up the walk to Austina's front porch.

I scurried after Anna. "Can you give me some of that Amish mojo?" I whispered out the side of my mouth as I knocked on Austina's front door.

"Angie, I have no idea what you are talking about." She chuckled.

Sure she didn't.

I whistled for Oliver, and he abandoned the bush he was surveying and galloped up the steps onto the porch. When he reached my feet, I scooped him up into my arms.

Austina flung open the door. "You came. Thank God." She said this not like a curse, but as if we really were answer to prayer. I hoped that proved to be true. Austina yanked on my arm and pulled me into the house. She had about fifty pounds on me, so I flew forward like a rag doll. Anna leapt over the threshold just before the librarian slammed the door shut.

Austina caught her breath. "I'm sorry. Anna, are you all right?"

Anna smoothed her apron over her skirt. "I am."

Austina let go of me. "I didn't want that sheriff's department spy to hear one word of our conversation. I know he will report everything he hears back to the sheriff."

Her comment gave me pause. She knew the sheriff and I were dating. How did she know I wouldn't repeat what I heard to Mitchell?

"It's okay. No limbs were lost. Right, Anna?" I hoped to lighten the mood and set Oliver on the floor.

Anna wiggled her fingers. "Everything is still in working order."

Austina rubbed her bloodshot eyes. "I have tea all ready for us in the living room."

Anna, Oliver, and I followed Austina down a short hallway into a small living room. Now that I was inside the house, I noted that it must have been a historic home. The woodwork was ornate and expertly restored. Austina had put a lot of love into her home. However, the love of the house itself could not be compared with her obvious love of books, which, from what I could tell, went way beyond her occupation.

In Austina's living room, more striking than the high-polished floors and sparkling wood paneling was the sheer number of books. There were books on every flat surface, even on the sofa. Some had scraps of paper or bookmarks sticking out of them. Austina moved a stack to the floor at the end of the couch. "Please sit down." She gestured for Anna and me to sit in the place she had just cleared off.

Oliver sat at Anna's feet—he knew she was his best shot at procuring a butter cookie from the tea tray.

Amid the books on the coffee table, there was just enough room for the tray. The teapot and cups were decorated with books. I sensed a theme.

"Since you're here, am I right in thinking that you plan to help me?" Austina asked as she sat in an armchair across from us.

"We're here to hear you out," I hedged, ignoring Anna's scowl as I spoke. My Amish friend was all ready to start snooping. I couldn't help but feel responsible for how much she'd come to enjoy investigating. Before I moved to Holmes County, Running Stitch's quilt circle had led a much quieter life, free of dead bodies.

Austina poured three cups of tea. "You have to help me. My mother isn't well. She's at Heavenly Gardens, the nursing home downtown."

"I didn't know that about your mother," Anna said.

Austina flinched at Anna's surprise. "I would have taken care of her if I could. I even tried for a little while, but it was impossible with my work schedule, and I need my job. Her condition needs twenty-four-hour care. I can't give her that at home."

Anna leaned forward and patted Austina's knee. "No one is judging you," she said as she settled back into her seat and picked up a cup of tea. "We all have to make tough choices when someone we love is unwell."

Tears welled in Austina's eyes, and she swiped them away with the back of her hand. "I hate being like this. I'm not a weak, weepy woman, but whenever I think of my mother learning of what happened and what people will be saying about *me* to her, it breaks my heart."

"Then we will do whatever we can to make sure she doesn't find out," Anna said.

I shot a look at Anna. She had to know that was a promise we couldn't keep.

Apparently, Austina agreed. "You can't stop the aides at the nursing home from talking," she said.

Anna sipped her tea. "You'd be surprised. Most of the aides at Heavenly Gardens are nice Mennonite girls. They will respect your wishes."

Austina didn't seem as sure.

Anna examined the teacup in her hands. "I love your tea set. I do love books."

Austina smiled. "Books are my life, as if you couldn't tell. I work with them all day and read them all night." Austina picked up the teapot. "Would you like some more tea? It's Lady Gray. That's my favorite. I knew after this morning I would need some Lady Gray to keep me going."

Anna set the empty cup back onto the tray and nodded.

I noticed Austina didn't have a television—at least, as far as I could tell. There might have been one in another room, but I was willing to bet Austina spent a lot more time reading than doing anything else.

"I'd like to have such a tea set," Anna commented as she watched Austina expertly pour the tea from the book-covered pot.

I glanced at Anna in surprise. To have a decorative tea set was so un-Amish of her. "You would?"

Her eyes slid to me. "Angie, don't be scandalized. There are many nice *Englisch* things that I would like to have. I can recognize the convenience and pleasure that they bring. That being said, I won't have them. The point of being Amish is wanting something but choosing not to have it in a show of obedience to your church district and to *Gott*."

Austina handed me a cup of tea. "Then you must have amazing willpower."

Anna shook her head. "Our obedience comes from *Gott* and is for *Gott*."

The librarian frowned. "Even obedience to someone like Bartholomew Beiler? Who makes ridiculous rules that only make his church members miserable?"

Anna cupped her teacup in her large wrinkled hands. "Bartholomew Beiler was an unhappy man who spent most of his life making sure that the people living in his district were as unhappy. This is true, but his way was not the Amish way. *Gott* wants us to find joy in the simple pleasures of life and in our work. Bartholomew never understood that."

I picked up a teacup and blew on my hot tea. "Why was he so unhappy?"

Anna shook her head. "Since I am not a member of his district, I don't know. Bartholomew's district is very tightly knit and quiet about their ways. Few know what happens there."

I cleared my throat. "Austina, can you tell us about what you found when you went inside the bookmobile this morning?"

She examined me. "By asking that, does it mean that you will help me find out the truth?"

I felt Anna watching me from her side of the couch. "If I can help, I will. If there are Amish involved in this, the quilting circle ladies and I will have a better chance of getting answers than the sheriff's department will, no matter how well liked Sheriff Mitchell is among the Amish. He is still a police officer, and it's hard for them to trust him."

Austina chewed on her lip. "And you don't mind upsetting the sheriff, or how uncomfortable it might be for you?"

I do mind, I thought, but I said, "You have enough on your mind. Let me worry about Mitchell."

Chapter Eight

"Now, can you answer the question?" I asked.

Austina cleared her throat. "I stepped into the bookmobile. I placed my bag on the desk right by the door as I always do and turned on the light. Then—" She closed her eyes as if to block out the image. "Then I saw him. At first I thought he was sleeping in the middle of the bookmobile. I remember thinking, 'What crazy Amish guy is taking a nap in my bookmobile?' It wasn't until I was right above him that I realized it was Bartholomew Beiler, and that he was dead." She rubbed her forehead as if remembering the gash on the bishop's head in the same place.

"Was the door to the bookmobile locked?" Anna asked.

I leaned back. I might as well let her ask the questions.

Austina thought for a moment. "I suppose it was. I used my key to unlock the door, but I didn't try the doorknob before turning the key. I assumed that it was locked because I very clearly remember locking it last night before I left."

I bit the inside of my lip. That wasn't good news for Austina. If there was no sign of forced entry, it made her and anyone else who might have access to the key a suspect.

"Who had keys to the bookmobile?" I asked.

"I always carry mine with me, but there are two spares in the workroom back at the main library. We keep the library workroom locked at night, so if someone took one of those keys, it would have had to be during the day."

"Could a non–library worker slip into the workroom and swipe the key without a staff member noticing?" Anna adjusted her glasses on the tip of her nose and leaned forward.

I looked heavenward. I was pretty sure a year before Anna hadn't used the word "swipe" as part of her working vocabulary. I was to blame for this, and for pulling the quilting circle into these murder investigations. However, it seemed the roles were reversed this time around. This time, it was Anna who was the most gung-ho about the investigation.

The librarian shook her head. "Not likely, but I refuse to believe any of my coworkers could do this. They've never even interacted with Bartholomew. He refused to set foot in the library building because he was convinced it was the home of the devil, or some such thing."

I frowned. "Okay, so not everyone liked the bishop, but what about you?"

"What do you mean?" Austina asked.

"Who didn't like you?"

She bent her head over the teacup in her lap. "I don't know why it matters."

"It matters," Anna said, catching on. "Because maybe someone killed the bishop to frame you."

Austina's mouth fell open. "Isn't there an easier way to get back at me rather than killing someone?"

"I would hope so," I said. "But in my experience most killers think they have no other choice, even if there are many options they can't or refuse to see. Who doesn't like you, Austina?"

Austina shifted in her seat. "I—I don't have many friends. I mean, close friends. I know I'm loud and opinionated and rub most people the wrong way, especially at work. I know that's not good news for me."

It wasn't. I wouldn't lie to her and tell her anything different. "What about that woman who yelled at you at the bookmobile yesterday. She seemed pretty upset."

Anna raised her eyebrows in surprise. Rachel and I hadn't told the other ladies about this development.

"Pretty upset" was putting it mildly. That woman had been positively unhinged.

Austina wouldn't meet my eyes. "Bunny."

Oliver lifted his head from his paws and looked around as if expecting a rabbit to hop around the sofa. When no bunny appeared, he lay his chin back on his folded paws.

"Bunny?" I asked.

Austina took a deep breath. "The staffer who I got fired."

"What? Back up." I waved my hands. "You got someone fired and didn't tell me? Was this recent? Why didn't you tell us that the moment we walked through the door?"

She swallowed. "It happened about two weeks ago. She was my assistant on the bookmobile. I worked with her every day. Actually, we worked side by side for nearly five years and never had a problem."

"The coworker you got fired was named Bunny?"

"Yes." Another sigh. "Bunny Gallagher."

"That's her nickname, right?" I leaned forward in my chair.

"No, it's her real name. I know because I was her supervisor."

"Of all the names in the world, her parents chose Bunny?" I asked.

Anna shook her head as if she couldn't understand it either.

"I suppose so," Austina said, sounding tired.

"So what happened? What changed?" I demanded.

"I found out she was stealing fine money from the bookmobile. I felt there was something fishy with the amount we were collecting. We never made huge amounts on fines, but I felt like we weren't collecting as much as we usually did."

"Maybe patrons were getting better about returning stuff," I offered.

"That's what I thought at first, but I was suspicious enough to set a trap."

"A trap?" I began to pace.

"Bunny had no idea what I was up to."

"So how did Bunny steal the money?" Anna asked.

"When collecting fine money from the patron, instead of adding the fine to the cash register, she pocketed it. It took so long to discover because she would waive the fine on the computer, so each night the cash register and the library's computer system would reconcile. I should have realized it earlier. It's one of the oldest tricks in the book when it comes to library fraud."

"Library fraud?"

"It happens," she said seriously.

"Where can I find Bunny?" I asked.

Austina was quiet for a long moment. "She has an apartment on Jackson Street in Millersburg. In the building that used to be a hardware store." She rattled off the address.

Bunny Gallagher lived in Millersburg on Jackson Street a block from Double Dime Diner. If she lived that close to Double Dime, she might be a frequent customer. The Double Dime was the place I went for half my meals and all my non-Amish gossip, so I might have even seen her there. In any case, Linda, the one and only waitress at the diner, would know who she was, whether she was a regular or whether she'd stopped by just once. Linda knew everyone who walked through the diner's glass door.

While Austina stared into her teacup, Anna and I shared a look.

"Does anyone work on the bookmobile with you now?" Anna asked.

She blinked and straightened in her armchair. "Sometimes Amber Rustle will join me if I know I have a very busy day ahead of me, and the main library can spare her."

"Amber?"

"Do you know her?" Austina asked.

I knew Amber. Her best friend had been murdered last December, and I had helped unravel the crime. It was the last murder investigation I had been involved with. I had hoped it would be my last, but considering I was now sitting across from a murder suspect, that appeared unlikely. Amber was also the college-aged daughter of one of my fellow township trustees, Jason Rustle. Jason would not be pleased to hear his daughter was caught up in another murder. I wouldn't be surprised if he ordered her to quit her part-time library job on the spot.

I nodded to Austina. "Her father is a fellow township trustee."

"That's right. I had forgotten."

"Going back to when you arrived at the bookmobile this morning, did you hear anything? Was there any indication that anyone else was there?"

Austina's voice quivered. "Do you think the killer may have still been nearby?"

For a brief moment, tough Austina appeared so frightened and vulnerable that I felt bad for her. What I didn't know was whether she was afraid for her safety—or that she might not get away with murder. Anna might have been convinced that Austina was innocent, but I still wasn't sold on the idea.

I shook my head, hoping to ease some of her anxiety. I wasn't an expert on dead bodies, but I have seen my share, and the bishop looked like he had been dead a while. "I don't think so."

She blew out a breath. "Good," she whispered. "It

would be so much worse to think someone was watching me when I found Bartholomew—worse even than finding the body itself."

Shortly after that statement, Austina slumped back in the chair as if the gravity of her situation had fallen on her shoulders.

"What will you do now?" Anna asked Austina.

"What do you mean?" the librarian asked.

"The police have taken away the bookmobile. Will you work at the main library until it is back?"

Tears welled behind Austina's glasses. "No. I've been put on unpaid administrative leave until this business with the murder is cleared up. I don't know what I am to do now, or even what I should do this afternoon."

Anna set her teacup back on the saucer on the tea tray. "Austina, you need to get some rest. Angie and I will go now and let you do that."

"Wh-wh—" I started to protest. I had so many more unanswered questions to ask Austina about the bookmobile, the library, and Bartholomew Beiler. Anna gave me a "be silent" glare better than any shushing librarian I had ever seen, and I snapped my mouth closed.

Anna stood up. "I'm sure Angie will be in touch."

Austina walked us to the door. Despite Anna's disapproval, I asked Austina one more question. "What about yesterday when Rachel and I met you?"

She nodded. "You mean when I was arguing with the bishop in front of God and everyone?"

I nodded. "There was a young teacher there with the

children. I saw her in the doorway of the school. What is her name? Do you know her?"

She nodded. "She's Phoebe Truber. She is the teacher of the school in Bartholomew's district. All the children that go to that school are members of Beiler's district."

"I know Phoebe," Anna said. "She's a sweet girl. Shy, but sweet."

"She seemed upset," I said.

Austina placed her hand on the doorknob and turned it. She didn't pull it open just yet. "The bishop and I were yelling at each other in her schoolyard. It would have upset any teacher to have something like that happen in front of her pupils."

I knitted my brow. Something about the teacher's expression had struck me as odd. "I think there was more to it than that. Does she check out books from the bookmobile? Is she one of the young women that Bartholomew accused you of corrupting with your books?"

Austina's face hardened for the first time. The irate librarian's scowl that Rachel and I had seen during her argument the day before now returned to replace her weepy expression. "I can't tell you that. I can't tell you the titles of any books my patrons check out."

I frowned. "You can't even tell me if she uses the bookmobile?"

Austina shook her head. "No, I can't, and I don't know what this has to do with finding out who killed the bishop." She opened the door.

Anna and Oliver stepped outside. Oliver returned to the garden to finish his inspection.

"I am very grateful for what you are doing for me,

Angie," Austina said. "I know it can't be easy for you to become involved, considering your relationship with the sheriff. But I am grateful. Remember that, no matter what."

No matter what *what*? I wanted to ask, but I didn't get a chance—she then shut the door in our faces.

Chapter Nine

Inside my car, Anna buckled her seat belt. I was still outside the car, trying to convince Oliver that he'd already sniffed every single plant in Austina's front yard. I waved at Deputy Anderson in his department-issued cruiser. He scowled back. I clearly wasn't on the deputy's favorites list right now, if I ever was. He must have asked himself on a daily basis how his hero the sheriff could be dating me. Some days, I wondered the same.

After I got Oliver settled in the back of the car and gave one final wave to Deputy Anderson, I asked Anna, "What do you know about Bartholomew Beiler? How was he perceived in the Amish community?"

"He was not well liked. His community adhered to his rules because he was the bishop, but he was a harsh man. Many young people from his community have left Amish life or joined a different district. It doesn't happen often, but it seems to me it's happened much more often with Bartholomew's followers than with other districts in the county."

I started the car and eased out of Austina's driveway. "So his community is shrinking?"

She frowned. "*Ya*. At a certain point, it won't exist if the young people keep fleeing. Without the younger generation, there won't be any more children to be raised that way."

"Was Bartholomew worried about that?" I asked.

"He had to have been. And maybe that was why he was cracking down on the books his members read. Maybe he blamed the *Englisch* influence on his church members for his dwindling numbers." Anna rested her hands on her quilting basket on her lap. "He should have really been blaming himself for holding on to them too firmly. If a man's will is gripped too tightly, it is crushed. That man either becomes broken or dangerous, or both."

I shivered. "Is that from the Bible?"

"*Nee*. It is from my own thoughts. I have seen it many times and have come to this conclusion myself." She gave me a sideways smile. "Don't tell my son of my deep thoughts. He will tease me."

I chuckled, happy to have her joke break the tense mood in the car. "Jo-Jo doesn't need an excuse to tease anyone."

"That is true."

"Do I know anyone who left Bartholomew's community?"

"Jeremiah Leham," she said.

I braked hard at a stop sign at the entrance to Austina's neighborhood and stared at Anna. "Sarah's husband?"

Sarah Leham was another member of my quilting circle. She was a sweet woman, always willing to lend an extra hand at Running Stitch despite her busy life as an Amish mother and wife of a vegetable farmer. She was also a notorious gossip. "Wow. Do you think Sarah knows about the murder by now?"

Anna gave me a "duh" look, which made me smile because it didn't go with her prayer cap. "*Ya*, she knows. I wouldn't be surprised if she heard about it before you left the crime scene. Since Sarah didn't come straight to the shop like she usually does when events like this happen, maybe she didn't hear your part in the discovery. When she finds out you found the body, she will pepper you with a million questions. I hope you are ready."

I was ready. I had been on the receiving end of Sarah's barrage of questions before and had survived, for the most part.

Anna smiled. "Mattie can mind the shop for a little while later. I think it's time we paid a visit to Sarah and her husband."

"It's like you can read my mind," I told Anna.

She snorted. "Don't spout your *Englisch* mumbo jumbo at me."

I laughed and turned the car in the direction away from town and toward the Lehams' farm.

The Lehams ran a large farm on the outskirts of Rolling Brook, five miles east of the center of the township. I had been there only a handful of times. It seemed whenever we had quilting circle meetings Sarah was eager to escape the farm and come into the shop.

Sarah and Jeremiah had five children. Since the Lehams were New Order Amish, their children went to the local public school in Millersburg, and they even rode the school bus there. However, like all Amish children, the Leham children's schooling stopped after the eighth grade.

As my car rolled up the long gravel driveway, Sarah beamed. She came down the porch steps and met us. I climbed out of the car, and the thin Amish woman said, "Angie, Anna, I didn't know you were coming over for a visit. Do you have some news?" She was always ready and willing to hear the latest township gossip.

"We do have news," Anna said.

Sarah grinned from ear to ear. "I suppose it's about Bartholomew Beiler," she said with more enthusiasm than I would've expected. She skipped up the front steps. "Come on in!" She held the door open for us. "I was about to start putting lunch on the table for Jeremiah."

I checked my phone for the time. It was barely ten thirty, but I knew farmers like Jeremiah usually got up at four a.m. to work the farm. Clearly, I would never make it as a farmer. Waking up before eight was painful enough.

Oliver sniffed the floor of Sarah's porch and seemed to be satisfied there was no scent of a feathery friend in the home. Together, we followed Sarah into the house.

Sarah led us straight through the front room and into the spacious kitchen. The kitchen was like every other Amish woman's kitchen I had been in. The floor was made of wide-planked wood. The natural gas–powered appliances, including the oven and refrigerator, dominated the space. As New Order Amish, the Lehams had indoor plumbing, but I knew some of the stricter communities, probably including Bartholomew's, didn't allow it.

Sarah wiped her hands on the edge of her apron. "We're having vegetable stew and corn bread. I've made enough to feed the whole district. Will you stay and eat with us?"

My stomach rumbled with hunger. The meal smelled wonderful. "Sure," I said. "It's never too early for soup, right?"

Sarah grinned. "That's right."

Anna plucked a wooden spoon from the hook on the cabinet. She dipped it into Sarah's stew and blew on it before taking a taste.

Sarah watched her closely while Anna considered the flavor.

"It is *gut*," Anna declared, setting the spoon in the sink.

Sarah's shoulders relaxed, and she beamed at Anna as if she had just announced Sarah had won grand prize at the county fair. "*Danki*, Anna."

"It could use a little more sage next time. Since herbs should go in right at the beginning, it's too late now for that."

Sarah laughed good-naturedly. "I knew I wouldn't escape with a cooking compliment from you that easily."

I started setting the table using the clean silverware piled on the counter.

Sarah picked up a soup bowl and ladled some of the steaming soup into it. "Jeremiah will be happy that you are here. You will want to ask him about his old bishop, I imagine."

"Anna said that you would have heard about Bartholomew Beiler's death by now," I said.

Sarah laughed. "I heard all about it. Jeremiah's

younger brother stopped by to tell us. He's ten years younger than my husband and still in the old district. It's all that anyone in that community is talking about."

"I'm sure it is," I said. "What's his brother's name?"

"Levi. Levi still lives with Jeremiah's elderly parents." She frowned. "They live a few miles from here outside of Berlin. We don't see them often. Even after all these years, my husband's parents are still hurt that Jeremiah left the district to marry me."

"That's why he left?"

She nodded and filled the next bowl of soup.

"That's pretty romantic of him," I said.

Sarah giggled and set the bowl on the counter next to the other full one.

"Even though it would upset his parents, Levi came here to tell you of the bishop's death?" Anna asked.

Sarah nodded. "He was upset but relieved too. He said now that the district must choose a new bishop, they might finally have a chance to have a kind leader."

Did that mean the murderer had had the same thing in mind? I shivered. I tried to push the idea aside, because if Levi was so happy with Bartholomew's death, he may very well be the one who committed it. One thing was for sure. I needed to talk to Jeremiah's younger brother myself.

"Did someone come in the shop and tell you about it?" Sarah asked. "I'm sure it is the main topic of conversation throughout the county. I'm sorry that happened to the bishop, but there won't be many who will cry over his passing. He was a cruel man. You should have heard some of the things he said to Jeremiah's family about our district, Anna." She frowned. "And about me." She shook her head once as if dismissing the gloomy thoughts. Soon, she returned to her normal cheerful self.

"We didn't hear about it from someone visiting the shop." Anna filled glasses of water from the tap.

"I was there," I said as I set one of the soup bowls at the table.

Sarah dropped her ladle and it splashed in the soup pot. "You were there?"

I told her about the events of the morning.

Gingerly, Sarah fished the ladle out of the pot and rinsed it off in the sink. "I've been away from the shop too long. Jeremiah has been bringing in the last of the harvest and taking it to market. It won't be long before the first frost strikes. Jeremiah is always edgy this time of year and worries about what crops we can harvest in time. It is difficult to see what is left behind or lost on the field."

"And getting the latest gossip," Anna teased.

Sarah laughed, and her cheeks flushed. "*Ya,* maybe that too."

I finished setting the table. "Do you know when the frost will be?"

Sarah nodded. "A hard frost is predicted for the end of the week. Jeremiah should be back soon." She clapped her hands, which made Oliver jump from the warm spot where he'd curled up in front of the oven. "You should see our bumper pumpkin crop. We've never had one like it before. I haven't seen you ladies, so I haven't been able to tell you. We're opening the field up as a pick-your-own-pumpkin patch. It's the first time we've done it. But we have so many extra pumpkins, we don't know how else to move them."

"Like for Halloween?" I asked, surprised. The Amish forbade the celebration of Halloween.

Sarah sniffed. "Of course not. It's for harvest time. People buy pumpkins for things more than carving jack-o'-lanterns."

"Oh, right," I said quickly. "That's the *Englischer* in me talking again."

That got her to smile, as she wiped crumbs from the counter with a dishtowel. "Angie, you and the sheriff should bring Zander here to pick his pumpkin. It would be a nice little family outing."

I wrinkled my brow.

Anna shook her finger at me. "Don't scrunch up your pretty face like that. It might get stuck that way. I know what you're thinking," Anna said.

I folded my arms across my chest. "What's that?"

"That you're not a family," she said. "You will be someday. Mark my words—you and the sheriff will get hitched."

I bit back a chuckle because I knew it would only encourage them, and I needed to bring this line of conversation to a halt. "First of all, I can't believe you really just said 'get hitched.' What 1970s Westerns have you been watching?"

Anna sniffed. "I don't watch television, but if I happen to be in an *Englisch* business while it's on, it's not my fault if I see it. *Bonanza* isn't bad."

I barked a laugh. "But in reference to your 'get hitched' comment, the only hitching I know about in Holmes County involves attaching a buggy horse to a post."

"Humph!" Anna replied. "I know these things. It

might take longer than an Amish courtship, but I can always tell when a couple was meant to be."

I was about to argue more when Sarah chimed in, "I think Anna is right, Angie." Sarah carried the stewpot across the kitchen and set it on a cast-iron trivet in the middle of the table. "If you and the sheriff were going to break up, you would have last Christmas when your ex-fiancé was here trying to win you back. The boy tried every trick in the book, but you still chose the sheriff."

She didn't need to remind me about that. I blushed to myself thinking how I behaved when Ryan was visiting Holmes County. "Mitchell wasn't the reason I didn't marry Ryan."

They both gave me a disbelieving look.

"Okay, he wasn't the *only* reason. My decision had to do more with wanting to be here with all of you."

Anna smiled. "You are a sweet girl, but you should—"

The back door to the house creaked open and Sarah's husband, Jeremiah, strode in. His appearance saved me from hearing what Anna thought I should do. Which was a good thing, because chances were high I wouldn't have liked it.

Chapter Ten

Jeremiah Leham, a short, broad-shouldered man with a brown beard that hung an inch down from his chin, smiled when he found Anna and me sitting at the pine kitchen table. "I thought it was your car parked out front, Angie. *Gude mariye*, Anna." He gave Anna a nod.

Anna sipped water from her glass. "*Gude mariye*, Jeremiah. How are the pumpkins?"

"*Gut. Gut.* I suspect that Sarah has already told you of our plans for the patch this year." He smiled lovingly at his wife. "There's not much she can keep a secret."

Sarah swatted her husband with a dishtowel. "Hush, you. Wash your hands, and Anna and Angie will join us for afternoon supper."

"*Wunderbar*," Jeremiah said, walking over to the sink. "It will be *gut* to hear the news from town."

Anna and I sat on either side of the table, I right below the kitchen window. Sarah sat on the end. As he dried his hands on the dishtowel his wife had swatted him with, Jeremiah settled at the opposite end from his wife. He dropped the dishtowel on his lap and used it as a napkin. Jeremiah bowed his head and said the blessing in Pennsylvania Dutch. I caught only a couple of words: *Gott* for God, and *maahl* for meal. Anna had been trying to teach me the Amish language, but it was slow going. Having grown up in Texas, I took Spanish in school. Who knew someday I would live in a part of the United States where a background in German would have been more useful?

When the prayer ended, Jeremiah lifted his head. "I have heard about Bishop Beiler's passing." His voice was solemn, but I wouldn't describe it as sad or upset, as I would have expected, considering he was talking about a member of his former district.

"Angie was there," Anna said.

"Oh?" Jeremiah asked.

I quickly explained what my mom and I had witnessed in the bookmobile. "Who would want to hurt the bishop from your old district?"

He blew on his soup spoon. "Everyone in my old district disliked the old bishop in some way or another. He was a hard man. To him, life was meant to be about work and suffering. There was no joy in his heart. He believed the more you worked and the more miserable you were, the closer you were to *Gott*. It was something I could never believe. If *Gott* loves us so much, how could he want us to suffer?"

I blew on a spoonful of stew. "Even still, it must have been hard to leave."

He was quiet for a moment. "It was the hardest thing I've ever done." He smiled at his wife. "But I have never regretted my decision. I know this is the path that *Gott* wanted for me."

Sarah beamed in return. Her cheeks were a pretty shade of pink.

Jeremiah was different from Rachel's quiet husband, Aaron, who barely spoke, but I supposed a man would have to be a talker to be Sarah's spouse. That's the only way he'd have any hope of having his opinion heard.

I sipped from my water glass. "So if everyone disliked the bishop, why was he still the bishop?"

Everyone looked at me openmouthed.

I held up a hand. "I know how it works—a bishop is bishop until he dies or can't serve any longer—but if there is no vote of confidence, how can he lead?"

"That is the *Englisch* view," Jeremiah said. "We don't elect our leaders and toss them away after four years for someone new. He remains the leader because *Gott* chose him."

My forehead wrinkled. "How did he do that?"

At first I didn't think Jeremiah was going to answer the question, but finally he said, "Usually, unless a bishop, deacon, or other elder becomes too ill to serve his community, he serves in that position for the remainder of his life. When it is time to choose a new church leader, the men of the church are put forward and given hymnals. One of those hymnals contains a Bible verse on a slip of paper. No one knows which hymnal it is because they are mixed up. The man who opens the hymnal and finds the verse becomes the next church leader. And that was how Bartholomew became bishop."

"You leave it up to chance?" I asked.

He shook his head. "Members of the church can nominate the men to be given a hymnal. My old district is very small, so for the position of bishop only four or five men will be put up for the position."

"So that gives someone a one in four chance to be bishop," I said thoughtfully.

He nodded over his soup spoon.

"Back to my original question. Who might have wanted to hurt the bishop?" I asked.

Jeremiah was quiet. "I don't know."

Something about his tone told me he had some ideas, but didn't want to share them.

"You left the district to marry Sarah?" I asked.

He frowned. "That was not my only reason. That is a very personal question."

"I'm sorry," I said quickly.

"It is a personal question, but I will answer it because it might help you understand. I left the district because of the bishop. He was far too strict." He glanced at his wife. "When I started courting Sarah, he didn't approve and said that I needed to find a girl from my own district. He was especially upset because Sarah came from a New Order church. I never considered leaving the Amish way of life, but I knew that Bishop Beiler's way wasn't how it had to be. Courting Sarah and being around the members of her district, like the Grabers"—he nodded at Anna—"taught me I could still be Amish and lead a less confining life. My parents were disappointed, I know, but I left the district, and Sarah and I were married not long after I was baptized as a member of her church."

"Do you think anyone from his district might have hurt him?" I said, rephrasing my original question and hoping for a different result.

"Killed him, you mean?" His brows merged together.

I nodded.

He pushed his bowl away from him. "*Nee*. The people in the district are *gut* people. If they didn't like how the bishop ran the district, they would simply leave or keep their mouths shut. That is the Amish way."

I frowned. I wanted to believe Jeremiah, but his words were at odds with a dead bishop.

Chapter Eleven

After we left the Lehams', I drove Anna home to her family farm. Jonah, his wife, Miriam, and their three children lived in the main house on the farm, and Anna lived in the small *dadihaus* her late husband had built when he'd turned over the farm to his only son to manage.

Gravel crunched under my car's tires when I pulled into the Grabers' driveway. Anna sat next to me in the front seat. Oliver was in her lap.

I parked the car and got out. Anna opened her door, and I lifted Oliver to the ground so that she could exit.

Anna beamed. "I forgot. We have a surprise for you."

I wrinkled my brow. Anna's cheerfulness at the surprise had me suspicious. "What kind of surprise?"

"You will—"

Before she could finish her statement, a large brown, tan, and white hooved blur galloped toward us. Her ears flew back in the wind and her face split into a goaty smile.

Oliver yipped in joy to see his old friend.

My mouth hung open. "Petunia? What is she doing here?"

"She's ours now," Anna beamed. "The Nissley family sold the auction yard and moved to Kentucky. They decided to leave Petunia behind. When Jonah heard about it, he offered to take her. You know how kindhearted my son is."

Now that she mentioned it, I thought I remembered hearing something about Gideon Nissley selling the auction yard, but I never would have guessed he would leave his beloved Nubian goat behind. Petunia had been a faithful companion to him during some very difficult times.

As if she read my mind, Anna said, "Gideon said he couldn't take her with him and was so grateful we could give her a home. The family planned to live in town there, and there was no place for a goat. So here she is."

"Here she is," I said.

Petunia bumped my hand, requesting an ear scratch. I kindly obliged, charmed that after a year had passed the goat still remembered me. Sure, our relationship had been rocky, and she had knocked me on my behind more times than I would like to count, but she meant well.

Oliver ran in tight circles of canine bliss and the two animals bumped noses. Their joy was short-lived when they were interrupted by a *Gobblegobble!*

"What's that?" I cried and scooped up Oliver before he ran away in fright. It sounded like the noise was on top of us.

In my arms, Oliver stared into the tree branches

above and whimpered before burying his face in my chest. I tilted my chin up. Above us, there had to be at least fifteen full-sized turkeys in the oak tree. My mouth fell open.

Anna groaned. "The turkeys. How did they get out again?"

"Again? This has happened before?"

"More times than I can count. My son got it into his head that he would farm turkeys." She shook her head. "We finally sold off all the geese, who gave us nothing but trouble for months, and then these creatures arrive. You would have thought my son would have learned his lesson after the debacle with the geese."

"You'd think," I said. Anna and I both knew better. Jonah was always trying to find a get-rich scheme. If it wasn't geese and turkeys, it would be something else. I hoped for my bird-fearing dog that my childhood friend would stay away from winged creatures for his next livestock choice.

The turkeys watched us with their black eyes. From up in the tree, they had a closer resemblance to birds of prey than poultry.

"How did they get up there?"

"They flew, of course," Anna said.

"Flew?"

Anna took her quilting basket from my car and shut the door. "They are birds. They have wings, don't they?"

"So do penguins," I said.

Gobble. Gobble. Gobble. Squawk.

Apparently, the turkeys didn't like being compared to penguins.

Oliver shivered in my arms, and Petunia stepped

between us and the posse of turkeys. There was a flutter of feathers, and the largest of the birds, a tom, jumped to the ground. He fluffed his wings.

"Dear Lord!" I screeched as the giant bird sized us up. Fallen leaves crunched under his talons.

Jonah came running from the barn and held a finger to his lips. He held what looked like a fishing net in his hands. My eyes went wide. This wasn't going to end well. Oliver shook in my arms.

Jonah's twin nine-year-old sons, Ethan and Ezra, ran quickly behind him. The boys were grinning. They loved every moment of their father's crazy schemes. I saw the silhouette of Jonah's wife, Miriam, in their front screen door. She folded her arms across her chest. Not everyone in the family approved of Jo-Jo's antics.

I started to back away. Oliver would be safer if I hid him in the back of the car.

"Stay there," Jonah mouthed at me.

"Are you kidding?" I mouthed back. The turkey was bigger than the inflated balloon that bobbed through downtown Manhattan during Macy's Thanksgiving Day Parade. His beady black eyes bore into me as if he knew I'd had a turkey sandwich for lunch the day before. For all I knew, it might have been his mother.

Jonah threw the net over the bird, and the tom went crazy. Feathers flew everywhere. I ran around the side of my car with Oliver clutched to my chest. My dog was shaking so hard. I opened the car door and put him inside. Petunia jumped in after him. Great. There was a goat in my backseat. I shut the door with a shrug. Petunia would comfort Oliver. I would worry about the hoof marks on the upholstery later.

Jonah pulled on a rope that ran through the net, and the turkey flipped on his back as the net closed around him. His brethren in the tree gobbled in protest. If Jonah wasn't careful, he'd have a Butterball mutiny on his hands.

The twins whooped and hollered as they watched their father wrestle with the bird. Above, the giant tom's family gobbled and squawked with a vengeance. Jonah yelled at his sons to bring the wheelbarrow over. With the help of his boys, he rolled the bird into the wheelbarrow. They took care not to hurt the thrashing bird.

I winced. "Is the turkey okay?"

Jonah wiped his brow. "He will be fine. We will cut him out as soon as we get him to his pen."

The once giant bird appeared pathetic all tangled in the netting. Poor turkey. I almost decided to become a vegetarian—you know, after the holidays.

"There are more in the tree," I said.

Jonah sighed, looking up. "Yeah, I know. The *Englisch* farmer we bought the turkeys from said their wings had been clipped. I guess he was wrong."

I stared up at the looming turkeys. "What are you going to do about them?"

"They will come down eventually. They have to eat. I have the twins watching the tree."

I didn't say it, but Jonah could not have picked two less reliable bird-watchers. I wouldn't be surprised if the twins kept scaring the turkeys back into the tree whenever they made a move for the ground.

Jonah peered in the window of my car. "Did you know Petunia and Oliver are in there taking a nap?"

"Yep," I said, as if it was the most natural thing in

the world to have a French bulldog and Nubian goat asleep in the backseat of my SUV.

"Okay, then." Jonah hooked his thumbs around his suspenders and turned to Anna. "I told you I would give you a ride home from the shop, *Mamm*, when I came into town this afternoon," he said to Anna. "You didn't have to make Angie drive all the way out here."

"We were in the neighborhood," Anna said, picking up a small scrap of cloth that had flown out of her quilting basket amid the turkey chaos. "Angie and I were visiting Sarah and Jeremiah Leham."

The corners of Jonah's mouth twitched, as if he was holding back a smirk. "Is that right? Was it a social call?"

"*Ya*, it was," his mother replied. "Sarah is a member of the quilting circle, and we hadn't seen her in a few days because they are so busy with the final vegetable harvest of the year."

"Oh," Jonah said with a full-blown smirk. "I thought that just maybe you were there to pump Jeremiah for information about his former bishop, who happened to turn up dead this morning."

"Well, all right." Anna grinned, and for the first time I saw from whom Jonah got his mischievous streak. "That too. It doesn't hurt to ask a question or two. You know, Sarah is always eager to talk."

"Especially since I had the misfortune of finding the body," I said.

"What?" Jonah yelped, no longer joking around.

"I guess I didn't technically find it. Austina Shaker was already there when Mom and I arrived on the scene. I called the cops, though." I said this like it was no big deal.

Jonah gaped at me. "Your mom was with you. That's hard for me to picture."

The turkeys muttered among themselves above. I didn't have a great feeling about that many birds looming over us like vultures. "Can we go inside and talk about this? The turkeys are freaking me out."

Jonah nodded and joined me at the car to get Petunia and Oliver out. It took some coaxing, but finally Oliver and Petunia hopped out of the SUV. Oliver wasn't happy when Jonah said that Petunia wasn't allowed in the main Graber house, so he decided to stay out in the buggy barn with her, as far away from the turkeys as he could get.

When I walked into the Grabers' house, Miriam scowled at me. Miriam always scowled at me; I wasn't her favorite person. She suspected her husband was once sweet on me. Maybe Jonah and I did have a crush on each other when we were ten, but it would have never worked out, even if I hadn't moved away to Texas at that age. He was Amish. I was "English." I knew he wouldn't change his way of life, and although my aunt became Amish to marry my uncle Jacob over fifty years ago, I knew I couldn't make the same commitment.

Miriam spun around and waltzed back into the kitchen. She wasn't the chatty sort.

Jonah stepped out of his work boots and left them beside the front door. "I feel like there is more to this story than you finding a dead body. You should be used to that by now." He walked across the maple floors in his black socks and sat on the hearth. There wasn't a fire there yet, but I knew there would be soon. Winter wasn't far away.

I sat on the plain brown sofa, which faced the large picture window looking out on Jonah's grazing fields. Near the split-rail fence, the family's two draft horses nibbled on the browning grass. "I kinda sorta promised I would find the killer."

Jonah clicked his tongue and shook his head, looking much like one of those draft horses after a long day of plowing.

I pointed at Anna. "Your mother put me up to it."

"Pish," Anna replied, settling down next to me on the couch. She tucked her quilting basket in between us. "I just gave you a nudge. You know that you would have agreed to it even if I hadn't been there."

She was probably right, but I wasn't going to let her know I thought so.

"I don't like this." Jonah propped his elbows on his knees. "I don't like it one bit. Angie, you were doing such a great job of staying out of trouble, and now this?"

"You're one to talk. Do I need to remind you about the turkeys outside? Besides, I don't purposely get into trouble. It sort of finds me."

He shook his head. "What does the sheriff think about this?"

"He doesn't know yet." I wagged my finger at him. "And don't you go telling him. He has enough on his plate without worrying about me."

Anna opened her quilting basket and pulled out a

nine-block piece of cloth that she was piecing. The intricate quilt topper was pinned, but the individual pieces needed to be sown together. "Since we have that settled, I'm happy you're here, son. I think you can help us too."

"Me?" Jonah gasped. "Oh, no—not me." He shot a worried glance in the direction of the kitchen. He lowered his voice. "I'm already in hot water over the turkeys."

I knew he was concerned that Miriam might overhear. His wife would not approve of Jonah helping Anna and me with a murder investigation. If Miriam had her way, Jonah wouldn't speak to me at all. Although I couldn't blame her for being upset about the turkeys.

Anna positioned her glasses on the end of her nose and threaded her needle. "Then I suppose Angie and I can handle the investigation ourselves."

Jonah's shoulders slumped. "What do you want me to do?"

"We will tell you in time, but I'm glad you are on board."

Jonah sighed.

"Do you know Phoebe Truber?" I asked.

Jonah frowned. "Not very well. She's a member of Bartholomew's district and a schoolteacher. Why do you ask?"

"Ever since we left the crime scene, I've been thinking of her. I saw her for the first time yesterday outside the bookmobile." I went on to explain how Phoebe had been watching from the schoolhouse while Bartholomew and Austina argued.

Jonah leaned back against the side of the fireplace.

"She was probably just concerned about them fighting in front of the kids."

I shifted in my seat on the sofa. "Maybe, but she looked really upset. She's so young. And she looked fragile, really—I think that's the right word."

"She's not that young."

"She's not?" I asked.

"She's about our age—definitely over thirty."

"Really, and she's not married?"

Jonah grinned. "You are over thirty and not married."

I rolled my eyes. "I'm not Amish either."

Anna moved her needle in and out of the fabric. "*Gott* does not wish for all his children to marry. Some can serve him better alone. Maybe he wishes her to remain a schoolteacher. She would not be able to do that as a married woman."

"Excellent point, Anna," I said, giving her son a beady look.

Jonah grinned in return.

I stood. "I should get back to the shop. Mattie is going to be wondering where I am."

Anna started to get up, but I waved her back into her seat. "I can find my way out."

Jonah followed me outside anyway. The screen door slammed behind us. "Angie, I don't like this at all."

Oliver and Petunia galloped around the barn. They were the ultimate odd couple, but seeing them together again brought a smile to my face. Depending on how soon Petunia knocked me on my behind with one of her loving head butts would determine how long that smile lasted. "I don't plan to take your mom on my snooping expeditions, if that's what you're worried about."

"It's not. *Maam* can take care of herself. I'm worried about you. I don't think you should get mixed up in Bartholomew's district. They are a private bunch."

I gave him a look and unlocked my car with the key fob. Above us the remaining turkeys in the tree gobbled and chattered. To me it sounded like they were planning a counterattack to rescue their tom turkey.

Jonah ignored them and said, "They are more private than the Amish people you are used to. They wouldn't like an *Englischer* snooping around. I don't want you to get hurt."

I smiled and patted his arm. "Thanks for your concern, Jo-Jo, but I won't do anything stupid."

He snorted. "At least ask me or someone else to come with you if that changes."

"I will," I promised.

Miriam stepped into the doorway, her hands wringing the tea towel with so much force I imagined she thought it was my neck.

"Look out!" one of the twins screamed.

I dropped my hand from Jonah's arm and saw Petunia and Oliver run at us at full tilt. The tom turkey that the twins had supposedly returned to his turkey pen was chasing after the goat and dog. His broad wings were fully extended, making him look like an enraged harpy. The twins raced after the turkey with their net.

I whipped open the driver's-side door and Oliver catapulted his squat body into it. I dove in the car after him.

Petunia spun around ready to defend her canine friend.

I was halfway down the driveway when I dared look in the rearview mirror. The tom turkey stood in the middle of the driveway flapping his wings. Petunia glared at him, and Jonah and the boys were bent over at the waist laughing themselves silly.

Oliver whimpered from the passenger seat.

I gripped the steering wheel. "Oliver, I don't think we will be visiting Petunia again until Jonah gets those turkeys under control."

He lay on the seat and placed his chin on his paws and sighed. He missed his hoofed bestie already.

Chapter Twelve

A mile down the road from the Grabers' farm, my cell phone rang. The readout told me it was Mitchell.

"Howdy," I said into the speakerphone.

"I love it when you talk Southern to me." There was laughter in his voice, but he sounded tired too.

"Any leads on the bishop's murder?" I asked.

He groaned. "You're as bad as the district attorney. It's only been a few hours."

"You know, I've been thinking." I tapped the steering wheel. "Maybe it wasn't a murder. Maybe the bishop tripped and landed on his head."

"Then how did the bishop get inside the bookmobile without a key?" Mitchell asked. "There was no forced entry."

"I haven't gotten that far yet."

"It doesn't matter anyway. I would have agreed it could have been an accident, if there weren't two wounds."

"Two?" I straightened up in my seat. "I only saw the one."

"There was the gash on his forehead, and that may

have knocked him out and incapacitated him. But there was also a much larger wound on the back of his head. It was bashed in."

I grimaced. Seeing one wound was bad enough. It was a good thing I missed the second one. "Couldn't it still be an accident?"

"The medical examiner will know for sure, but I doubt it. He would have had to knock his head on something and then reel back and smash the back of his head on something else. That's way too coincidental for me."

"Did you find the murder weapon?"

"No. The culprit must have taken it with him." He paused. "And then there is the gasoline."

"Gasoline? What are you talking about?"

I could almost hear Mitchell's thoughts on the other side of the phone. He sighed. "We found a canister of it behind the bishop's body. Our theory is that whoever killed him planned to cover it up by torching the bookmobile. With all that paper, the vehicle would have gone up in flames pretty fast."

I gasped. "If that's true, why didn't the killer do it?"

"Don't know. Maybe someone came, maybe he heard something and got spooked."

"This just confirms that Austina couldn't have done this. She would never burn her beloved bookmobile, not to mention all those precious books. No way, no how."

"Angie," Mitchell said.

I recognized the frustration in his voice. I stopped at a stop sign and decided to change the subject. "So, what's up—you know, besides murder and attempted arson?"

"You are going to have to stop by the station to sign your statement this morning. I called your mom and told her the same thing. She wasn't too pleased."

"I bet." Bartholomew's wasn't my first dead body—I knew the drill—but this would be all new for my mother. She was probably considering what to wear to the sheriff's station. "Anything else?"

"I just want to make sure you don't have any crazy ideas about meddling in this investigation."

"What do you mean?" I asked.

When all else fails, play dumb.

"You know exactly what I mean." He made an exasperated sound. "Angie, this is going to be a tricky case, and I told you about the arson to prove to you how dangerous the person behind the bishop's death must be. Not to mention, Bartholomew was from a particularly closed-off Amish district. His community is much more wary of outsiders than the other districts you've dealt with. They don't look kindly on the police asking too many questions."

"Even if those questions lead to who killed their leader?"

"Even then."

"All the more reason for me to help out. I might be able to get closer to them than you can."

"No, you won't." His tone left no room for argument.

I ignored that. "Sure I will. I have before."

"That's what I'm telling you. This time it's different. They won't want to talk to any English person about their community, especially a woman."

I didn't say anything.

"You aren't going to pay any attention to this conversation, are you?"

"I always pay attention to what you have to say, Mitchell. I don't always follow your advice, but I always hear it."

He groaned. "That doesn't make me feel any better."

There was murmuring on the other side of the line.

"I'm on my way," Mitchell said, muffled. "Listen, I have to go. We can discuss it tonight after dinner."

"After dinner?" I asked, confused.

"Dinner at your parents. Did you forget?" Some of the humor was back in his voice.

"No, but I told Mom that you probably wouldn't make it because of the murder."

His voice softened. "Thanks for giving me an out, but I want to see you. The case has hit a dead end at the moment, and I will have to eat."

"Dead end?" I asked, trying not to sound too eager.

I must have failed. Mitchell gave an all-suffering sigh.

"Mom will be so happy you're coming." I chewed on my lip, wondering whether this was the time to mention my mother's matrimonial designs on us. Probably not. He was under enough stress. "All right. I'll see you there, but we can't talk about this in front of my parents. My mom is already freaked out about the murder as it is."

"If only you were as easily freaked out, then I wouldn't have to worry about you being chased down by a crazed killer."

"That won't happen."

"Oh, yeah?"

"Okay, that won't happen this time."

He groaned. "Love you. Bye." Then he disconnected.

Wait, what?

Did he just say, "Love you?" What did that mean?

"Love you" was not "I love you." "Love you" was what you signed an email to a friend. Did he say, "I love you," and swallow the "I"? Or was it "Luv you," which was even worse?

Back in Dallas, I would have called one of my girl-friends to dissect the conversation over and over again, but since I had moved to Ohio, I had lost touch with most of those friends. They had been friends with Ryan and me as a couple, not with me as an individual. And my Amish friends certainly wouldn't understand this debacle. If Mitchell and I had been Amish, we would have been mar-ried by now with two sets of twins. Mitchell's "love you" was the last thing I needed to have on my mind.

Pushing those thoughts aside, I gave Mattie a quick call and asked her how things were at the shop.

"Everything is fine," Mattie insisted. "I just about have everything together for tomorrow's quilting class."

"Great, and in that case, I have another errand to run. I think I will be gone another hour—two at the most."

"You are snooping, are you?" she asked.

"Umm." She knew me so well.

She sighed. "How did the visit at Austina's go?"

I gave her the quick version, ending with my agree-ment to find Bartholomew's killer.

Mattie sighed, sounding a lot like Mitchell had a few minutes before. "I'm not even going to bother to tell you what a dumb idea this is."

"Great," I said. "What can you tell me about Phoebe Truber?"

There was silence on the line. "There's not much to tell. She older than me. She's a shy girl. Honestly, I was really surprised when I heard she was chosen to be the teacher at Hock Trail School. She didn't seem to have it in her to control a roomful of kids."

"What do you mean?"

"She's too timid. I can't imagine her telling anyone what to do." She paused. "Maybe she is different with children than she is with adults. I saw her at a couple of socials when I was in *rumspringa*. I can't remember if I ever saw her speaking to anyone."

"Did you ever speak to her at one of those socials?'

"*Nee*. She was so much older than me, and her nose was always in a book."

My eyebrows shot up. "What kind of books?"

"Novels, I guess. I never asked her about it. I didn't know why she came to anything if all she wanted to do was read."

Maybe because she could read when she was outside of Bartholomew Beiler's district.

Phoebe had to be one of the young women that Bartholomew didn't want visiting the bookmobile. But why wouldn't Austina tell me? I knew there had to be more to it than protecting her patrons' privacy. Had Phoebe committed murder in order to be able to keep reading? That seemed a little extreme, but this new knowledge made me more certain that I needed to pay the schoolteacher a visit. It was almost two now, but by the time I reached the schoolhouse, far out on the outskirts of Rolling Brook, classes would be out.

"You're going to talk to her, aren't you? About her bishop?" Mattie asked in my ear.

"Yep. You must be a psychic," I said.

"A what?" my assistant asked.

"Never mind," I said. Aaron would never forgive me if I put thoughts about the paranormal world in his younger sister's head.

"I don't think she will say anything to you. Like I said, she's really shy."

"It's worth a shot, and people like to talk to me."

Mattie snorted and hung up.

Since Mattie had the shop well taken care of, I made a U-turn in the middle of the country road and headed away from downtown Rolling Brook in the direction of Hock Trail School. The only way I was going to satisfy my suspicion that Phoebe Truber was involved was to talk to her myself.

The schoolyard was quiet. I shouldn't have been surprised. I knew the district's parents must have kept their children at home today, after the news of Bishop Beiler's death spread through their community. Maybe Phoebe wasn't even at the school, but as I told Mattie, it was worth a shot.

I shifted my car into park.

Oliver lifted his chin from his paws and sighed.

"We might as well double-check," I told him and got out of the car.

There was something eerie about being at the last place I had seen Bartholomew alive, even if the book-mobile wasn't there. In my head, I could hear him and Austina arguing. He had been angry—really angry—and so insistent. Yet Austina had been equally firm.

A brisk breeze sent the swings in the playground swaying back and forth, and I shivered. Oliver stayed close to my legs. He must have sensed the eerie feeling too.

I walked up the three steps to the schoolhouse. The front door was ajar. "Hello?" I called in a singsong voice as I pushed the door open.

In the middle of the schoolhouse, the red-hot mouth of the potbelly stove was open, and Phoebe knelt in front of it, tossing paperback novels into the flames two by two.

Chapter Thirteen

"What are you doing?" I cried as she tossed another book into the stove. The novel instantly set ablaze, its pages curling inward as the flames ate them away.

A wooden crate of paperback books sat beside her on the floor. More kindling, it appeared.

Phoebe let out an *"Eep"* and dropped the stack of paperbacks in her hands. She spun around as if expecting to see a monster. Instead, she found me. She fell on her hip so close to the stove, I thought she might singe her dress. "What are you doing in here? You aren't supposed to be here."

I rushed forward and yanked the crate of books away from her.

"What are you doing? Those are mine." She sat up and scooted herself away from the stove.

"Then why are you burning them?" I nudged the crate of books behind me with my foot.

Her face crumbled. "I have to. They killed the bishop."

I picked up one of the novels. There was a young

couple on the cover watching a sunset together. It was a romance, very sweet, very . . . non-killeresque. I held up the book. "This killed the bishop?"

She stumbled to her feet and closed the stove's door. "Yes. Those books are the reason the bishop is dead. Without them, he would still be alive."

"Because he didn't want his district members reading them?"

Her mouth fell open. "How did you know that?"

I dropped the paperback back into the crate with the other books. "I was here the day before he died."

She stared at me, blinking.

"I was here when he was fighting with Austina about the bookmobile visiting his district. You were here too. I saw you in the doorway."

She brushed dust and soot from her black apron. There was a lot of soot gathered there. I wondered how many books she had burned before I showed up. Phoebe cleared her throat. "I remember. So you must know that's why he died. Austina argued with him about allowing books in the district. When he still wouldn't let her bring books in, she killed him." Her voice shook as she said this.

"Austina didn't kill the bishop over library books."

She folded her arms. "Then she must have had another reason, because she did it."

"How are you so certain? Did you see something?"

"*N-nee*, I didn't see anything myself, but it's what everyone is saying."

I scowled. "That doesn't make it true."

She pointed a soot-blackened finger at me. "I know who you are. You're the township trustee who helped

Aaron Miller get permission for his pie factory last year."

I frowned. "I didn't have that much to do with it."

"You shouldn't be in here. This is a school for Amish children." She stood and brushed soot off her hands. "Give those books back to me and leave."

I kicked the crate farther behind me with my heel. "I'm not going to let you burn them."

"They're mine and I can do whatever I wish with them."

I gave the crate another back kick and it banged into the edge of the door frame. "I suppose that's true, but there are a lot of easier ways to dispose of those books rather than burning them. Your stove will never keep up with this many books."

She folded her thin arms over her chest. "That's none of your concern."

"If you don't want them, let me take them for the library book sale. Maybe then they can do some good."

She bit her lip. "So that someone else can buy them? They are evil. They cannot do any *gut* for anyone."

"If that person isn't from your Amish district, what do you care if someone else buys and reads them?"

She thought on this for a moment. "Fine," she said, nodding. "Take them. I don't ever want to see them again." She walked over to the chalkboard and started wiping away the math problems covering it.

"I hated long division in school. It always seemed to take longer than it should," I said in a more conversational tone.

She swiped an eraser across the board, completely wiping out one of the problems with a fluid, practiced stroke. "It is important that the children learn how something is done even if the answer to the question is obvious."

I nodded. "I think my dad would agree with you at that. He was always disappointed that I didn't have his passion for math. I have always been more attracted to art."

She didn't respond, and kept erasing. Strands of her bright red hair sprang out of her bun and out from under her prayer cap on the back of her head like rays of the sun.

There was a globe in the front corner next to Phoebe's desk. A paper nameplate was in the middle of the desk, and it read, MISS TRUBER.

Everything in the room was labeled in English, reminding me that some Amish children didn't learn English until they started school. Two blackboards covered almost the entire front wall. The first blackboard had the Beatitudes written on it. Although I hadn't attended church in many years, I recognized them because my aunt Eleanor made me memorize them. She said they were one of the most important passages to remember. My eyes fell on one verse: "Blessed are those who mourn, for they will be comforted." Was Bartholomew Beiler's family being comforted now? I realized I didn't know much about him or his family. I assumed he was married. He would have to be to be a bishop. Did he have any children? Who were they? Wouldn't his family be the best ones to know who might have wanted the bishop dead?

On the chalkboard, my eyes fell to the next line: "Blessed are the meek, for they will inherit the earth."

That was a perfect description of Phoebe. Her hands shook as she erased the other board.

She finished her task and gasped when she turned around. "What are you still doing here? You should leave."

"Not yet. I was wondering if I could talk to you about Bartholomew Beiler."

"Nee." She spun around and started to attack the second chalkboard. The verses disappeared with each swipe of her eraser. Her shoulders drooped, and she turned around to face me again. "You aren't going to leave until I talk to you, are you?"

I smiled. "Nope. I'm annoying that way, or so I've been told."

She sat in one of her students' desks facing away from me and toward the chalkboard. I sat at a desk in the same row a couple of seats away. The desks looked as if they came from public school circa 1970. I wouldn't be surprised if they did. The Amish were bargain hunters, and flea markets and school auctions were favorite places for them to shop. They were the ultimate recyclers before it was trendy.

My knees knocked onto the bottom of the desk. It was easy to forget how small children's school desks were. Sitting in that seat reminded me of my childhood, of the many times I would read in my lap or draw when I should have been paying attention to whatever the teacher was saying.

She didn't look at me, just kept staring straight ahead and said, "I've already told you why the bishop was murdered. Those books by the door are the reason he is dead. What more can I tell you?"

I folded my hands on the top of the desk. "How can you be so sure? Do you know something? Did you see something?"

She ignored my question and said, "I know you own Running Stitch. Everyone in the county has heard much about you since you moved here."

"I bet they have," I said, and shifted in my seat. I could already feel the bruises forming on my knees. "I'm sorry for your loss and the loss to your community. I know it must be devastating to lose such an important man."

Phoebe removed a white handkerchief from her apron pocket and dabbed her eye. "I didn't cancel school today, not officially, but none of the children showed up. I can't say I blame their parents for wanting to keep their children at home. It's so terrible."

"Was the bishop giving you a hard time because you borrowed and read books from the library?"

Her head snapped up. "Did Austina tell you that?"

"No." I shook my head. "I just figured it out. Why else would you use them for kindling?"

"I wasn't reading anything bad—I promise you I wasn't. If I had known it would drive Austina to kill the bishop, I would have stopped reading. I didn't want this to happen over some silly book I hid under my pillow at night."

"Why are you so sure it was Austina?"

"Who else could it be?" She braced her hands on the desktop. "Who else was angry with him? You were here the last time they fought. Didn't Austina look angry?"

I thought back to that afternoon. More than angry, Austina had appeared defiant, and maybe a tad bit superior. The bishop had been the furious one.

"So no one in the district was angry at the bishop?"

She didn't answer.

"You saw the bishop fight with Austina. Whether you like it or not, the police are going to want to talk to you. They are going to ask you the same thing."

She stared at her hands. "The only person I know of is Gil Kauffman." She whispered the name.

"Who's that?"

Still without looking at me, she said, "He lives in the district. He wanted to marry the bishop's daughter. The bishop supported him, but the bishop's daughter wanted to marry someone else." She took a breath. "The bishop finally relented, and her engagement to the other man was announced the day before the bishop died."

"Who was the other man?"

"Levi Leham."

I nearly fell out of my chair—or I would have if I wasn't wedged so tightly into the tiny desk that I could barely breathe. "Levi Leham? He's marrying the bishop's daughter?"

She nodded. "He was. The wedding was supposed to be this weekend. Now it will be postponed."

Why hadn't Jeremiah and Sarah shared this little kernel of information with me? It wasn't like Sarah to keep a secret about anything, especially something this interesting.

"What's the name of the bishop's daughter?"

There was a pause, and for a moment I thought she wasn't going to answer. Then she said, "Faith."

"Faith Beiler," I said. I didn't know her.

Just then the door to the schoolhouse flew open.

Chapter Fourteen

A redheaded Amish man who looked to be in his early forties stomped into the schoolhouse. His red beard was streaked with white, giving it a peppermint look, and was much longer than my friends in the New Order wore theirs. From the beard, I knew immediately that he was married. It was pretty easy to tell the married men from the unmarried men in the Amish world. Beard, married. No beard, not married. I also surmised, from the shade of his hair, that he was related to Phoebe.

"Phoebe, what are you doing here?" the peppermint-bearded man demanded. "We need you to come home right now. I told you there was no point in teaching to—" The man pulled up short when he saw me. "Who are you?"

"Who are *you*?" I shot back, realizing that I had been asking that question a lot lately.

"I'm Phillip Truber, Phoebe's brother." He stood next to the potbelly stove and dug his fists into his hips.

I ungracefully wiggled out of the student desk. "Angie Braddock. I own Running Stitch, one of the quilt shops in town."

"Quilts? We have no need for quilts. Why are you here?" He looked from me to his sister and back.

"I stopped in to talk to Phoebe to see how she was doing," I said. "The death of Bishop Bartholomew Beiler has been very upsetting."

"You know her?" Phillip's voice cracked like a whip as he directed the question at his sister.

"I—I—" Phoebe stammered.

"We met yesterday, when the bookmobile was visiting the school," I fibbed.

"You're one of those librarian people?" he spat. His face grew as red as his beard.

Since when was that a bad thing?

He glared at his sister's soot-covered apron and skirt. "What on earth have you been up to?"

Phoebe swallowed. "I stoked the fire in case any of the children came here." As her voice shook, I realized that she was afraid of her brother.

I eyed him more closely. He was tall, at least six-three, an unusual height for an Amish man. He had buttoned his navy blue work shirt all the way up to his throat, just as Bartholomew Beiler had worn his the day I met him. It appeared to be part of the confining dress for Bartholomew's district.

I had been in Amish Country long enough to notice some of the subtle differences in the clothing. Jonah would never wear a shirt that tightly buttoned. He'd complain about not being able to breathe. Jonah may have been Amish, but he wasn't afraid to speak his mind. Thankfully, he grew up in a New Order district that allowed him to do that . . . within reason.

"I told you this morning the children would not

come here," Phillip snapped. "Why did you waste firewood to start a fire?"

It wasn't firewood, I thought, but held my tongue. I guessed Phillip would be all for the book-burning party.

"It's time to go." He threw open the door.

Phoebe gathered up her cloak and large black bonnet from one of the many pegs that lined the left side of the schoolroom.

Phillip glared at the crate of novels by the door. "Whose are these?" He glowered at his sister.

I hurried forward and picked up the crate. "Oh, those are mine. I'm in charge of the library book sale that was scheduled for the end of the week. I'm not sure if it's still going to happen now, considering, you know . . ." I smiled brightly. "But I'm always gathering up books to sell for such a good cause."

Phillip gave his sister a suspicious look, as if he knew exactly who the books belonged to. If Mattie, who was from a completely different Amish order, knew Phoebe was borrowing books, then he must have known as well.

I carried the crate through the door. "I should be going. Nice visiting with you, Phoebe. If you want to talk, just let me know."

"She doesn't have anything to say to you," Phillip snarled from the top of the steps.

That's what you think.

After leaving the schoolhouse, I swung by the sheriff's station to sign my statement. I was in and out within thirty minutes. I was beginning to become a bit of a pro at it. Mitchell wasn't there. When I reached Running Stitch, Mattie was closing up shop.

She walked out the door and said, "I have to help out at the pie factory tonight. One of Aaron's bakers called in sick, but tomorrow I want to know everything. You were gone forever."

"You got it," I promised.

Before heading to my parents' house for dinner, I stopped at home to change. My mother was the sort that expected folks to dress up for dinner. I blamed this on her obsession with *Downton Abbey*.

Dodger gave Oliver and me a dirty look when we walked into the house. He was angry that we had left him alone all day. Oliver took a downward dog stance in penance. Dodger boxed at his canine brother's nose, and soon all was forgiven, the two rolling on the floor together.

I set the crate of books from the schoolhouse next to my front door. I sighed and felt sorry for Phoebe. I too had been a shy girl who kept her nose in a book growing up. Eventually, I grew out of my shyness. My mother would credit that to forcing me to participate in beauty pageants. To tell the truth, she was right. I hated them so much that I had to assert myself to make her give up the dream of having a future Miss America for a daughter. I shuddered at the thought.

Instead of the evening gown my mother would have preferred for dinner tonight, I opted for black slacks and a silver sweater. Even though they didn't go with the outfit, I chose to wear my cowboy boots. They'd help me get through the night.

Before we left, I whistled for Oliver by the back kitchen door to let him out into the backyard. Once upon a time, Oliver had a doggy door to come and go as he pleased, but when a deranged arsonist used it to try to kill me, I had Mitchell nail it shut. Since then, my landlord had installed a new door altogether. "Time to go outside," I said in a singsong voice.

Oliver sighed, looking at Dodger, but finally waddled to the back door.

I did not allow Dodger outside unsupervised. The cat got in all sorts of trouble when I was watching; who knew what trouble he could cause when I wasn't paying attention?

Oliver stopped on the threshold and growled.

Oliver wasn't a growler. When it came time to fight or flight, he was the first one to hightail it out of there.

In the fading light I scanned the yard, but I didn't see anything out of the ordinary.

The house behind mine had some overgrown brush that grew up right alongside my back fence. Maybe there was a cat or chipmunk hiding back there? "It's okay, Ollie," I said. "You need to go potty, so we can go to Grandma and Grandpa's."

Oliver growled deeper in his throat, and I knew something was wrong. I took a step out the door, and Oliver bit into the pant leg of my dress pants, holding me there, unless I was willing to let him tear a hole in them. Was someone out there spying on me, or preparing to rob me? I knew Oliver wouldn't bite me like that unless he was truly concerned. I froze.

Something in the bushes moved, and it was a lot bigger than a chipmunk. The form stood, and I could just make out the shape of a person. I thought it was probably a man or a very tall woman. It was too dark to know for sure. Nor could I tell if the intruder was

Amish or English. The sun was setting and the back-yard was almost completely in shadows this late in the day.

Oliver let go of my pant leg, indicating the person must have disappeared. I grabbed a flashlight from the kitchen cupboard and stepped into the yard. Oliver slunk behind me, fierce guard dog that he was. I crept to the back fence. "Anyone there?" I asked.

No answer.

I didn't want to yell too loud and make the neighbors think I was crazy. They still kept their distance from me as a result of the fire in my backyard last year.

I clicked on the flashlight. "Come out if you're there."

Nothing.

I shone the light on the ground under the shrubs where I had seen the figure stand up. There were two footprints there. The shoe size was larger than mine, and I have big feet, so my visitor had definitely been a man. The shoes were pointed directly at my back door. A chill ran down my spine. Someone had been watching the house.

I turned around and bolted back to the house. Oliver beat me there—he could really book it when he was spooked. I slammed the door after us and threw the bolt.

By the time I was on my way to my parents' house, I almost had myself convinced that I'd imagined the dark figure beside the back fence. I had a more difficult time explaining away Oliver's strange reaction and those pesky footprints.

Who could the intruder have been? Certainly not my

elderly landlord or his wife. My landlords would have had no reason to spy from the bushes when they could just let themselves into my house when they pleased.

Could it have been a kid taking a shortcut through my yard? I had never seen anyone do that before. My rented house was on a Millersburg side street in a quiet neighborhood of modest homes. There were lots of children in the neighborhood, but then, the size of the footprint suggested it was a grown man.

I thought about telling Mitchell when he showed up at my parents' house, but then he would have wanted to leave dinner right away to check it out. After the day that I'd had, I didn't think I could stand the fit my mother would have over another canceled meal with Mitchell and me.

Oliver whimpered from the backseat. Dodger meowed in his carrier. If someone was staking out my house, I certainly wasn't going to leave my cat home alone to face him. Oliver pressed his nose up against the cat crate's metal door, trying his best to squeeze through the mesh to comfort his young charge.

When I turned into my parents' driveway, Mitchell stood outside of his SUV, parked in front of my parents' house under a streetlamp. I shifted the car into park. The sheriff met me at the car and opened my door for me.

I climbed out and smiled. "What a gentleman you are."

He shrugged. "I try."

In the dim streetlight, I saw there were dark circles under his eyes. The bishop's murder was taking a toll on him. There had been too many murders in Holmes

County lately, and every last one of them fell on Mitchell's broad shoulders. It appeared he was beginning to feel their collective weight.

I patted his arm before opening the back door to my little SUV and let Oliver out. He hopped to the concrete and stared impatiently back at the car as I pulled Dodger's carrier from the backseat. The cat meowed loudly in annoyance. He didn't like the carrier, but I had to transport him that way. If I let him loose in the car, he would try to climb on my head. I knew this from experience.

Mitchell stared at my hand holding the carrier. "What's wrong? What's going on?"

I cocked my head. "What do you mean?" I asked innocently.

Mitchell's brow knit together. "Something happened. You wouldn't bring Dodger to your parents' house if something didn't happen. Your mother flips out when he sharpens his claws on her leather sofa."

That was true.

I balanced the weight of the carrier in my hand and closed the car door. I might as well tell him, I thought. "We had a little issue at home, and I didn't want to leave Dodger there by himself."

He took the cat carrier from me and blocked my path to my parents' front door. "What kind of issue?"

I would have enjoyed his closeness if he weren't so irritated with me at the moment. I sighed and told him about the Peeping Tom.

Mitchell's knuckles turned white as his gripped the handle of the cat carrier more tightly. "Angie, why didn't you call me? And you went out there to look for footprints?" He ran his free hand through his thick dark hair flecked with silver. The silver gave him a distinguished, trustworthy look. There was more of it than when I'd first moved to Holmes County a year before. I assumed that was because of the rise in the murder rate in the rural county and not because of me, but I could have been wrong.

The front door opened. "Angie!" My dad bellowed from the front door. "What are you two lovebirds doing out there? It's too cold to canoodle outside."

I felt my face grow hot. *Thanks, Dad.*

The tiniest hint of a smile curled the right corner of Mitchell's mouth.

Oliver galloped toward the sound of my father's voice. "There's my boy," Dad cooed as he scratched Oliver between the ears. Dad let him inside and waved us to follow.

"Are you coming?" I asked Mitchell.

"I'll be there in a minute." His voice was hard as he unclipped his cell phone from his belt.

I took Dodger's carrier from his hand and our fingers brushed. He was far too distracted to notice.

Chapter Fifteen

A s soon as I stepped through the front door, Mom pointed at the carrier. "Why did you bring your cat?"

"You know I take Dodger to Running Stitch too. Why not bring him here to see his grandparents?" I knelt in the foyer and opened the carrier. Dodger shot out like a silver-and-white bullet.

Mom pursed her lips. "He'd better not scratch my sofa, Angela. Do you remember what he did to the settee the last time he was here? It's still out for reupholstering."

Dodger meowed a protest. It could have been a swearword. I wasn't sure; I wasn't fluent in Cat.

"He'll be a perfect gentleman," I said, and then added, "I hope."

Mitchell entered the house after he finished his call. Ever the proper hostess, Mom took his coat and hung it in the foyer closest. In the great room, Mitchell sat next to me on my parents' nine-foot sofa. The sofa was huge, but he sat close enough so that our legs touched.

I relaxed into the seat. He wasn't mad. Well, that

probably wasn't true—he was still mad, but he wasn't mad enough to give me the cold shoulder. I'd take it.

Mitchell touched my arm and whispered, "I called Anderson. He's headed to your house to check out the scene."

I squeezed his fingers. "Thanks," I said, although I had my doubts that Deputy Anderson could find the footprints in the trees even if there was a neon sign pointing them out.

"Don't thank me yet. I still want to know why you didn't call me right away." His face darkened.

Uh-oh. I was in trouble.

"Angie, dear." My mother placed a wineglass in my hand. "You must taste this. Our chef recommended it as the perfect pairing with the mushroom puffs."

I wasn't much for drinking, but I took a big gulp to settle my nerves.

Mitchell arched an eyebrow.

"I'm still surprised you hired a chef," I said, assuming that was a safe topic of conversation. My mother was known to cook a gourmet meal herself.

Mom sniffed. "You can't expect me to cook after the morning we had." She started to hand an identical wineglass to Mitchell.

Mitchell shook his head. "Thank you, Daphne. I'm sure it's delicious, but I still have to work later tonight. I will taste those mushroom puffs, though."

Mom set the glass back on the silver tray. "I suppose it's about that awful murder. I'm still reeling from this morning's grim discovery. I had to take a sleeping pill as soon as I returned home to block the image. A hot bath helped too."

Dad flopped on his giant leather recliner. It was the one piece of furniture in the room that Mom had allowed Dad to pick. He had one just like it in their house back in Dallas. Dad was a simple guy when it came to his creature comforts. He knew what he liked and stuck with it. "I wasn't pleased when Daphne told me what she and AngieBear found."

"Understood, sir," Mitchell said, looking a tad nervous. He could face down a killer, but he became anxious when talking to my dad. It was adorable.

Dad balanced a small plate of mushroom puffs on his round tummy. "Do you have any leads into who might have done this?"

I was grateful to Dad for asking the question. It saved me the trouble.

"Not yet." Mitchell popped a mushroom puff into his mouth, maybe to keep himself from saying any more.

"Dinner is served." A young man in a white chef's uniform complete with puffy hat stepped into the living room. He looked like he came out of central casting for *Top Chef*.

"Wonderful," my mother said.

She hadn't been joking about the chef.

The chef preceded us to the kitchen.

"Where did you find a chef like that in Amish Country?" I asked my mom.

"He works for one of the larger hotels in Berlin. I happened to hear he had the night off from the hotel, and here he is."

"You happened to hear?" I shook my head. My mother had the uncanny ability to get what she wanted. She really missed her calling as a party planner.

The dining table was elegantly set. It was so not Amish. White plates with gold rims, silverware polished to a high sheen, and blooming white hydrangea in round glass vases marched down the center of the table. I wondered where my mother found the spring flowers in October. I didn't bother to ask. Mom had her ways.

Mitchell didn't react to the fancy table settings. My heart fluttered that he had the ability to move as the sheriff in a rural Amish county and still be one hundred percent comfortable in a setting like this with my parents. That would come in handy if there was ever a wedding. Not that I was counting on a wedding with the sheriff, but I knew if there was one, my mother would hold it to high Texas society standards even in the middle of Amish Country.

"Is this how you grew up?" Mitchell whispered behind me. He was so close to me that his breath tickled the hairs on the back of my neck.

I shook my head. "This is all for show." I paused. "For you," I said out of the side of my mouth. "She must like you if she's gone to all this trouble. The chef is new."

He brushed the back of my arm with his fingers. "I want her to like me."

"I thought we would have a harvest-themed dinner tonight. Chef Roy has put together a lovely menu." She glanced at Mitchell. "I hope you like squash."

"Love it," Mitchell said as he stepped around me into the room.

She beamed.

I arched an eyebrow at Mitchell. Since when had he started to love squash?

Mitchell took the seat across from me as if he ate like this every night.

The chef brought out a squash soup for the first course. It was sort of like liquid pumpkin pie. I had to stop myself from inhaling it. Now I knew the chef to talk to if I ever had my mouth wired shut.

Mom set her spoon on the edge of her bowl like a lady. My mother has never been tempted to inhale food. After a few delicate spoonfuls, she was done. On the other hand, my father was using the yeasty dinner roll to soak up every last drop from his dish.

"Angie," my mother said. "Is there any news about the book sale?"

I shook my head. "I haven't heard anything. Austina is sort of preoccupied. I'm not sure it will even go on." I tried hard to keep the relief out of my voice.

"That can't happen." Mom pursed her lips "What about all the work we've done?"

I stopped my spoon an inch from my mouth. "What work? We've only known about the book sale for a day. I haven't done anything for it."

"You may not have, but I have. I spoke with Willow Moon from the Dutchman's Tea Shop this afternoon, and she's on board."

"On board? On board for what?" I asked as the chef brought out small salads of lettuce, apples, and cran-berries.

"For the book sale." My mother forked a single cran-berry. "She's ready to work. We have some great ideas we'd like to share with you."

Mom and Willow Moon had joined forces? Was there a more frightening combination?

Across from me, I caught Mitchell smiling into his salad. The jerk.

"Refreshments are a must," Mom went on. "And I thought Willow to be the perfect person for the job since her tea shop is so popular, and just down the street from the Millers' factory."

It was true that the Dutchman's Tea Shop was a popular stop for tourists and locals in Rolling Brook, but it wasn't because of the tea. The tea was awful. Willow prided herself in making her tea concoctions and pawning them off on unsuspecting guests. Each tea flavor was worse than the last. I still shuddered when I thought of her Witch's Bite tea from last Halloween. She wouldn't serve that one again, would she? Some customers claimed it had burned off their taste buds.

Mom sipped her wine. "Between her tea shop and the baked treats from the Millers, I believe we will have plenty to serve."

My salad wasn't looking nearly as appetizing as it had two minutes earlier. "Mom, Willow will make some type of awful tea that will send everyone to the hospital."

Mom waved my concern away with her fork. "Her tea isn't that bad. The strawberry flavor she made this summer was delightful, if a little too sweet."

It was like drinking hot strawberry preserves.

I shifted in my chair. "Couldn't you have asked someone else?"

The chef brought out the next course: chicken with a squash risotto and acorn squash. The squash theme was going all the way. Maybe that's why Mom picked Willow. Willow was big into themes too.

"Not in Rolling Brook," my mother said, "and this book sale should be a Rolling Brook event."

Typically, I would agree with her on this point, but not today.

I sighed in defeat. "At least let me make sure the book sale is still on. I planned to stop by the library tomorrow. I will check to see what the plan is now." I paused. "Now that Austina is out of commission."

I felt Mitchell watching me. He knew that wasn't the only reason I wanted to visit the library. I made a point not to look at him. If I happened to question some of Austina's coworkers while I was there, what harm was that?

Mitchell's phone rang.

"Excuse me," he said. "It's one of my officers."

Mitchell was gone for a long time. Long enough for the chef to serve dessert, which was a squash cake. By that time I was squashed out. He returned as Dad polished off his piece of cake.

Mitchell stepped into the dining room, but did not sit. "I'm so sorry, Kent and Daphne, but I'm going to have to leave a little early because of police business."

Dad started to stand.

Mitchell waved him back into his seat. "No, there's no need for you to get up. I had a lovely evening. Thank you."

Dad wiped his mouth with his napkin. "We understand, James. We're happy you could join as long as you could."

"What about dessert?" my mother asked.

Mitchell looked at the squash cake. "I'm sorry I will have to miss it." He didn't look that sorry to me.

"I'll walk you out," I said.

Mom set her folded napkin on the table. "I'll send a piece of squash cake home with Angie for you."

When we were outside, Mitchell said, "Squash cake? That squash cake is all yours. Please don't save it for me."

I smiled. "But I thought you loved squash."

He adjusted the collar of my blouse. "What I love is to be on your mother's good side. She's still not sure about me. If she had her way, you'd be married to Ryan Dickinson by now and living in Dallas with your own personal chef."

I hooked my arm through his, leaning close for the warmth. I should have grabbed my coat before coming outside. "Mom has accepted my decision by now. Besides, last I heard Ryan was engaged to someone else in Texas. He didn't waste any time."

Mitchell turned to look at me. "Is the only reason you stayed with me because Ryan has a new lady friend?" His blue-green eyes sparkled in the glow of the streetlight.

I smirked. "You know that's not the only reason."

He grunted and unlocked his SUV with his key fob.

"What's the callout about? Is it about the murder or the Peeping Tom at my place?" I couldn't stop myself from asking.

"Neither. Someone has been joyriding through the county and knocking over mailboxes."

I grimaced. "That's terrible, but why does it need your attention? Can't Anderson and other deputies handle it?"

"They can, but all the mailboxes are Amish. I want to make sure that's not intentional."

"You think someone is targeting Amish homes?" I rubbed my arms and wondered whether any of my friends had lost their mailboxes to the bandits. "That's awful."

He nodded. "And it's the last thing I need right now with a murderer on the loose. I don't want us to be distracted by these jokesters—probably teens—and miss something on the bigger case." He gave me a quick kiss on the lips. "Don't think I will forget about the peeper either."

"I wasn't worried. Take care, Mitchell."

"Always." He kissed my cheek.

I grabbed his hand. "Can I ask you a question?"

He laughed. "Like I can stop you?"

I smiled. "Does it bother you that I call you Mitchell instead of your Christian name?"

He arched his brow. "My Christian name?"

"My mother was concerned. She thinks it's odd I don't call you James."

"Ahh." His aquamarine eyes sparkled.

I search his face. "Does it bother you?"

He wrapped me in a hug and whispered in my ear. "I like it."

I shivered.

Mitchell released me. "Tell your mother I like you calling me all sorts of names."

My face heated up and I pushed him away. "Go find those mailbox bandits."

Laughing, he climbed into his car.

Chapter Sixteen

A fter leaving Mattie alone in Running Stitch the entire day before, I was at the shop bright and early
on Thursday morning. Before Mattie arrived, I had the
shop set up for the class with the chairs in the circle,
and the fabric packets Mattie made the day before for
each pumpkin on each chair.

Oliver and Dodger curled up together snoozing in
Oliver's dog bed by my *aenti's* rocking chair.

The fabric's autumnal colors made me crave a
pumpkin spice latte, but there was no Starbucks in
Rolling Brook. The closest thing to it was the Dutchman's Tea Shop, and I didn't want it that badly. I was
afraid of the surprise ingredients my cotrustee would
throw in, like a ghost chili pepper.

Mattie stepped into the shop just as I was about to
open. "Angie, I'm impressed." She placed the huge
tray of Amish cookies from her family's bakery on the
long table next to the percolating coffeepot. "You have
everything ready."

I smiled. "All I did was move the chairs together and

put on the coffee. You're the one who cut all the pieces. That's the hard work."

"I wasn't going to say that." She laughed and hung her cloak and bonnet on one of the pegs on the wall.

The shop was open for business, and the class was set to start at eleven. It wouldn't be long before class members would begin arriving. Our regulars liked to arrive early to share township gossip and the treats the Millers' bakery provided for the classes.

The bell on the door jangled, and I looked up from counting money in the cash drawer to find Willow Moon standing in the doorway. Willow wasn't your typical Amish Country resident. She was about sixty and had close-cropped hair that was dyed lavender. She hung a crystal around her neck and wore her signature gauzy blouse that seemed to float midair around her.

Willow clapped her hands in front of her chest, and her blouse fluttered. "Angie, thank goodness you're here. I've been dying to talk to you about the book sale. Your mother and I have been on the phone this morning, already hammering out all the details."

Mattie shot me a look. She understood how a conversation between those two women could be dangerous.

Willow removed the short crocheted cape from her shoulders and tossed it on one of the pegs.

"Mom mentioned she asked you to help out, Willow. We really appreciate it—"

"It's no trouble at all." The crystal hanging from Willow's neck sparkled as she moved. "I thrive on township events like this, and there is no better cause than the library. What a wonderful way for the trustees to partner with the English and Amish communities in Rolling Brook."

I had to agree with her. "Yes, but I'm not sure there will be a book sale, because of the murder. I doubt the library will let Austina be involved. They have put her on unpaid leave," I said.

"Murder? Bah." Willow waved away this concern. "The library won't let that stop them. I spoke with the library director this morning, and she was thrilled we still wanted to host the book sale."

"She was?" I asked.

"Certainly. The library doesn't want what happened to cloud their services to the county." She paced around the room, touching all the fabric lining the wall as she went. "It is unfortunate that we no longer have the bookmobile, but the library has a delivery truck they use to move books between the branches. The director said we could use that to transfer the book sale books out to the pie factory."

Mattie held the edge of her black apron. "It's still going to be held in the parking lot of my brother's factory? Does my brother know this?"

"Not yet, but he will," Willow promised. "I'm headed straight to the bakery after I leave here."

I closed the cash drawer. "I had planned to go to the library today to talk to them about the book sale, but it sounds like you handled everything."

"Oh, no," Willow said. "You should. In fact, we should go together. When do you plan to go to the library?" she asked.

"After my quilting class this morning. It will be finished by one."

"Oh dear, I have a hair appointment at one I can't reschedule." She patted her short pixie cut. "I'm thinking of going a dark purple for autumn. Maybe plum."

"Really, it's okay. I can go by myself if you think it's necessary," I said. Thank goodness for that hair appointment. "I think plum will bring out your eyes."

She beamed. "Really?" She fussed with her hair. It didn't move.

I wondered how much mousse held it in place.

"And yes, I do think it is necessary for you to go. You can snoop about the murder. Do you think Austina murdered that bishop?" Willow asked.

I blinked at her rapid change of subject. "No, of course not," I said, but even I recognized the doubt in my voice. "Her motive is too ridiculous. Murder over library books? That's pretty far-fetched, don't you think?"

"You of all people should know that people in this township have been murdered over less."

Willow was right. I did know that, but I still couldn't believe Austina was responsible. Why would she put her career and her very life in jeopardy for library books?

The bell on the door jangled and the first of our students arrived. Lois, one of our regulars, who was wearing her signature green plastic-framed glasses, beamed. "Look at those cookies. You always have the best spread, Angie."

I laughed. "That's thanks to the Millers' bakery across the street."

"Are you joining our class today, Willow?" asked Shirley, who came in next and who wanted to make a quilt for her daughter's wedding—even though her daughter was about to celebrate her first anniversary with her husband.

Willow shook her head and sent her blouse flying into her face. "No, I'm afraid I have to return to the tea shop." She pointed at me. "Angie, I want a full report about your visit to the library. I will be at the Prim and Curl until four."

"Four? I thought your appointment was at one?" I asked.

She waved her hand. "Beauty takes time, my dear."

"There's something else my mom and you have in common," I muttered.

"Oh, I know, didn't I tell you? Your mother and I have an appointment at the Prim and Curl together. Daphne said that she's been looking for a new salon since she moved here, so I invited her. We thought it might be a good time for us to plan more of the book sale."

Heaven help me. With Mom's and Willow's powers combined, I was in deep trouble.

"In that case, I will stop by the Prim and Curl before your appointment ends."

She beamed. "I'll tell Daphne."

If she tells my mother that there is a far-off chance I will be there, I had better show up, because Mom will expect it.

After Willow left, Mattie stood in the middle of the circle of quilters. "Ladies." Her voice quavered.

The rest of the ladies had arrived for the class. Anna

usually led the classes, but she was helping Jonah on the farm that morning. I hoped she wasn't stuck turkey wrangling. Thankfully, Mattie agreed to step in.

Mattie opened her mouth again, but no words came out, and her hands shook.

Mattie was a star at helping customers one-on-one, but my shy assistant didn't enjoy being the center of attention. In fact, when she volunteered to substitute teach the class for Anna, I had been surprised. I'd been proud too. She had changed a lot since she started working for me the year before. She was more confident and self-assured. Both are qualities valued in the *Englisch* world, but less so in the Amish, and I often wondered what Aaron, her older brother and Rachel's husband, thought of his younger sister's transformation.

I was about to step in and get the class's attention, when Mattie straightened her shoulders. "Ladies, are you ready to begin?" This time, her voice was strong and commanding. I wondered whether she was channeling a little bit of Anna's persona for inspiration.

The chattering settled down and the ladies still at the cookie table quickly found their seats. Mattie beamed at them. "Let's start with the filling." Mattie held up the pumpkin she'd made the week before as an example.

I beamed too.

As class progressed around me, the students chattered. Midway through, Mattie gave the students a break to replenish their cookies and coffee. The pumpkins came along nicely. I thought this might be our cutest project yet for the class.

I grinned to myself, but that grin was soon wiped off my face when I saw Martha Yoder walk by my main window and peer in. She caught me watching her and pivoted around, heading straight for Authentic Amish Quilts next door. Would there ever be peace between the two of us?

I returned to the refreshment table in time to catch the tail end of what Lois was saying. "I can't help but wonder if the killer was really trying to get back at Austina. She's prickly for a librarian. Shouldn't librarians be friendlier?"

"I've never thought of Austina as prickly," Shirley countered as she filled her plate with cookies. She selected two peanut butter ones. "Though she is no-nonsense."

Lois adjusted her glasses on her nose. "Maybe that's why the staff at the library disliked her so much."

I filled my mug with hot water from the carafe. "They don't like her?"

"Can't stand her," Lois said. "In fact, I've heard them grumble about it in public."

Shirley clicked her tongue. "That's shameful."

"What's the complaint?" I asked.

"Much of what Lois said, I suppose," Shirley answered. "Austina ruffles feathers."

I picked up a snickerdoodle—my favorite—and munched on it thoughtfully. Maybe the ladies were right. What if the killer was some irate employee, such as crazy Bunny, who offed the bishop to frame the librarian. But then again, that seemed like a long way to go. As far as I knew, Austina was alone in the bookmobile almost every day since she'd fired Bunny, so she spent very little time with the rest of the library staff. In any case, it was a lead worth checking out, and I was happy to have this extra nugget of information before I visited the library that afternoon.

Break was over and the ladies returned to their seats.

Two ladies to my right were sewing the tops of their pumpkins. I took a seat on the edge of the circle and worked on piecing a quilt that my quilting circle would quilt later that month for a client. Christmas orders for quilts were coming in fast and furious. Of all the business ventures I had undertaken to promote the store, the custom-made Amish quilts were the most profitable.

"If you ask me, another Amish person bonked the bishop over the head."

"Why?" Shirley asked around a bite of peanut butter cookie.

Lois lowered her voice. "It had to be an Amish killer. My guess is one from his very own district. No one else cared enough to kill him."

I leaned closer to hear whether they had any suspicions as to who the actual Amish killer could be, when my needle dug under my fingernail. I yelped, sticking my finger into my mouth.

"Angie? Are you all right?" Mattie asked.

The entire class stared at me, and I felt my complexion flush. "Sorry. I guess I was distracted while I was doing the last touches on this quilt piece." I held it up to show the shades of purple.

"It's lovely," one of the class members said.

"Take care not to get blood on it," another advised.

"Right." I stood up hastily and headed to the small bathroom in the back of the shop.

In the tiny restroom, I let the cold water from the tap run over my bleeding finger.

Was Lois right? I couldn't get her last statement out of my head. "It had to be an Amish killer. My guess is one from his very own district. No one else cared enough to kill him."

Chapter Seventeen

After the quilting class ended and the last few members had left with quilted pumpkins and Rachel's cookies in hand, I told Mattie I was going out for a bit.

My assistant pointed at Dodger, who was now awake and scaling the wall of fabric bolts. "Don't leave him here with me."

I plucked the cat from the wall and nuzzled him under my chin. "He's not so bad."

Dodger purred.

"*Ya*, he is." Mattie pressed her lips into a thin line. "The last time you left him here, he shredded two pincushions."

"He thought they were cat toys," I said in my cat's defense. "They were shaped like little birds."

Mattie threw up her arms. "Okay, fine, but if he eats anything, it won't be my fault."

"I never said it would be."

I gave Dodger one more snuggle and set him on my aunt's rocker by the picture window. From there, he had a clear view of all the happenings up and down the street. I hoped he would have more interest in that than in terrorizing Mattie and destroying my shop.

Over his gray shoulder, he gave Mattie a smug smile that only a cat could master.

Mattie scowled in return.

Two more buggies went down the street toward the pie factory.

"There seems to be a lot of traffic headed to your brother's factory," I said.

Mattie came to stand next to me in front of the window. "The grand opening is tomorrow. Aaron asked some families in our district if they would like to sell their produce there."

"Like a little farmers' market?" I asked. "That's a great idea."

Mattie nodded. "He hopes it'll be successful enough to do once a week."

"Why haven't I heard about this before?"

"It wasn't actually his idea. Willow suggested it after the bookmobile was driven away from the factory."

"You mean after the bishop was killed."

She nodded.

A wagon full of pumpkins moved down the street. Jeremiah Leham was in the driver seat.

"It is a good idea," I said.

"Aaron hopes it will help people forget about what happened there in the bookmobile."

I plucked my jacket and Oliver's leash from the peg on the wall. "I'll check it out when I get back from the library."

Oliver licked Dodger's cheek and waddled over to me.

"The devil cat and I will take care of things here," Mattie grumbled.

I grinned. "I knew I could count on you."

Oliver and I headed out the door.

From Austina's description, I had a good idea of where Bunny's apartment was since it was near the Holmes County Courthouse and the Double Dime Diner, but to be sure, I punched the address into my GPS. The automated woman's voice chirped at me to go right.

Oliver growled at the device suction-cupped to my windshield. He hated the GPS woman, especially when she was recalculating.

The woman's voice led me right to my destination. Bunny's apartment building was in a flat-faced, nondescript structure I had never taken any notice of before. Austina had said it had been a hardware store in another life, but I couldn't see that. Now it was divided into apartments. I parallel-parked on the street and got out of the car. I looked up at the window, and a curtain moved.

"Angie!" Jessica waved to me from across the street.

One of my closest friends, Jessica Nicolson owned an antiques shop called Out of Time that was directly across the street. I removed Oliver's leash from my hobo bag and clipped it on his collar before crossing the street. His made an irritated snuffling sound. He was not a fan of the leash unless we were going on a *real* walk.

Jessica leaned her broom against her shop window and knelt in front of Oliver. "I've missed you, old guy."

Oliver snuffled again. He didn't like being called

old. Maybe we were both going through a little midlife crisis?

Jessica chuckled as if she understood. "Angie, I haven't seen you in a while. Is the sheriff keeping you busy?" She wiggled her eyebrows.

"Please," I muttered.

That only made Jessica laugh.

"Are you here to pick up your mother's candlesticks? The UPS man just dropped them off. I gave her a call, but she said she had a hair appointment and would come later in the week."

I shook my head. "I didn't know about the candlesticks, but I can take them for her if you want. I'll be seeing her later this afternoon."

Jessica shook her head, sending her shoulder-length strawberry blond hair waving back and forth. "No, that's all right. I'd much rather lure her into the shop. I received a gorgeous Edwardian platter that I plan to tempt her with."

"You're terrible."

"You know she loves it."

It was true. There were few things my mother loved more than interior design. Beauty pageants would be one. And I supposed Dad and me, but I suspect we tied for third.

"And I've been having a blast helping her find pieces to furnish the new house. It's refreshing how she wants to use antiques instead of put together pieces from Ikea." She gave a mock shiver.

I didn't say anything. My entire house was outfitted in Ikea. It fit my budget. Most of the money I earned I put back into the shop.

"So if you're not here for the candlesticks, why are you here? Not that I don't love a visit from you and Oliver, but you have on your Mission Impossible Angie face. I'm thinking this isn't a social call."

"What's my Mission Impossible Angie face?" I asked.

"It's a face where you look all determined. You squint a little too." She squinted at me as if imitating my expression. "If you're not careful, your face will stay that way."

Great. I had a face that gave away when I was investigating. I tried to force my eyes not to squint. "You sound like my mom."

"Like I said, she's a smart woman. I see you're trying not to squint. You can't fight the Mission Impossible Angie face," she said as she picked up her broom and began to sweep away the fallen leaves from the sidewalk in front of her shop.

"So what is the mission?"

I sighed, giving up. "What can you tell me about the building across the street?"

"The apartment building?"

I nodded and studied it. I thought I saw the curtain move again, but that might have been a trick of the sunlight off the windowpane.

"I can't tell you much of anything. I don't even know who owns it. It seems to me the tenants are a revolving door of renters. I always seem to see different ones come and go out of there."

"Do you know anyone by the name of Bunny Gallagher?"

She stopped sweeping. "Bunny? Is that a real name?"

"I'm afraid so."

She shook her head. "Nope, and I think I would remember a Bunny." She narrowed her eyes at me. "Why do you ask?"

"Did you hear about Bishop Beiler?"

She frowned. "Is that the bishop who died in the bookmobile?"

I nodded.

"No, wait." She held up hands in a universal stop sign. "Don't tell me that you're snooping into that crime."

I tried not to squint.

She pointed at me. "You are."

My shoulder drooped. "I found the body, and Austina, the librarian who is the primary suspect, asked me to look into it."

"I thought you were getting out of the murder business."

I placed a hand to my chest in mock horror. "I'm not in the murder business."

It was her turn to roll her eyes. "I wasn't saying that you committed the murders, but you like to solve the murders."

I knew what she meant. "Well, no one has been killed recently."

She shook her head. "Mitchell is not going to like this. Do you want to ruin the relationship you have with him?"

"No," I said defensively. "But Mitchell knew me as a snoop before he knew me as a girlfriend, so he should understand."

She pursed her lips as if she didn't believe it. "I'm coming with you."

"Coming with me where?"

"To talk to Bunny."

"You can't do that," I said. "Who will watch your shop?"

She waved away my concern. "It's the middle of the week and business has been slow. I think your mom is the only walk-in I've had in days."

I bit my lip.

"Don't worry. My online business is going gangbusters." She pushed open the door, tucked the broom inside, and turned the sign on the door that read, BE BACK IN TEN MINUTES.

"This might take longer than ten minutes."

She still held the door open. "Don't worry."

Oliver wiggled through the opening.

"Oliver," I called.

"It's best to leave him in there. Cherry Cat will want to see him anyway. My other two cats, not so much."

"You're right. It is going to be hard enough to convince Bunny to talk to us without Oliver in tow."

She locked the door and shook the handle a couple of times to make sure it was secure. "Let's ride."

At the apartment building, we stepped through a set of glass doors. There was another set of glass doors that were locked.

On the wall, there was an intercom. All we had to do was buzz the right apartment. Unfortunately, none of the apartment numbers had names attached to them.

Jessica slid her finger along the buttons. "Maybe we should hit them all like they do on television until some fool buzzes us in."

"I guess that might be worth a try."

She moved her finger toward the buttons, and I caught it just in time. "On second thought, let's not. What if someone calls the cops? I don't think Mitchell wants to spring me from Millersburg city police lockup."

She dropped her hand. "Good point."

As Jessica and I stood there trying to decide what to do next, a young man in a denim jacket jogged down the steps inside the building. He opened the glass door between us and the rest of the building. The young man held the door for us. "Do you need inside?" He held the door open widely.

"Thanks," I said as we slipped through.

He gave me a wink.

After he had gone, Jessica clicked her tongue. "Hasn't anyone ever taught him you shouldn't let people you don't know into a locked building? We could be killers."

"It's lucky then that we're not. The problem is, we still don't know which apartment belongs to Bunny."

Before the stairwell, there was a mail room to our left. I stepped inside and was happy to see that the mailboxes were labeled not only with the unit numbers but also with the occupants' last names.

Gallagher 2A. "Bingo," I said. If my understanding of the building was right, 2A was the apartment number with the moving curtain.

"You're a regular Sherlock." Jessica gave me a high-five.

I grinned at her.

There was no elevator, so we took the stairs. "Ready?" I asked.

"Ready," she answered, taking a fighting stance.

I groaned and knocked on the door. We could hear shuffling inside. When the door finally flew open, we were met with the business end of a shotgun.

Chapter Eighteen

Jessica and I dove to opposite sides of the doorway as if the shotgun had fired.

"Greg!" A woman's deep voice echoed through the apartment. "Put that thing away before you kill someone."

Yes, please. Great idea.

The large woman ripped the shotgun from the man's hand. "Your program is on the television, and I made you a grilled cheese. It's on the TV tray with a glass of milk."

He blinked at her as if he wasn't completely sure who she was. "Is there tomato on the grilled cheese?"

Her stern face softened just a fraction. It was a small crack in the tough exterior. "Yes. I made it just how you like it."

He beamed at her and clapped his hands as he turned and disappeared into the apartment.

"It's not loaded," she said to us after the man disappeared.

Good to know. Tell that to my heart stuck in my throat.

"It makes him feel more secure to have the gun," she went on. He's never had any bullets, though. I'm not dumb enough to let him have ammo." She examined us. "Whatever you're selling, I don't want it. Whatever charity you're raising money for, I don't care."

I was still trying to recover my voice after thinking I was about to have my head blown off. Thankfully, Jessica was more together. "Are you Bunny Gallagher?"

"What's it to you?"

I took that as a yes.

Jessica folded her arms. "We're friends of Austina Shaker and wanted to talk to you about her."

"Then you're no friend of mine." She started to shut the door.

I recovered enough to stick my boot in between the doorjamb and the closing door. I thought maybe she was going to slam the door on my foot, but was relieved when she stopped just short of crushing my toes. "Please. We want to talk to you about Bishop Beiler too."

"Are you from the police?" she asked. Thankfully, she didn't seem to recognize me from the scene outside the bookmobile two days earlier.

I opened my mouth, but Jessica was faster. "We're aiding the police with their investigation, yes."

I groaned. If it got back to Mitchell that Jessica and I were impersonating an officer, he would flip his lid.

Bunny sniffed and seemed to take this at face value. "I wasn't there when the bishop got killed. I was already fired by then."

"But you knew him," I said, trying not to look at the

shotgun in her hand. Even though she held it by the barrel, it still made me nervous.

She squinted at me. After a beat, she said, "Yes, I knew him. He stopped by the bookmobile to tell us to leave his district dozens of times. I would have been happy to leave his district be. It was Austina who insisted that we stay. She felt she was in the right, and no one was going to make her think otherwise, especially not some crazy Amish bishop. People like Austina can only see right or wrong. There's a lot of gray in this world, and we all have to make our way in it." She shot a glance over her shoulder.

Behind her, the television began to roar. Greg yelled something, presumably at the screen.

"I took that money because Greg needed it. He needs a lot of care, and my pathetic paycheck cannot cover it. You don't work at a library for the money," she said bitterly.

I decided not to mention that there were plenty of options other than stealing.

"I think now that they see that Austina has killed someone, they will give me my old job back." She gritted her teeth. "This time, I will demand a raise."

"You still stole from the library," I said.

"Stealing isn't as bad as killing someone," she said matter-of-factly.

I supposed that was technically true, but I wouldn't hold my breath that the library would reinstate her. "Did you have any contact with the bishop since being fired by the library?"

"No." She scowled. "Why would I? What do I care

what any of the Amish do. Bunch of bonnet-wearing freaks, if you ask me."

I balled my fists at my sides. *No hitting, Angie,* I reminded myself.

She gripped the barrel of the shotgun so tightly her knuckles turned white.

There was gunfire on the television, and Greg hollered again.

Bunny looked over her shoulder and back at us. "I'll be there in a second, you crazy old man!"

Jessica and I shared a wince.

"Where were you the night the bishop was murdered?" I asked, doing my best to sound like Mitchell.

She glared at me. "Not that it's any of *your* business, but I was right here with my husband. He will vouch for me."

Her husband was clearly senile. I didn't think he was much in the way of an alibi.

Bunny moved to close the door, but I didn't remove my foot from the threshold into her apartment. "Bunny, do you really think that Austina killed the bishop?"

She screwed up her mouth and then relaxed it. "I sure do. That woman is capable of anything. She fired me, and she knows the condition Greg is in. I hope she goes straight to jail—even if she didn't do it."

I clenched my teeth.

She shrugged. "The Amish I knew from the bookmobile didn't care a whit about Bishop Bartholomew Beiler. Can't say I blame them. He was a mean s—"

"We get the picture," Jessica said. "I think we should let you get back to your husband."

"Don't come back," Bunny said, and closed the door.

This time she meant business, and I removed my foot just in the nick of time.

"You almost lost a toe there," Jessica said.

"As bad as that might be, I think I'd be more upset if she'd scuffed my boot." I inspected my prized cowboy boot for any sign of trauma. It was okay.

I followed Jessica down the stairs and across the street back to her shop. She unlocked the door and let us inside.

I closed the door behind us and saluted Sir Richard, the suit of armor that stood by the door. At one time, my father had wanted to buy it from Jessica. Thankfully, my mother and good sense prevailed and he'd given up that idea.

"That woman is a piece of work," Jessica said.

I shivered.

"Where are you off to now?"

"The library," I said. "I hope to find out more about Bunny and Austina there."

"Do you still consider Austina a suspect?"

I chewed my lip. "I don't know. I don't want to, but . . ." I trailed off.

Jessica folded her arms. "If you don't believe Austina, at least not completely, then why are you involved in this case?"

"Because I want to believe her, and Sarah's family is tangled up in this mess too. Her brother-in-law is going to marry the bishop's daughter."

She frowned.

"I need to get going. I promised to meet with Mom and Willow at the hair salon later. They're there plotting the library book sale." I shuddered.

This made Jessica smile, as I knew it would.

I whistled for Oliver, but he didn't appear. I knew where to find him. I wove through the tangle of furniture and odds and ends. It was a wonder Jessica could find anything in the store. It didn't have any organization as far as I could tell.

Oliver was exactly where I expected him to be: behind the counter on the other side of the curtain that separated the main floor of the shop from Jessica's even more disorganized office and stockroom. He and Cherry Cat were curled up together in her cat bed. Oliver was a little too big for the small bed, so his back end spilled over the side. Cherry Cat was washing the top of his head as if he were one of her kittens.

Cherry Cat was Dodger's biological mother, so she and Oliver had had a close friendship ever since we adopted the little gray-and-white furball. Unfortunately, Dodger didn't inherit his mother's prim and proper ways. I finally gave up on curtains and resorted to miniblinds in my house after Dodger had shredded three sets. He could destroy them much faster than I could make new ones.

"Oliver, it's time to go. We're going on an errand but then we are going to see Grandma," I said in a singsong voice.

He lifted his head, knocking Cherry Cat under the chin. The solid gray feline hissed slightly, and Oliver whimpered an apology.

Jessica shook a finger at the cat. "Cherry Cat, don't you be mean to poor old Oliver."

Oliver squished up his flat face. There was that "old" word again.

"Oliver," I said, "let's go."

He gave a great sigh and then wiggled out of the bed. Cherry Cat fell to the side at the loss of her canine pillow. She didn't hiss, but gave me a withering look. I had seen the same expression on Dodger's face hundreds of times. Like mother, like son.

"Do you really think there will still be a book sale?" Jessica asked.

"Looks that way."

She frowned. "It doesn't seem right with everything that has happened."

I shrugged and silently agreed.

Chapter Nineteen

The main county library was on the outskirts of Millersburg on an access road. Beyond the library was woodland where Rachel's father, a rogue Amish man named Nahum Shetler, called home. Unease settled over me as it always did when I thought of Rachel and her father. I wanted Rachel to make peace with the man who'd abandoned her when she was a baby, but she wasn't ready to do that. I couldn't force her, even though I thought it would be good for her to do it. Months earlier, she had made me promise not to bring Nahum up in conversation. She said she would tell me when she was ready to talk to him. I was starting to think that time would never come.

The library's parking lot was covered with fallen leaves. An Amish man with a gas-powered leaf blower on his back blew them into a pile on the side yard, where another Amish man raked them into the bag. It wasn't until I was out of my car that I noticed that the man with the leaf blower was Jonah.

Beside me, Oliver cowered at the noise the leaf blower made. He slid to the car's floorboards and buried his head under the front passenger's seat. Poor guy. Leaf blowers weren't as scary as birds, but they came in a close second.

I unbuckled my seat belt and leaned over to pat his rump. "You'd better stay in here, Ollie."

He shivered in reply.

I grabbed my hobo bag from the backseat, cracked a window for Oliver, and got out of my car. He'd be fine in the car for a few minutes. The sun was out and the temperature held steady in the midfifties.

"Jo-Jo!" I called.

He didn't respond but continued to blow leaves.

"Jonah!"

Nothing.

I sighed and spotted a goat eating leaves under one of the trees. Petunia was tied to the tree with a long length of rope. An oak leaf hung from her bottom lip, and when she saw me she strained against the rope. I walked over to her. Nubian goats were not little pygmies. Her head was level with my waist. I scratched her between the ears. She accepted the caress, and then strained against the rope again in the direction of my car.

I patted her head. "Oliver is in there, but he's afraid of the leaf blower."

The goat blew air out of her mouth in a sigh, and the leaf still on her lips fluttered onto the grass.

Jonah remained oblivious, but his companion pointed to me with his rake. Jonah turned around and found me standing there with Petunia.

After what seemed like forever, he shut off the leaf blower.

"Thank you!" I shouted at the top of my voice as if the leaf blower was still going at full throttle.

Jonah joined Petunia and me under the tree. I wasn't too surprised to see Jonah on library lawn service. My lifelong friend would do any small job to make a dollar or two. He was always looking for ways to make money quickly. The leaf blower was new, though.

"What are you doing here?" I asked.

"*Mamm* didn't tell you about my new business venture?" Jonah asked.

"Umm, no, she didn't."

He rested the hose of the leaf blower against his right shoulder like a soldier standing at attention with his rifle. I kept the comparison to myself because, as an Amish pacifist, Jonah wouldn't like it. "You see," he said, "I've given up on the livestock thing to make my way in the world. The geese were a disaster, and I'm learning the turkeys aren't much better."

I was happy Oliver was in the car. He might have passed out just from hearing the word "turkey" after his encounter with Jonah's flock. "When did this new business venture start?"

He grinned. "This morning."

I rolled my eyes. Of course.

"We're clearing the library's lawn of leaves for free. This is so we can talk to folks and build up some business. Lots of people, such as yourself, have stopped us and asked. We already have our first paying job lined up."

I examined the contraption on his back. "That does not look like an Amish lawn tool," I teased.

"Sure it is," he said with a laugh. "It's gas powered, like my refrigerator, and it doesn't have any of the newfangled electricity that you *Englischers* are so fond of. Levi here is on the rake because he's not allowed to use the leaf blower." Jonah half covered his mouth. "Which is fine with me; raking by hand takes forever."

"Levi Leham?" I asked.

He nodded. "Levi and I make a *gut* team. He rakes while I blow."

Across the yard, Levi dropped a handful of leaves into the enormous brown paper lawn bag. I studied him. He was built much like his brother. He had a compact muscular frame, but he appeared to be taller than Jeremiah and his hair was a darker shade of brown. There wasn't any red hue to it that I could see peeking out from under his black stocking cap.

I frowned at Jonah. "You could have told me that you were in business with someone connected to Bartholomew's murder."

Jonah scoffed. "He doesn't have anything to do with the murder."

"How can you say that? He's engaged to the bishop's daughter."

Jonah groaned. "Is there anything that happens in the county that you don't know?"

"I make it my business to know." I folded my arms.

Petunia head-butted me in the hip. Not hard enough to knock me over, but she got my attention.

"And Petunia? Is she part of this business venture too?" I asked.

He grinned. "She is now. Miriam insisted I take her with me. We had a small incident this morning."

Petunia ducked her head as if ashamed. I didn't buy it and arched my eyebrows at my childhood friend.

Jonah tugged on his sandy beard. "Petunia broke into Miriam's root cellar and ate half of my wife's cabbage harvest before we caught her in the act."

"How many cabbages did she eat?"

"At least eight."

"I'm surprised she's not sick. Should she see a vet after eating that much?"

He shook his head. "I saw her eat barbed wire once."

I grimaced.

"Miriam will calm down. She always does, and the more I think about it, the more I believe that it was a *gut* idea to bring Petunia with us. The more leaves she eats, the less we have to bag out, and she attracts attention too. That's how we got the paying job. The man who spoke with us loves goats."

"Who doesn't love goats?" I asked.

"Miriam."

I refrained from asking what Miriam actually liked, but it was on the tip of my tongue. I eyed Petunia. "Are you sure that rope is secure?" Petunia had a reputation for being an escape artist.

"It's fine," he said with more confidence than I felt.

Levi joined us. "Jonah, that bag is full."

"They are filling up fast." Jonah pointed at the Amish buggy tethered to the hitching post on the other side of the parking lot. "We have another in the buggy."

Levi nodded and started toward Jonah's buggy and his horse, Maggie.

I stopped him. "You're Jeremiah's brother. I don't think we've met."

He gave me a level look. "We haven't."

"And Bartholomew Beiler was your bishop?"

Levi made a pained expression. *"Ya."*

Jonah shifted from one foot to the other.

"I'm sorry about your bishop."

He nodded. "It's terrible what happened. The whole district is a mess over it."

"How is Faith?" I asked.

His eyes snapped in my direction. "Faith? Do you know her?"

I took a step back. "Well, no, but I heard you were engaged to her. I'm friends with Sarah," I added, even though Sarah was not my source for this information.

His shoulders relaxed. "I should have known. I forgot that my sister-in-law is a member of your sewing group."

We were quilters, so we weren't exactly in a sewing group, but I didn't bother to correct him. "Sarah is a good friend."

"And a gossip." There was a hint of bitterness in his voice.

I didn't correct him here either. What he said may have been true, but I didn't care for his tone.

Jonah lowered the hose of his leaf blower from his shoulder. "I figured Levi needed to do something to keep him occupied during this difficult time, so I offered him this job cleaning up leaves with me."

"I'm grateful to have it," Levi said. "There is so much gloom and doom in the district right now. It is nice to escape it." He looked at me. "And Faith is struggling. Anyone in her position would be. She lost her father and her bishop in the same moment." He stared at the library. "It does seem strange that I would be working outside of the district today, but work is *gut* for the soul. That's the lesson Bishop Beiler always taught. He did not abide idle hands."

"I've met a few others from your district recently," I said.

"Who?" he asked.

"Phoebe and Phillip Truber. I met them at the school on Hock Trail."

I felt Jonah watching me.

Thankfully, Levi didn't ask me why I had been to the school.

"Do you know them?"

He didn't answer.

"What about Gil Kauffman?" I asked, suspecting I was pushing my luck.

He scowled, proving me right. "We have a small district—everyone knows everyone." He stepped away and resumed raking. I could take a hint. The conversation was over.

Jonah cleared his throat. "What brings you to the library? Don't tell me you don't have enough to read already."

I lifted my chin as if offended. "A true reader never has enough to read."

He laughed.

"Actually, I'm here to talk to some of Austina's co-workers."

Jonah sighed. "Angie."

"I promised I would help her." If I lifted my chin any higher, I would get a crick in my neck.

Levi threw his rake on the ground. "Are you talking about that librarian who killed the bishop?"

"She's a librarian who's a suspect for the bishop's murder."

He scowled at me again. "How could you help someone who did such a horrible act?"

"I don't believe she did it." I held my ground.

"But are you sure?" Levi asked.

I squirmed under his scrutiny. The truth was, I wasn't sure. Before the murder, Austina had been merely a friendly acquaintance. It wasn't like the time that my best friend, Rachel Miller, had been accused of murder and I knew with every fiber of my being that she was innocent. But I did not know Austina as well, so I couldn't be one hundred percent certain. Doubt is a dangerous rope to walk.

Jonah saved me from answering and slapped Levi on the arm. "These leaves aren't going to rake themselves. Let's get back to work." He fired up the leaf blower and any further conversation was impossible.

I gave him a grateful smile.

Chapter Twenty

I stepped into the library building. There were two workers talking to a patron at the circulation desk. I recognized them but didn't know them well. The woman must have recognized me too, because she said, "Amber is in picture books."

Even though it was the main county library, it wasn't large. It encompassed one big room, and the staff could see every section from children's to audiobooks from the circulation desk.

I found Amber kneeling in front of one of the three-foot-high picture book shelves. She sorted a stack of colorful books on the carpeted floor in front of her. Seeing those books, I suddenly had a pang that I didn't have a child to read them to. At thirty-five, I would have thought I would have children by now. My ex-fiancé had wanted to put marriage and children off even though we had been together six years before he proposed to me. It was for the best. I couldn't imagine dividing a child between Ohio and Texas, where Ryan still lived. I pushed the glum thoughts aside. Thirty-five was just a number, and I had time.

And it wasn't like I didn't have a child in my life. Mitchell's nine-year-old son, Zander, was a hoot. Many times, when Mitchell had an emergency call and Zander's mother, Hillary, wasn't available, he would drop Z by my house or the shop to keep an eye on him.

I wouldn't go as far as to say I was a parent figure to Z. He had two loving parents already, but we had become good buddies over the last few months. If he was no longer a part of my life, it would almost be as difficult to bear as if I'd lost the sheriff.

Amber smiled up at me. "Hi, Angie. I didn't expect you today. You were here earlier in the week to pick up your holds. Did you finish them already?"

I shook my head. "Not yet."

Last Christmas, Amber's best friend was murdered, and I had helped bring the killer to justice. Through the experience we had become friends, and I visited her every time I came into the library to feed my reading habit, which was at least once a week.

Her smile dissolved. "You're here about Austina."

I nodded.

She twisted her mouth. "I wondered if you would be involved in it. I heard you and Austina found the body."

I leaned on the short bookshelf. "What can you tell me about Austina?"

She shot a glance at her coworkers at the desk. "Let's go outside and talk." She stood up with her stack of picture books and placed them on top of a metal library cart standing a few feet away. "I'm going to take my break," she said, loudly enough for the staff at the desk to hear.

The man working at the desk nodded absentmindedly. The woman didn't even turn from her computer screen.

I followed Amber out the front door. Outside, I expected to find Jonah and Levi still there, but they had left.

"Oliver is hiding in my car. He was afraid of that leaf blower," I explained. "Is it okay if I take him out to walk around a bit?"

She shook her head. "Oh, sure—go ahead."

As I went to my car to let Oliver out, she went over to a red picnic table under a huge oak tree. The tree was half bare but still had more leaves to drop. Jonah and Levi would have to come to the library again to finish the job. She wrapped her arms around herself and shivered.

I reached into the back of my car and grabbed the wool blanket that I always kept there. It was the same blanket I had given Austina after I'd found her with the body. The blanket was covered with Oliver's fur, but I didn't think Amber would mind.

Oliver tentatively jumped to the pavement and pressed his nose to the blacktop as we walked across the parking lot. I suspected he was looking for evidence to prove the evil leaf blower was really gone. He whimpered and looked at me. He must have caught a whiff of Petunia. He sighed when he realized she was gone. Oliver trotted after me to the picnic table.

Amber smiled at him. "Nice to see you, Oliver."

He sniffed the toes of her riding boots in return.

I handed Amber the blanket. "Thanks. I guess I should have stopped and grabbed my coat before coming out here." She smiled. "But this will work just fine."

I sat on the top of the picnic table next to her. The

wooden surface felt like sitting on an ice cube. I shifted in my seat and put my feet on the bench.

"So what can you tell me about Austina?"

Amber snuggled under the blanket. "There's not much to tell. I worked with her, probably more than a lot of the others in the library. I've been filling in at the bookmobile a lot lately."

"Since she fired Bunny," I said.

She gripped the blanket closer to her shoulders. "You know about that?"

"Austina told me, and I just spoke with Bunny a little while ago. There was a shotgun involved."

Amber's mouth fell open as she listened to my tale. "I knew Bunny was cuckoo for Cocoa Puffs, but geez . . ."

"I came to that determination too," I said. "Is there anything else you can tell me about her?"

She shook her head. "Not really. Like Austina, she worked exclusively on the bookmobile. I might see her every once in a while at an all-staff meeting, but it was pretty rare."

"You didn't work on the bookmobile before?"

She lifted her legs and folded them underneath her, cross-legged. "Not until after Bunny was fired, and I started my new position."

"New position?"

She grinned. "I'm not a shelver anymore. I'm a library assistant. I can do all sorts of new stuff like catalog books and run circulation reports." Her eyes glittered at the thought of circulation reports. Clearly Amber had a different relationship with statistics than I did. "I'm thinking of going to library school after college."

"That's great, Amber. You'll make the perfect librarian."

"Thanks!" She beamed. "I think my dad is happy I finally settled on something. He can't stand indecision. I changed my major at least five times. The last time I changed it I thought he was going to pop a blood vessel."

I knew her father's impatience firsthand from our work as township trustees together. We spent many hours in meetings, usually on opposite sides of an argument.

"But back to Bunny. Like I said, I don't know her, but she's kind of oafish. Big-boned, my grandmother would say, because it's somehow nicer than heavy. In my mind, someone named Bunny would be more a cheerleader type. You know, bouncy and perky. Bunny reminds me more of an ox."

I grimaced.

"She was fired a couple of weeks ago. I don't know why. That stuff is confidential."

Oliver jumped after a leaf blown across the grass by the cool breeze.

"She stole fine money from the bookmobile," I said.

"That would do it. It's an unforgivable sin in the library world." She shook her head as if she couldn't imagine anyone doing such a thing. "I don't know how she and Austina worked together, trapped in the bookmobile for all those years. Even though I didn't see them often, it was clear they didn't like each other."

"What makes you think that?" I shoved my hands into my coat pockets.

"The looks they shot each other behind the other's back, or the way they grumbled about each other under their breaths. Our director even tried to separate them by looking for another staff member to work on the bookmobile, but no one volunteered. No one wanted to work with Austina or Bunny."

"Okay, so Bunny definitely had a problem with Austina. What about anyone else on staff?" I asked.

She shook her head. "I can't think of anyone else at the library who had a problem with her. No one was around her enough. Other than Bunny, I had the most contact with Austina, and that was just lately."

"Was Austina difficult to work with?"

Amber picked a fallen leaf off the table and twirled it between her fingers. "She's all right. She treats the bookmobile like her private domain. I'm still learning the ropes there, so I don't argue with her."

"But you weren't on the bookmobile the day before Bartholomew died."

She shook her head. "I would only go out with Austina if she was visiting the large district. The Beiler district is so small that Austina could handle it herself. I stayed back and worked here. We're short-staffed all over the library system because of budget cuts, so the director wants me to fill in where I'm needed the most."

Oliver rolled in the grass at our feet, and Amber smiled at his antics.

"That makes sense. Did you ever see the bishop?"

"Once. Here at the main library."

"He came here?"

She nodded. "He wanted to speak to the library director. I suppose it was to complain about Austina and the bookmobile. I can't think of any other reason he would walk into the library. You should have seen the sneer he had on his face when he was here and saw all the books. He hated them." She shivered. "How can anyone hate books?"

"I don't think it is so much the books that Bartholomew hated, but the ideas they hold."

She twirled her leaf. "That makes it somehow worse."

"Did he talk to the director?"

"No." She let the leaf fall to the grass. "It was a Saturday, and the library director never works on the weekend. We told him he was welcome to come back and talk to her another day, but he never did."

"When was that?"

"About a week ago. I hadn't thought about it much until now." She hopped off the picnic table. "I'd better get back to work. I only get a fifteen-minute break."

"One more question."

She turned to look at me with her eyebrows raised.

"Do you know where the keys to the bookmobile are in the library workroom? Austina said there were two there."

She nodded.

"Have they gone missing?"

"Not that I've noticed. I saw them there today."

"Did you see them the day the bishop was killed?"

Amber thought for a moment. "I think I did, but I can't be one hundred percent sure. Why?"

"Someone got into the bookmobile, and I want to know where that key came from."

"Let me ask around to see if anyone noticed them missing. I'll text to let you know."

I smiled. "Tha—"

But my thank-you was cut off when a familiar-looking mustard yellow sedan sped into the parking lot.

"Uh-oh," Amber muttered.

My sentiments exactly.

Bunny stopped her car directly in front of the book drop by the front door. She paused just long enough this time to slam her car door before storming inside the library.

Amber ran for the library. Oliver and I were two paces behind her.

I ushered Oliver through the glass doors. The library had a no-dogs policy, but I didn't think the library staff even noticed, with Bunny standing in front of the circulation desk with her hands on her hips.

"I want to speak to the director."

The young man at the desk licked his lips. "She's left for the d-day. She should be back tomorrow."

"I want to talk to her about getting my job back now that Austina is gone and killed someone. I'm the most qualified. I know how to run the bookmobile better than anyone."

A patron sitting at one of the computers quietly got up and bolted out the door. An Amish mother in the reading area with her child scooped up the child and did the same. I couldn't say I blamed them. Bunny looked like she was about to pop.

"And I want a raise," Bunny snapped. "You should pay me at least as much as Austina was making."

"You will have to take that all up with the director, and like I told you, she's not here," the young man said, still stammering.

Amber stepped forward. "We're going to have to ask

you to leave or we will call the police to escort you out."

Bunny spun around and glared at Amber. Tiny Amber was a third Bunny's size, but she held her ground and glared back for all she was worth. She really would make a terrific librarian.

There glare-off was interrupted when Bunny caught sight of me. "What are you doing here?" She gave me her death glare. "Don't you have your own life? Why are you so focused on mine?"

"I didn't come here to talk to you, Bunny. It's a public library. I had no idea you would be here," I said calmly.

"Likely story, after you come to my house and practically accuse me of murder." Spittle flew from her mouth.

Amber turned to me with wide eyes.

Sirens broke into the air.

"Did you hit the emergency button under the counter?" Bunny asked the trembling man at the circulation desk.

"Y-yes," he said.

"I can't believe this." She threw up her hands. "I come in here asking about my job and every last one of you overreacts."

As if we were the ones overreacting.

Bunny stormed out of the library and walked into two approaching police officers. Amber and I went to the glass door to watch. Oliver and the male library worker were hiding in the children's section somewhere.

The officers who arrived were from the Millersburg Police Department, not the sheriff's office. I was grateful for that. It would take longer for it to get back to Mitchell that I was on the scene when Bunny was arrested for disorderly conduct.

Even through the glass door we could hear Bunny yelling at the officers about being fired and Austina the killer librarian.

Amber shook her head. "She's not doing herself any favors."

"No, she's not," I agreed. And I thought I officially had my prime suspect for Bartholomew's murder.

Chapter Twenty-one

The Prim and Curl was on Clay Street, which ran perpendicular to Jackson Street, the main drag that ran through the center of Millersburg.

I snapped a leash on Oliver's collar despite his snuffling protests and decided to park in front of the courthouse and walk to the hair salon. It was a short walk.

Outside of the salon, my father was sitting at a park bench throwing scraps of donuts to the two mourning doves at his feet. Oliver saw the mourning doves at the same moment I did and dove under the nearest bush.

I waved at Dad and he shooed the birds away. One took off, but the other hopped a few feet away and didn't even bother to flutter his wings. That second dove must have really liked donuts. I couldn't say I blamed him; they had sprinkles.

I waved at Dad. Then I knelt on the sidewalk and reached into the bushes to pull Oliver out. It took a couple of tugs—he'd really wedged himself in there—but finally I grabbed him around the middle and yanked for all I was worth. After a second, he came flying out and into my arms, and I landed hard on my tailbone in the middle of the sidewalk.

Oliver was unharmed as I cradled him in my arms. We sat there panting for a moment, I from exertion, he from fear. When I had enough energy, I struggled to my feet and hobbled over to my father on the bench.

He grinned at me as I sat down. "Tough day?"

"It was okay." I told him about it, leaving out the part about being greeted at Bunny's door with a shotgun. There was no need to add that worry to my father's concerns, especially while my mother was redecorating. There was only so much a man could take.

I eyed the box of donuts, now resting on his ample shelf of a stomach. "How many were in there?"

"A dozen?" he said.

"You don't sound so sure of that."

He grinned. "Maybe a dozen plus."

I arched my brow. "And now there are three."

"I shared them with my friends." He pointed at the mourning dove that hopped in place. "I suppose Oliver would be upset if I called this winged creature a friend, but it's the truth." He reached over and patted Oliver on his back.

A few crumbs peppered the ground and the mourning dove pecked at the scraps all the while keeping a keen eye on my father. I suspected the bird was hoping for a larger offering. Oliver remained transfixed in his state of terror and he buried his head deeper into my armpit.

"Mom inside?" I pointed a thumb behind us to the salon.

He nodded. "She's been in there for hours. At this rate, I expect her to come out with a different face."

I chuckled. "What are you doing out here?"

He stared down at the donut he held delicately between his thumb and forefinger. It was a chocolate cake donut, his favorite. I was more of a maple cream stick kind of girl.

Dad sighed. "I didn't have anything else better to do."

I scooted closer to my dad. Since he'd retired, he had yet to find his footing in life after work. It was a huge adjustment for him to work every day for forty years and just stop. I knew he was having trouble finding a direction. He was of retirement age, but he could still work if he wanted to. His company was sorry to see him go, but he decided to retire so he and Mom could spend half of the year in Ohio with me.

"What about the woodworking Jonah was teaching you?"

He grimaced. "I discovered I'm not very good at it. When Jonah gave me a lesson, I almost cut off my thumb. Don't tell your mother I spent a small fortune on all those power tools."

"Oh, Dad." I sighed.

Dad bumped my shoulder. "Don't give me that look. It's bad enough I have to deal with your mother pitying me."

I rested my hand on Oliver's warm back. He'd finally stopped shivering. "I'm not pitying you, but I hate to think you're bored on my account."

"I would not trade seeing you for my job. Being here with you even if I am bored out of my skull is better than being in Texas away from you."

I kissed his cheek.

"Donut? It cures all ills." He shook the box at me.

I held out my hand, and he popped the maple cream stick into it. He got me.

"That's my girl."

I took a big bite, and the donut exploded in my mouth in a wave a sugary goodness. I suppressed a groan and told myself if I counted the donut as my lunch, then it wasn't that bad to indulge. I licked cream from the corner of my mouth. "You're not helping my diet."

"Diet?" Dad snorted. "Why do you need to be on a diet? You're perfect just the way you are."

I smiled. "Thanks, Dad."

"So, I have told you what I'm doing here. What brings you here?"

Oliver wiggled his nose out from under my arm. I suppose the smell of fresh cream stick overcame his fear of the mourning dove. I broke off a corner of the donut and fed it to him, careful not to give him any cream. Too much sugar wasn't good for him. Truth be told, the dough part of the donut wasn't great for him either, but my pooch was an emotional eater and he needed baked-good comfort at the moment. He got that from me.

After swallowing his morsel, he reburied his head.

"I need to talk to Mom and Willow about the library book sale. Mom drafted Willow to be our third coconspirator. Honestly, I'm hoping to turn the entire thing over to them. They're more than capable, and I have enough on my mind."

"Like the murder."

I nodded.

He polished off the remainder of his donut in one

bite and meticulously wiped his silver goatee with his napkin. "I hope you aren't getting involved in the investigation. I know you found the body, and that must have been terribly upsetting, but your involvement should start and end there."

I pursed my lips. "I have been asking a few questions. Nothing more than that. Austina is my friend, and I can't believe she would do this."

"And how does James feel about you asking questions?"

I scuffed the bottom of my boot across the grainy sidewalk. "He's not a fan."

"Ahh," Dad said, breaking the sound into four syllables. "Well, I won't tell you not to get involved because it sounds to me like you already are and I'm sure James will do his fair share to discourage you. But I do want you to promise me one thing."

I looked at him. "What's that?"

"I want you to be careful. Be careful for me."

"Always."

He sighed and picked up the last donut. My dad was an emotional eater too.

I patted my father on the knee. "Want to come in with me?"

He glanced at the door. "No, thank you. I was in there for five minutes when we first arrived. I barely came out with my life."

I stared at the glass door. "What happened?"

"You'll see."

On that ominous note, I stood up. The mourning dove finally flew away. Not that Oliver witnessed its departure. He was too busy hiding from it. I faced the bench to peer through the salon's large storefront window. Inside there was a flurry of activity as hairstylists and manicurists fluttered around the room with hair dryers and nail polish in hand. I couldn't see my mother or Willow. It wasn't a place I was eager to take Oliver into after his encounter with the mourning dove. He had no fear of people, but the busyness of the place might grate on his fragile nerves.

Dad seemed to understand my hesitation and said, "Leave Oliver out here with me. I'll keep close watch on him while you go into the battle zone."

I agreed and handed Oliver to my father. Even though the mourning dove was long gone, Oliver wasn't taking any chances. He curled into a tight ball on my father's lap. As I walked away, I heard my father whisper, "Here, have a donut—it will take the edge off."

I pretended I didn't hear that.

Chapter Twenty-two

A s I opened the front door of Prim and Curl, the scent of hair dye and spray hit me like a flatiron to the face. I waved the cloud away from my nose and narrowed my itchy eyes. I would need a shower after visiting this place. I sneezed.

A perky young girl sat at the reception desk. "God bless you! Welcome to Prim and Curl. We're here to make you beautiful." She delivered these lines with flawless precision, and I wondered how many times she had repeated those very words.

"I'm looking for Daphne Braddock. I was supposed to me—"

The phone rang and she held up one finger to me, indicating I should wait. "Prim and Curl. We're here to make you beautiful." That line again.

I peeked around the corner. The place was packed. Not surprisingly, there wasn't an Amish person in sight. I glanced at my watch; it was a little after three.

The receptionist began tapping on her keyboard with the tips of her improbably long fingernails, which were painted a bright pink. "Yes, Velma," she said. "I can squeeze you in for a nail appointment next week. Let me check availability." There was a pause. "I'm so sorry, but the only availability we have next week is Thursday."

While Prim and Curl Girl was occupied, I skirted around the dividing wall that separated the reception area from the rest of the salon.

She waved frantically at me to come back, but I ignored her. I didn't have all the time in the world, and I wasn't going to stand there and listen to her negotiate an appointment time with Velma for the next half hour.

No one noticed me as I scanned the room for my mother and Willow. I didn't see them, so I tapped the nearest stylist on the shoulder.

She looked at me, and I wiggled my fingers at her. "Can you tell me where I can find Daphne Braddock or Willow Moon? I'm Daphne's daughter. I was supposed to meet them here." Two ladies across from us laughed uproariously at something another stylist said. The sound was deafening in the already tight space. "Wow, this place is jumping."

The stylist used a round hairbrush on her client's hair. "It's to die Thursday."

"To die?" I made a face.

"Not *die* as in dead. *Dye* as in hair. Two Dye Thursday is when we have two hair coloring treatments for the price of one. It's a special promotion we do every month. As you can see, it's very popular. It's kind of like a get-your-hair-done-and-treat-a-friend thing." She stepped closer to me as she moved around her client's head, brushing out and brushing down. It looked exhausting. As much as my curls drove me crazy, at least they were low maintenance. I didn't even blow-dry my hair unless I was willing to walk around all day as a puff ball.

"You're all done," she said to her client. "I'll meet you at the counter."

"Thank you," the client said. "You're a miracle worker, Delia."

Delia smiled, displaying perfectly straight white teeth. "The pleasure is all mine." She turned to me. "Can I interest you in Two Dye Thursday?" She stood on her tiptoes as if trying to get a good look at the top of my head. "You could use a little something to cover the beginning of those grays."

I clapped my hand on the top of my head. "Grays? What grays? I don't have gray hair."

"Just one or two. I can pluck them out for you."

I backed away from her with my hand still firmly on the top of my head. "No, no plucking. And I'm not dying my hair either." My hair was one of my features I was most pleased with—it was long, blond, and wildly curly. It was my identity.

She smiled. "Sorry. Occupational hazard. I always drive my family crazy over the holidays because I want to fix their hair." She lowered her voice. "Do you know I actually have a cousin who has a mullet? He's had it for decades." She shivered. "I would disown him if I could."

Her comment brought to mind the difficult practice of Amish shunning. I supposed what Delia wanted to do to her cousin wasn't that much different.

"Your mom is in the back of the shop. She and Willow are under the shake-and-bake."

"They're where?" I decided that Delia the hairstylist spoke in riddles, and I wasn't privy to the game.

"It's my little name for the dryers. It's to the left." She pointed to the back of the salon with her hair dryer. "At the back of the salon there is a room where the dryers are. That's also where we do the mani-pedis. It's a little calmer back there."

I thanked her and headed to the back of the salon. It was much quieter there. Two manicurists worked on clients in one corner of the room, and I found my mother and Willow sitting side by side under matching heat lamps.

Mom held a yellow legal pad on her lap that was almost completely covered with writing. Willow also had a legal pad, but hers was blank. Clearly, she let my mother serve as secretary. Good move. Mom took meticulous notes.

"Hey, Mom," I said over the whirl of machines.

Mom peered at me over her legal pad. "Angie, you're finally here! Willow and I were discussing whether or not you would ever show up."

"Thanks for the vote of confidence," I muttered.

My mother went on as if she hadn't heard my grumble. "We have some amazing news about the book sale."

There was a small black manicurist's stool a few feet away from me. I kicked it with my foot over to where my mother and Willow sat. I thought I would have to sit down for this conversation.

"After leaving your shop this morning," Willow said. "I stopped by the Millers' bakery. It took convincing, but Aaron agreed to allow the library book sale to continue as planned tomorrow and Saturday. He also is going to have a farmers' market in conjunction with the book sale and the grand opening for his pie factory."

"Mattie told me."

Mom clapped her hands. "Excellent. We have Friends of the Library and other volunteers bringing the books from the library this afternoon."

"And we have a tent being set up in the factory parking lot as we speak," Willow added.

I started to stand. "It sounds to me like the two of you have this all sorted out. You have it well in hand. I will let you take it all over."

"Oh, no," my mother said. "You are not going to weasel out of helping us."

"I wasn't trying to weasel," I whined. My mother brought the whiner out in me.

Mom tapped her freshly manicured fingernail on her legal pad for emphasis. "Yes, you were. I could tell by the way you were inching toward the exit. We need you."

"Why on earth would you need me?"

Willow smiled. "Because you being there will put the Amish at ease." Her eyes glittered. "And it will be a perfect chance for you to snoop."

I was about to argue with her when Delia came back. "Ladies, your color should be set. My assistants will come back to wash you out."

I took that as my cue to beat a hasty retreat.

Delia grabbed my hand midair. "Your cuticles! They are a disaster."

I wrenched my hand away and peered at my nails. They weren't that bad.

Delia clicked her tongue. "You could really use a decent manicure."

I hid my hand behind my back. "My nails are fine."

"Delia's right," my mother chimed in. "Give her a manicure, Delia, and put it on my tab."

Her tab? My mother was running a tab at Prim and Curl? Did my father know about this?

Delia smiled. "Luckily, I had a cancellation, so I can squeeze you in right now."

"Delia is a master," Willow said. "You won't regret it. I don't know how she does it."

The hairstylist blushed. "I'll do my best." She picked up my hand. "I think I will have to do some serious filing. I'd better get out my big file."

"Your big file?" My nails were cut short, but I didn't think they looked that bad. Although I had to admit, they weren't as lovely as they had been when I lived in Dallas. In my old advertising office, manicures had been a way of life to keep up with fashionable ladies in the department. I ended up in the seat across from Delia and had my fingers dipped in a bowl of soapy water.

Delia held up two bottles of nail polish. "Pink or red?"

I sighed. "Can I have blue?"

She smiled. "You got it."

Chapter Twenty-three

I left Prim and Curl with a serious headache from inhaling all the fumes and an amazing manicure. Mom was right. Delia was a genius when it came to nails. After I collected Oliver from my father, I walked back to my car.

I was busy admiring my nails on the stroll back. "Umph," I grunted when I walked into someone. I looked up from my manicure and found the elderly Nahum Shetler standing in front of me. I hadn't seen Nahum face-to-face in several months. His face was deeply wrinkled from hours in the sun, and his Amish beard grizzled, giving him a wild, untamed appearance that I had once compared to Rip Van Winkle's after waking from his twenty-year slumber.

Nahum curled his lip at me. "You!"

"Hello to you too," I said.

Oliver hid behind my legs.

The Amish man scowled.

Nahum is always such a nice guy, I thought sarcastically. I still marveled at how he could be Rachel's biological father. She was the sweetest person on the planet, and he could double for Gollum from *The Lord of the Rings*. This proved the nurture over nature theory.

His frown deepened. "How is my daughter?"

"Rachel?" I squeaked.

He folded his arms. "She is the only daughter I have."

I swallowed. "Rachel is fine."

He looked away from me. "I am glad she is well. Knowing that is all I need."

I swallowed. "She and her husband are opening the pie factory in Rolling Brook this weekend." I mentally clapped a hand over my mouth. Rachel would kill me if she knew I'd spoken to Nahum about her.

"I've heard about that. I thought of going, but she won't want me there."

"Do you want to talk to her? She is your only daughter."

"Don't meddle in things you can't possibly understand." He clenched his teeth.

I bit the inside of my bottom lip, holding back a smart retort. "She needs to know her father," I said. I couldn't help myself.

He held on to the end of his unruly beard. "What do you know of it? Did she tell you she wanted to talk to me?"

I shoved my hands in my jacket pockets. "Not exactly."

He tossed his beard onto his shoulder. "Then she does not."

"You could have a relationship with her if you chose to," I said, keenly aware that I was breaking my promise to Rachel by getting involved in her relationship with her father. "Rachel was an innocent baby when you sent her to live with her mother's family. She had no choice in the matter. Now, as an adult, she has a choice to see you."

His dark eyes narrowed. "You seem to think *you* always know the right from wrong. It will be a sad day for you when you find out the truth."

I had a feeling we weren't talking about Rachel any longer. "What are you talking about?"

He leaned in, and I could smell stale coffee on his breath. "I have heard you're poking your nose into the death of Bartholomew Beiler."

I didn't say anything, but I took a step back out of range. I bumped into Oliver, who shuffled out of the way.

He smirked. "So it is true. Not that I doubted my sources."

"You have sources?" My eyebrows rose. "Who would those be?"

"Your friend the librarian isn't so innocent," he said in a harsh whisper.

My body tensed. "How do you know that?"

"I know because I saw her coming from the library van late at night. She was there close to after midnight, and then she drove way."

I swallowed. "It's called a bookmobile."

"Does the name matter?" He snorted. "She came out of the vehicle where Bartholomew died, long before you found her and reported it to the police."

A chill ran down my spine.

"I see I planted a tiny kernel of doubt in your mind. It's a terrible thing, doubt. It is sure to grow whether we choose to feed it or not."

"Have you told this to the police?" I asked.

His eyes narrowed. "I have no use for your *Englisch* rule of law. Maybe I will, maybe I won't." He smiled. "But you can tell them. You should tell them, shouldn't you? Will you tell your sheriff who you seem to care so much about, or will you keep it a secret to protect your friend? Have I put you in a tough spot?" He stepped around me and walked away.

I stared after him, knowing I should call Mitchell that very second. It was important information in the case, but part of me wanted to talk to Austina first. Maybe she could explain why she was at the bookmobile so late at night. Why hadn't she told me? Didn't she ask for my help? How could I help her if I didn't have all the facts?

I picked up Oliver and hurried back toward my car at a light jog. What I didn't ask Nahum was what he was doing around Rachel and Aaron's pie factory at night.

I headed back to the shop. Running Stitch was quiet when I arrived. We didn't have any customers. Mattie asked if she could go to the pie factory to help her brother prepare for the grand opening the next day. I let her go. I had a lot to think about—mainly about whether I would tell Mitchell what I'd just learned from Nahum.

As she was tying on her bonnet, Mattie said, "You should come down to the factory after you close the shop for the day. Aaron is having a tasting for the fall pies. He wants to have some new offerings for Thanksgiving and wants to showcase them this weekend too."

I perked up. "Pie tasting? Now you're speaking my language."

She laughed. "Come after the shop closes. I'll tell him to wait for you."

I rubbed my hands together. "Excellent."

She smiled and left.

Even with the promise of pie, I couldn't shake the uneasy feeling that had settled over me when I ran into Nahum in Millersburg. I knew I should call Mitchell and tell him what I knew. I didn't want our relationship to be built on anything other than trust. I had already had one engagement fall apart. I didn't want my relationship with the sheriff to end in the same way.

I pulled my cell phone out of my pocket and decided that, if he answered, I would confess everything. If he didn't answer, well, I'd tried, right?

The phone rang twice and went directly to voice mail, indicating that Mitchell had silenced it. He could be in a meeting or in the middle of a takedown; I never knew. In any case, my conscience was cleared. I tried to tell him about Austina and the bookmobile, but he wasn't available to hear about it. I told myself this was the kind of information that shouldn't be left in a voice mail.

At four thirty, I locked Dodger inside Running Stitch— Oliver and I would pick him up on the way home—and made our way up the street to Miller's Amish Pie Factory. The bakery, the Millers' first business, was already closed for the day and the lights were out.

I kicked at a leaf on the sidewalk, and Oliver galloped after it. I wondered whether I should tell Rachel about my conversation with her father. He didn't want to talk to her. If I told her that, it would hurt her. That's the last thing I wanted. I only wanted Rachel to be happy. I thought making peace with her father was the best way for her to do that, but was I right? Rachel appeared to be happy on the surface, but there had been a melancholy cloud hovering over her the last year, ever since her father had resurfaced.

Sugartree Road was lined with small maple trees bursting in fall color and looked like red-orange torches guiding Oliver and me up the sidewalk. A buggy clopped up the street, and I waved to the driver. It was another shopkeeper. The quaintness of Rolling Brook struck me. It was not the sort of place where you would expect murder to occur, but it had, and more than once.

Instead of going in the front entrance, I went around back to the parking lot, so that I could have a view of the book sale setup.

As promised, the volunteers had set up a white tent there for the library book sale, as well as half a dozen Amish farm stands for the farmers' market Aaron was trying out that weekend. I hoped it would help. A weekly farmers' market would bring lots of business to Rolling Brook. I could see the advantages that it would bring, both as a business owner on Sugartree Street and as a township trustee.

Beyond the book sale tent and the farmers' stands there was a thick tree line. I could easily imagine Nahum watching the bookmobile from those trees. For a second time, I wished that I had asked him why he had been there. Not that I thought he would have told me.

I opened the back door and stepped into the factory. The door immediately opened into a long, narrow room. There were windows on either side of the room that peeked out onto the factory floor so that those visiting the bakery could watch the production. On the other side of the glass, huge vats of milk, sugar, and spices stood in galvanized containers. The Amish bakers measured ingredients out and poured them into giant mixing bowls that could swallow a person whole.

Fluorescent lighting filled the viewing room and the factory floor. There was electricity, yes, but not as much as you would see in an English factory. The Millers' Amish district allowed them to use electricity where it was required by English law, in order to follow FDA regulations for preparing and selling food. The milk and other dairy products were in refrigerated cases. There was no motorized conveyer belt. The Amish workers walked from station to station rolling the materials and ingredients they needed on carts.

Aaron, Rachel, and Mattie were all in the viewing room. A long folding table was set up and there was a line of ten pies on it.

They weren't alone. There were three other Amish people with them. Two middle-aged women whom I recognized from town, but I didn't know their names. The third person I knew. It was Phillip Truber, Phoebe's brother, who had stormed into the schoolhouse the day before, and he didn't look happy to see me.

Chapter Twenty-four

Phillip continued to scowl as I hovered in the doorway. I hadn't come to the pie factory to deal with the bishop's murder. In fact, I was looking forward to escaping from it for a bit. My thoughts were so muddled when it came to Austina's case.

Mattie waved me over. "Angie, you're just in time. We were about to start the tasting. I told Aaron to wait for you."

I shook myself and forced myself to pay attention. There was pie that needed tasting, and by golly, I was up for the challenge. I could always think better after a dose of sugar. It was my brain food.

Oliver's toenails clicked on the laminate floor as we moved across it.

I grinned. "Thanks for inviting me. You know I can always be counted on to taste your baked goods, Aaron."

Rachel's quiet husband nodded. "*Ya*, I do know this."

I nodded at Phillip. "Nice to see you again."

His scowl deepened. "Is it?"

Rachel frowned. "Do you know each other?"

"I met Phillip yesterday when I was talking to his sister Phoebe."

"*Ya*," Phillip said. "Angie was at my sister's school." He pressed his lips into a disapproving line.

Aaron's frown matched his. He probably suspected that I had been meddling again, which I had been.

Rachel's brow wrinkled. I knew dozens of questions were flashing through her head, but she wouldn't ask me until we were alone and away from her husband. Aaron had come a long way since I had met him, but he still wouldn't want his wife—or his sister, for that matter—involved in a murder investigation, even if the murder occurred on his property.

Rachel said, "Phillip works here."

I raised my eyebrows in surprise.

Aaron nodded. "Since I can't be two places at one time, I hired him a couple of weeks ago to oversee the operations in the pie factory."

"He used to work in a smaller bakery in Wayne County," Mattie said.

I wished she had told me all this yesterday.

Phillip nodded. "The pie factory is much closer to my home. I'm grateful for that."

I had so many questions running through my head, but I forced myself to be quiet. I hoped Mattie had the answers. I planned to grill her later.

Rachel picked up a knife and started cutting into the pies. The scents of pumpkin and cinnamon filled the room.

Oliver danced at my feet.

"I know that pumpkin and apple are the traditional

pies for the holidays, but I wanted to offer a signature pie from the factory. We will sell it in the shop too. I'd like it to be one we have each year. It's a celebration of the factory finally opening." Aaron met my eyes. "We could not have done that without you, Angie. You know my family and I are so grateful."

I grinned. "I find it my duty to protect everyone's right to pie."

Rachel and Mattie laughed. Aaron smiled. As far as I knew, he never laughed, but a smile was a victory in my opinion.

Phillip folded his arms and scowled. Clearly, he was not enjoying this, and he probably would have bolted the moment I walked into the factory if it hadn't been his job to stay there.

Mattie handed each of us a notecard and a pencil. "After you taste them all, number your favorites one to ten."

Rachel lined up the cut pieces on the table. Five small pieces from each pie. I chose the pumpkin fluff first. I had been eyeing it since I'd set foot in the factory. The first bite dissolved in my mouth. It was like a whipped pumpkin dream.

I took two more bites, swallowed, and pointed at it with my fork. "This one. Definitely."

Mattie laughed. "You haven't even tried the others."

"I don't have to. I know this is it." I set down my plate and picked up the next sample, an apple cinnamon roll pie. "But I will try the others in the name of product research."

The apple cinnamon was wonderful too. Actually,

each pie was delicious, but nothing beat the pumpkin fluff in my mind. When I thought no one was looking, I went back for seconds of that one.

"Trying to steal an extra slice of the pumpkin fluff?" a voice asked.

I froze with the pie knife suspended in the air.

Phillip Truber took the knife from my hand and cut me a generous piece. I was definitely counting this tasting as my dinner tonight.

I accepted the plate from him. "Thanks. I could eat the entire pie myself, and I'm definitely getting one of these for my dad when they go into production. I can already hear his lips smacking. I inherited my sweet tooth from him."

Phillip watched me. "You talk a lot."

I shrugged. There was no denying it.

"The pumpkin fluff is my recipe," he said.

I raised my fork to him. "My compliments to the baker."

Rachel, Aaron, and Mattie were on the other side of the room near the cash register, tabulating the votes.

He nodded. "Thank you." He started to stack dirty plates and silverware into a plastic tub. He didn't look up from his work when he asked, "Why were you visiting my sister's school yesterday?"

I shoved another forkful of pie into my mouth.

"I know it has something to do with the bishop's death." His brow furrowed. "You couldn't possibly believe that my sister had anything to do with it. Are you the reason the police came to my house later that day?"

I swallowed and wished I had a glass of water. "The police came to your house?"

"Ya." He glared at me. "They wanted to talk to Phoebe too. I can only assume that that is your fault."

I took a breath. "I suppose in a way it is."

He narrowed his eyes in surprise that I would admit to it so readily.

"I saw Phoebe on Wednesday when I stopped by the bookmobile. When I got there, Austina and the bishop were arguing."

"She wasn't in the bookmobile," he said, a little too sharply.

"N-no, but it was parked right outside her school-house, so she witnessed the argument. She was in the doorway of her school."

His shoulders relaxed. "That is not my sister's fault."

"Of course it's not, but I had to tell the police she was there. Maybe she saw something I missed. I'm sorry the police came to your house, but they have to investigate Bartholomew's murder."

His eyes narrowed. "But you do not."

I didn't say anything.

His eyes slid my way. "You have a reputation in the county as being nosy."

"Oh, well, then you've found me out." I forced a laugh.

His shoulders relaxed just a little bit more.

"Did your bishop know you were working here?"

His guard was back up. "What does it matter?"

"This is a New Order business with electricity, and a lot of machinery . . ." I trailed off.

"This is a *gut* place for me to be," he snapped. "I have to care for my wife and for my children. This job allows me to get them everything they need."

It was a strange sentiment from an Amish man, especially one from such a strict district. Typically, they believed that God would provide.

As if he'd read my mind, he said, "*Gott* provided me this job."

I set my empty plate on the table. "So the bishop didn't approve?"

"What does it matter now? The man is dead."

"Someone killed him," I said.

"I have work to do," he said, brushing past me.

I watched him go, wondering what he wasn't telling me.

Chapter Twenty-five

"Pumpkin fluff is the winner," Aaron announced. "Very *gut* work, Phillip."

Phillip nodded at his boss. *"Danki."*

Aaron offered one of his rare smiles, this time for his baker. "I knew it was a *gut* decision when I hired you."

Phillip walked over to him so that they could discuss the pies.

Oliver waddled over to me, licking his chops.

"Hey," I said. "I hope you're not eating pie."

Rachel smiled. "I gave him my pie crust—none of the filling, I promise."

I looked down at the little black-and-white dog, and he cocked his head at me, making his black ear higher than his white one. Then he stood on his hind legs and licked my hand.

"What am I going to do with you?" I wagged my finger at Oliver and then at Rachel. "And what am I going to do with you?"

She chuckled.

I suddenly felt very tired. "I'd better head home. It's been an especially long day."

Rachel pointed at my hand. "I see you got your nails painted."

"My mother."

Rachel grinned as if that was explanation enough. "I'll walk you out."

I waved to everyone else, and Rachel and I headed for the exit.

I zipped up my jacket when we got outside. In the parking lot, the large white tent for the book sale looked like a ghost of a house, and the farm stands cast long shadows on the pavement. A cold breeze whipped through the tent, causing its end to flap open.

Oliver whimpered and I bent to pick him up. The movement of the waving tent flaps was a little too bird-like for his taste.

I shivered, wishing I had worn a warmer jacket. It wouldn't be long until it was time to get out the hats and mittens. I wasn't looking forward to it. I loved Ohio, but the winters were a little more than I had bargained for. Last winter I would not have gone out at all if the sheriff and Zander hadn't forced me to go sledding. I packed a pretty mean snowball, after all.

"I'm surprised that Aaron will allow the book sale to go on as planned after what happened."

Rachel frowned. "After almost losing the pie factory last year, he is reluctant to give the township trustees any excuse to close him down."

It was my turn to frown.

She squeezed my hand. "It is all right, Angie. Aaron knew what he was doing when he allowed the book sale to go on. You don't need to fix it."

"Okay, but if any of them give you a tough time, you would tell me, wouldn't you?"

She smiled. "So you can knock their heads together."

"Something like that."

Rachel wrapped her cloak around her arms. "I saw you talking to Phillip. What was that about?"

"The bishop."

She nodded. "I thought that was it. Did he tell you anything?"

I shook my head. "Not really."

Rachel rested her hand on her cheek. "He's a great baker, and Aaron is very happy with his work." She frowned. "But he's not the friendliest man. Aaron said this does not matter because he is working in the factory, which is away from the public." Rachel touched my shoulder. "What is it, Angie? Is something else wrong?"

I smiled at my best friend. When I lived in Dallas, I had many friends. As my mother's daughter and Ryan's fiancé, I had been part of the social scene there, whether I wanted to be or not. But none of the friendship held the same sincerity that I found with my friends in Holmes County, especially the one I had with Rachel. That was probably why my heart broke over her relationship with her father.

"Sort of," I said. "I learned something today that I need to tell Mitchell, but I haven't yet."

She studied me. "Why haven't you told him?"

"I'm not sure." That wasn't completely truthful. I knew I didn't tell Mitchell because it made Austina look bad. In my mind, Bunny was the much more likely killer. A year earlier, I wouldn't have been conflicted at all about keeping that information from him, but things had changed. I knew my loyalty should be to him over Austina.

"What did you learn?" Rachel stamped her small feet against the cold.

Here was the other tricky part. If I told Rachel, her father would come up in the conversation. She asked me not to bring him up again, but maybe it would be all right in this case since it was related to the crime.

"Someone told me he saw someone leaving the bookmobile on Wednesday morning long before my mom and I found Austina there with the body."

"Who did this person see?"

"Austina."

She winced. "Does the person think Austina killed him?"

I nodded.

"Then he should go to the police. If he goes, then you don't have to worry about telling the sheriff yourself."

"I'm not sure he will. He's Amish."

"Who is it? Do I know him?"

"Um, kind of. He's your father."

The light dulled in her eyes, and the curiosity I had just seen there vanished.

"I need to talk to your father again," I said. "He might know more about this case. And when Mitchell finds out, he will definitely want to talk to him."

"Why are you telling me this?" Rachel wouldn't look at me. "There's nothing to stop you from talking to him."

"I don't want you to hear it from a third party or think I'm meddling in your life."

"Angie, you have nothing to worry about. I have made peace with my past," she said in her quiet way.

I wrinkled my nose.

"Don't give me that face. I have." She stood straighter. "Until you ran into my father last Christmas, I hardly thought of him."

"And now?" I couldn't stop myself from asking.

"It doesn't matter."

I didn't say anything.

She adjusted the cloak on her shoulders. "I can tell by the weight of your silence. You don't believe me."

"I want you to be okay. That's all," I said just above a whisper.

Oliver reached a paw out to her as if seconding my sentiments.

She held his paw. "I am okay. I have my husband, my children, and *gut* friends like you. I don't need anyone else."

I tried to imagine what it would be like without my father in my life. I didn't like the image. My dad was my rock. My mother tended to panic and wanted to fix things, so he was the one whom I leaned on when I was in trouble. It was my father who I told first when my engagement broke up. And it was my father who told me that he was glad and thought Ryan was a punk, which was the perfect reaction for the circumstances.

"Please, don't talk to my father about me. Promise me you won't. If you need to talk to him about Austina and Bartholomew, that is fine. You do what you need to do for Austina. But leave me out of it."

I opened my mouth to protest. Now would be a bad time to tell her I invited Nahum to the pie factory's grand opening tomorrow.

She looked up and met my eyes. There were tears in hers. "I'm asking you as my best friend—promise me."

It was the first time that Rachel had called me that. We weren't in middle school where we would trade bracelets or anything, but it still meant the world to me. Rachel was my best friend too. The corner of my own eyes began to itch. "I won't mention your name. I promise."

She smiled and went back inside the pie factory.

Chapter Twenty-six

The next morning, my alarm went off at seven and I groaned. Dodger jumped on my legs and walked the length of my body. I kept my eyes closed, as if to fool the cat that I was still asleep.

I had had a fitful night's sleep as my conscience nagged me that I needed to tell Mitchell everything that I'd learned. Finally, at two in the morning, I had sent him a text message telling him I had information about the case. Usually, Mitchell slept with his phone under his pillow, so he always heard it. Part of me had expected a call to clear my conscience. No call came. Instead of making me feel better, it worried me that he was out on the road somewhere or possibly in danger. It wasn't easy dating a cop; the nagging concern for his safety was always at the back of my mind. His first wife had warned me it would be like this. I hadn't wanted to believe her.

Dodger pawed at my nose, and I ducked under the covers. He smacked me in the face through the blankets like a boxer alternating between his right and left cross. He packed quite a punch for such a small creature.

I heard a whimper on the floor. I didn't know if Oliver was whimpering because Dodger was beating the stuffing out of me or because he was ready for breakfast too.

I shot up in my bed. "All right, already."

Dodger went flying across the room and hissed.

I leaned over the edge of the bed. "Are you okay?"

He gave me the evil eye. It appeared the only thing that was injured was his dignity. There would be payback, and it would come when I least expected it.

Oliver ran over to him, and licked him up one side of the face and down the other.

Dodger, now covered in doggy slobber, winced.

"Oliver, don't worry. He's fine."

Dodger mewed a complaint. I feared my slippers would be shredded while I was out today.

I pushed my curls out of my face and my cell phone rang. Maybe it was Mitchell. I reached across to the nightstand for my phone.

There was no caller ID. "Hello?"

"Angie, it's Sarah." Her voice was so soft, I could barely make out her words.

"Sarah, is everything okay?"

"*Ya.*" Her voice was still distant. "I need you to come over to my farm."

"Where are you calling from?"

"The shed phone down the road."

I was wide awake now. "Why? Has something happened? Are you all right?"

"I'm fine. My family is fine." She paused. "Most of my family. Levi is here and very upset. I'm afraid he might do something."

"Something like what?" I hopped out of bed.

"I don't know. He's so distraught. I'm afraid he might hurt himself."

I threw open my dresser drawer looking for something to wear. "Maybe you should call the police."

"*Nee*. The police can do nothing."

I grabbed a hair tie off of my nightstand. I was surprised that I actually had one left, and that Dodger hadn't batted it underneath the oven or my bed. "Did Levi say something?"

She lowered her voice even more. It was barely above a whisper. "Angie, he says it's his fault the bishop is dead."

I almost dropped the phone. "Don't let him leave. I'll be there as soon as I can."

I dressed at lightning speed. Oliver and I were out the door in two minutes. As I drove to the Lehams' farm, I couldn't help but wonder whether I was about to hear Levi's confession to the murder.

I called Mitchell on his cell phone. Again it went to voice mail, so I left a message. I was starting to worry. I almost called Hillary to find out whether she knew anything, since Mitchell would keep her informed because of Zander. Then I stopped myself. Things would have to become a lot worse before I called Hillary over Mitchell's whereabouts.

I called Jonah's shed phone too and left a message on his answering machine. I hoped he or Anna would hear it. I had a feeling that I would need them. Not for the first time, I wished my Amish friends carried cell phones. It certainly would make my life easier.

Sarah was standing on the wide front porch of her

house when I arrived. She waved at me. My typically carefree friend looked worried. She twisted the edge of her apron in her hands.

After getting out of the car, I opened the passenger door, and Oliver jumped out. He sniffed the ground, checking for birds. Thankfully, the Lehams were strictly vegetable farmers.

"Come on, Ollie," I said as I hurried to the porch.

I took the three steps at a run.

Sarah grabbed my arm. "*Danki* for coming, Angie. I didn't know what to do. Jeremiah isn't here. He's on a roofing job with my cousin. When the harvest is done, he works construction with my family."

"You're here alone with Levi?" I squeezed her hand.

She nodded. "All the children are at school. I'm happy for that. I would not want them to see their uncle in such a state. It was hard for me to see him this way. I was afraid to leave him to call you, but I knew this was more than I could handle on my own."

I hugged her. "I'm glad you did. You know you can call me anytime if you need anything."

"*Danki.* I know that." Her face was drawn with worry.

"Did you try anyone else?"

"I left a message for Anna on their shed phone, but I knew you would get the message faster."

I smiled. "I called Anna too. I'm sure she and Jonah will be over as soon as they hear the messages."

She nodded.

"Let's go in," I said.

She took a deep breath and opened the front door. To reach the kitchen, we walked through the living room.

The black potbelly stove in the corner of the room heated the entire house. Oliver went over to it and warmed his face.

We went straight to the kitchen, and he followed along too, probably in the hope he would get breakfast. We'd skipped it because we left in such a rush. Luckily I had enough time to fill Dodger's food bowl before I left. A hungry Dodger was a destructive Dodger.

There was no door between the living room and the eat-in kitchen, just a large archway. As I entered the room, I could see Levi sitting on the far end of the table with his head on the table and his arms wrapped around his head.

I shivered. He didn't seem to be breathing. I hoped he wasn't dead. Finding one dead body that week was already over my quota.

"Levi?" Sarah asked.

He lifted his head as if given a couple of jolts of electricity in his back.

His reaction made me jump. Okay, he was very much alive. That was one less worry. There were others. Levi Leham looked as if he'd gone on a bender. Depending on the district, some Amish were allowed to drink, but I seriously doubted alcohol of any kind was allowed in Bartholomew's district. And getting drunk was a big no-no in the entire Amish world. I didn't think any district condoned that. And Levi Leham was very, very drunk. "Who's that?" he slurred.

"It's my friend Angie—you met her yesterday." Sarah's voice was an octave higher than usual.

He blinked at me through bloodshot eyes. "You're that *Englischer* who's going to find out who killed the bishop." He snorted. "You found him." He dropped his head back onto his folded arms.

"I'll make some coffee," Sarah said.

"Good idea. Make it extra strong," I added in a whisper.

She nodded and went over to the stovetop.

I waited for Sarah to finish the coffee before I said anything more to Levi. I noticed the knuckles of his right hand were raw and cut as if he had punched a wall. I waved at Sarah and pointed at Levi's hands. She pursed her lips.

"Here you go, Levi." She put a steaming mug of coffee in front of him.

He lifted his head. The smell must have roused him. It was very strong.

He curled his right hand around the mug as if it were a lifeline. It made the cuts on his hands bleed.

Sarah clicked her tongue and went to the sink to wet a clean rag. "Let me see your hand."

Levi didn't argue. He gave it to her. She wrapped it around his hand three times and tied a knot in the middle of his palm. He didn't fight her, and covered the mug with his uninjured left hand. He'd yet to take a sip from it.

"What happened to your hand, Levi?" I asked.

He pulled the mug closer, right under his nose. "I hit a wall," he said dumbly.

"What kind of wall?"

"Barn wall." He grunted.

"Ahh, and where was that?" I tried to keep my voice low and friendly.

"At the Beiler farm."

I shot Sarah a look. She stood at the counter, drying breakfast dishes. Even in moments of crisis, Amish women had to keep busy. It was ingrained into them.

I scooted my chair closer to the table. "What were you doing there?"

He pulled the mug closer to himself, right under his nose. "I went there to see Faith. She's refused to see me ever since her father was killed."

"Why do you think that is?" I asked.

"Because I'm responsible for his death," he mumbled into his coffee mug.

"You hit him on the head?"

He looked up, meeting my gaze for the first time. I didn't break my eye contact and simply stared back. Finally he lowered his head and stared into the black abyss of his coffee. "*Nee*. I wasn't there when he died."

I flattened my palms onto the table. "Then why do you feel responsible?"

In my peripheral vision, I could see Sarah begin to dry faster.

His eyes were full of fire. "Because I was engaged to Faith, and Gil Kauffman is not. The bishop and Gil had planned for years that Gil and Faith would marry. Bartholomew was molding him to be the next leader in the district, but then Faith and I fell in love."

I froze. Was Sarah's brother-in-law about to tell me he had a motive for killing the bishop? The motive being the bishop had kept him from the woman he loved? That was pretty strong motive to murder someone. By the cuts on the knuckles, I knew Levi could be violent.

He surprised me by saying, "Bartholomew was a hard man, but he wasn't as horrible as everyone believed. It took some time, but he finally saw how miserable he was making Faith. He relented on his plan and allowed her to be engaged to me."

"How did Gil take that?" I asked.

He looked up at me with bloodshot eyes. "How do you think? He was furious and said that Bartholomew was betraying the district and letting his sentimentality rule his decisions instead of what *Gott* wanted. Gil only wanted to marry Faith to put himself in a better position to be bishop someday. He didn't love her, not like I do."

"Do you think Gil murdered the bishop?" Sarah asked, speaking for the first time since we entered the kitchen.

He dropped his head in his hands. "I know he did."

"You're sure?" I asked.

He nodded. "It's why Faith won't marry me now. She feels as responsible for her father's death as I do. She says it's fitting if she never marries, since she lost her father."

"And that's why you punched the barn wall."

He nodded miserably. "I know it was stupid to lash out like that, but I waited until after Faith told me and left the barn. I would never do anything to hurt or scare her." He gave us a pleading look.

I bit the inside of my lip. Like Levi, I had been cast aside by a fiancé. I understood how he felt. He was hurting, and on top of his injured hand, his pride had been badly bruised and his heart was broken.

Sarah set a mug of coffee, thankfully a less strong one, in front of me. I smiled my thanks. I was beginning to feel faint from the lack of caffeine.

Sarah clicked her tongue. "Faith has had a terrible shock. She will come around."

He shook his head. "She won't. She knew what she was doing. She even had a little speech planned out for me. She said it like she was reciting something she'd memorized."

I held my mug and let the warmth seep into my cold fingers. "Could someone else have told her what to say?"

"Who? Her father told her what to do most of her life and now he is dead."

Good question.

Sarah was more optimistic. "She will come around yet. She loves you. Give her time."

The front door on the other side of the archway opened.

"Sarah! Angie!" Jonah's voice rang through the house. Within seconds he was standing behind me in the kitchen. Jonah took one look at Levi and asked, "Levi Leham, are you drunk?"

I pushed back my chair and stood. "Levi has had a tough morning."

"Looks like it." He eyed me. "I got here as soon as I could. It looks like you have everything under control."

I nodded. "Levi and I had a nice chat."

Jonah arched his eyebrows but didn't ask. There would be questions later—lots of questions.

Anna entered the kitchen. "Jonah Graber, you flew into this house so quickly, you left me to tie up the horse." She smacked her son lightly on the back of the head. Then she turned her attention to Levi. "Looks to me like a broken heart."

A perfect diagnosis.

"Don't look so amazed, Angie," Anna said. "I heard about Levi's broken engagement at the market this morning. News travels fast in this county."

That was certainly true.

She ambled over and patted Levi on the shoulder. "Have you asked him everything you need to know?"

I gave her a half smile. Anna knew I had taken my conversation with Levi as an opportunity to investigate Bartholomew's murder. "For now. I might have a few more questions later, and the police will want to talk to him." I turned to her son. "Jonah, can I talk to you in the living room?"

My childhood friend, who knew me so well, frowned. "I'm not going to like this, am I?"

No, he probably wasn't.

Chapter Twenty-seven

Jonah and I went into the living room, and I shut the kitchen door after us. Oliver lay in front of the potbelly with his legs splayed as if he was an area rug.

I turned to face Jonah. "You told me if I was ever going into Bartholomew's district, I shouldn't go alone. I'm going now. Are you coming with me?"

His face fell. "I was right. I really don't like this."

"Jonah, I'm so close to finding out who the killer is."

He folded his arms. "Then call the sheriff."

"Do you really think anyone in Bartholomew's district is going to talk to a cop?"

"No," he said drawing out the word.

"Then we have to go."

"Angie, the people in that district are private. They won't want you there. They won't want me there either."

I folded my arms and matched his stance. "I'm going whether you come with me or not."

He dropped his arms and groaned. "Fine," he said, sounding much as he had when we were children and I had successfully talked him into doing something he didn't want to do.

I beamed. "We can take my car. It'll be faster than your buggy."

"All right," he said. "Let me just tell *Mamm*, so that she will drive the buggy back to my farm." He muttered something to himself that I couldn't make out when he went into the kitchen.

Ten minutes later, we were in the car on the way to Bartholomew's district. Jonah told me the way.

"When we get to the Kauffman farm, let me talk first," he said.

I took my eyes off the road for a second and gave him a look.

"I'm serious." He held on to his seat belt.

"Okay, but I'm going to talk. You can't tell me to be silent."

He snorted. "I would never dream of that." He pointed at the intersection ahead of us. "Turn here."

I paused at the intersection, if I could even call it that. It was more of a glorified running path through the woods. "Is my car going to fit through there?"

"Sure it will," Jonah said. "Buggies go in and out of there all the time."

"Are you sure?"

He sighed. "*Ya*. It's the quickest way to the Kauffman farm."

I turned my SUV onto the narrow road, and a tree limb scraped my roof. I winced.

My car's tires bounced in and out of the deep ruts in the dirt road.

I gripped the steering wheel. "This must be a nightmare in the winter. There is no way a snowplow can get back here."

"Bartholomew's church members keep to themselves as much as possible. Not being able to leave the district during the winter months isn't a big concern."

After about a mile, the road widened and the trees began to thin out. Through the thinning trees, I could see the outline of a narrow two-story house, and beyond that a large white barn.

"That's it," Jonah said. "That's Gil's farm. Actually, it's his father's farm. Gil will inherit it someday when he marries, and then his parents will move to the *dadihaus*."

I wondered whether that was another factor, wanting to take over the family farm, that motivated Gil to want to marry Faith.

There was a black mailbox at the end of the driveway. I turned onto the dirt drive.

"Stop the car here. They might not want your car too close to the house."

I shifted the car into park and removed the keys from the ignition. If Jonah was trying to make me apprehensive, he had succeeded.

The house was modest, and I could see an outhouse a few yards away from it. Jonah caught me looking at it. "Bartholomew didn't allow indoor plumbing in his district." He shivered. "Thankfully, my district is more civilized."

That made me laugh. Worrying about being "civilized" was so un-Amish.

I cracked a window before exiting the car. "Ollie, you stay in here, okay?"

He gave me a mournful look before snuggling under his blanket.

I slammed the door shut after me as a man stomped down the driveway to us. He had a steel gray beard, and his navy work shirt was buttoned up to the very top button. I knew right away he wasn't Gil. He was too old. I guessed it was his father.

Jonah waved and smiled brightly. "*Gude mariye*, Silas."

Silas's eyes narrowed. Jonah's charm hadn't worked.

He spoke to Jonah in Pennsylvania Dutch. I didn't understand what he asked him, but it wasn't a friendly greeting.

Jonah replied in English. "We'd like to talk to Gil."

"You have no reason to talk to my son." Silas balled his fists.

"It's about the bishop," I said.

Silas glared at me for less than a second. "Why do you bring that *English* woman here?"

I opened my mouth to say something, but Jonah stepped on my foot to stop me. I scowled at him. He knew not to step on the boots.

"She's right. We would like to talk to Gil about Bartholomew," Jonah said calmly.

"*Nee.* My son has nothing to say to—"

"*Daed*, I will talk to them." A voice came from the direction of a large barn, three times the size of the house.

Gil Kauffman looked much like his father, although he was clean-shaven. He wore his shirt buttoned up to his chin and had the same rigid posture.

The two men argued for a moment in hushed tones. Finally, Silas threw up his hands and stomped away.

Gil started in the opposite direction toward the barn.

"I have work to do," he said over his shoulder. "If you would like to talk to me, you can while I work."

Jonah and I followed him across the lawn.

"You'd better let me do the talking," Jonah whispered.

"Jonah," I hissed.

"He's not going to talk to you."

"We'll see about that," I said as I stepped into the dim barn.

By the time Jonah and I had entered the barn, Gil had a shovel in hand and was mucking a horse stall. The smell of manure and hay was almost overpowering.

"*Danki* for talking to us, Gil," Jonah said in his usual jovial way. "We stopped by because we just saw Levi Leham a little while ago."

Gil tightened his grip on the shovel handle. "What does that have to do with me?"

"Well," Jonah said, "he's concerned about Faith now that her father's gone."

Gil removed a metal pail from a nail in the side of the stall and set it on the barn floor. "He is going to marry her."

"Huh." Jonah rocked back on his heels. "I thought I heard you were going to marry Faith."

"I was," Gil said through clenched teeth, "but the bishop changed his mind. He told me Faith would be happier with Levi. How could he say that? He knew that Levi's brother left the district. How did he know that Levi wouldn't leave too and take Faith with him?"

"That made you angry?" Jonah asked.

"*Ya*," the other Amish man snapped. "It made me angry. Now the bishop is dead. It is only right."

I shivered at how calmly he said that.

"What do you mean?" Jonah asked.

"The bishop got what he deserved. It is *Gotte*'s judgment for going back on his word. He told me countless times that Faith and I were to marry."

Jonah removed his hands from his coat pockets. "Did you help with *Gotte*'s judgment?"

Gil did not answer.

"Where were you the night the bishop died?" I asked, speaking for the first time since we entered the barn.

Gil continued to muck the stall and said nothing.

Jonah repeated my question.

"I was here on the farm, all day and night." Gil dumped his shovel into the metal pail. "My parents and four younger siblings who were all here that night will tell you the same."

I had a suspicion that Gil's family wasn't above lying to the police just to keep the cops out of the district and off their farm.

"Could you have left in the middle of the night without them knowing?" I asked.

He went back into the stall for another shovelful. It was as if I didn't even exist. If this was what Amish shunning felt like on a small scale, I wasn't a fan. I ground my teeth.

Again Jonah repeated my question.

"My family will vouch for me. That's all you need to know." He pointed the business end of the shovel at Jonah and me. "Now you must leave."

I stepped back because I didn't want to get smacked with a shovel—and definitely not with a shovel covered in horse manure.

Jonah thanked Gil for his time, and he and I made a hasty retreat back to my car. When we reached it, I was relieved to see Oliver was safe and warm under his blanket in the backseat.

When I backed my car out of the Kauffmans' driveway, Jonah said, "What are you so upset about? We heard what he had to say."

"He completely ignored me."

"You're a woman and an *Englischer*. I told you they wouldn't talk to you." He seemed to put this as gently as he could.

"I just hate it when you're right," I grumbled.

He laughed as I turned back onto a paved road outside of Bartholomew's district.

Chapter Twenty-eight

After dropping Jonah off at his farm, Oliver and I made a quick stop at home, so I could shower off the scent of the Kauffmans' horse barn. I fed and checked in on Dodger too. The cat was not pleased when Oliver and I locked him in the house again. There had been no sign of the Peeping Tom so I felt Dodger would be all right. I didn't want to take him to the store, since I already knew I would be in and out all day helping with the farmers' market and the library book sale. I hadn't heard anything more about the book sale since I saw Mom and Willow at the salon the day before, but between the two of them, they had everything well in hand. By this point, I was the organizer in name only, which was how I liked it.

As we drove into Rolling Brook, my little SUV crawled behind an Amish man on a bicycle toting a cart filled with jars of fresh Amish honey. The man continued to pedal down Sugartree Street toward the pie factory. Oliver and I stopped at the shop. As we did, we were passed by a farmer carting cabbage in the same direction. It seemed Aaron had called on all of his Amish friends to make the farmers' market happen.

Oliver and I got out of the car. Across the street, Rachel bustled around the bakery, assisting her early-morning customers. There was no sign of Aaron. I suspected that he was already at the factory preparing with Phillip Truber for the opening. I hoped to swing by the bakery later. I heard one of Rachel's blueberry muffins calling my name.

I unlocked the front door to Running Stitch as my phone rang deep in the recesses of my hobo bag. I let Oliver inside and hurried over to the cash register. I slapped the bag on the counter, hoping it was Mitchell finally returning my call.

I fished in my bag and pulled the phone out in victory just as the call switched over to voice mail. I didn't have time to check the message before the phone rang again.

I held the phone to my ear without looking at the readout. "Mitchell?"

"No," an irritated female voice said. "This is Caroline Cramer."

Ugh. I should have let the second call go to voice mail too. "Hello, Caroline," I said, without enthusiasm.

"Please confirm whether or not this is true," she said in a clipped tone. "I have been told there is an unauthorized farmers' market happening on Sugartree Street this weekend."

Through my large display window, I watched another Amish cart roll by. This one carried jams and jellies in pint-sized mason jars.

I flicked on the shop lights. "There is a farmers' market happening, but it is not unauthorized." I held the phone away from my ear, but I could still hear her blow her gasket.

When her rant wound down, I placed the phone back at my ear.

"The Millers do not have permission to host such an event without township approval," she continued, and I imagined steam coming out of her ears like in a Wile E. Coyote cartoon.

"Wait a second," I said, with an edge to my own voice. "The Millers have nothing to do with this. They got approval from Willow. In fact, it was her idea!"

"Willow Moon is not the head trustee of Rolling Brook Township. She can't unilaterally approve such a thing."

"That's something you will have to take up with her." I locked my purse in the cabinet under the counter.

"I will. I attempted to call her, but she's not answering her phone."

Lucky me. If only I'd had the same idea.

"Willow said the farmers' market wasn't a problem." I propped my elbows on the sales counter. "She's been a trustee for a long time. I took her word for it, and I'm sure the Millers did the same."

"The farmers' market is a problem. We have rules and regulations in the township, and it's my job and the job of *all* the township trustees to make sure that they are followed to the letter of the law."

I rubbed my forehead. "I believe the purpose of the farmers' market is to bring more people to the library book sale. It just happens to be at the pie factory because the Millers have a big enough parking lot for the event."

She sniffed. "Then they are guilty by association. I would think after all the trouble that Aaron Miller got into last year over the pie factory, he would have been more diligent in checking if this was okay with the township."

Oh, please.

I took a deep breath, but before I could say anything, she continued her rant. "Furthermore, the book sale is different. That was cleared with us months ago, and I didn't see any reason to call a trustees meeting about the change of location. However, we need to have an emergency trustees' meeting to vote on this unauthorized farmers' market. Until then, I have half a mind to march down to the Millers' pie factory right now and shut the entire operation down."

At least it was only half her mind.

"Jason Rustle isn't available until noon," the head trustee said. "So we will have to meet then. I would like to handle this immediately, but we need all trustees there for the vote, and he insists he can't leave work early to take care of this. It seems I am the only one who takes my responsibilities as a township trustee seriously."

I stopped myself from beating my head on the cash register while I listened to her talk. "That's fine. We can even use my shop. The meeting will be at Running Stitch at noon." I leaned against the counter. "Please, don't go stomping into the farmers' market trying to shut it down until we meet. You don't want to make a scene in front of tourists, do you?"

She was quiet for a moment. "Fine. Since we have to wait, it gives me time to prepare. I will let the others know."

"I'll see Willow at the book sale. I'll tell her."

"Good. And tell her to answer her phone." She hung up.

Before I slipped my cell phone into my pocket, I noticed that I had a text message. Again, I hoped that it was from the sheriff. No such luck. It was from Amber Rustle. "I asked everyone at the library about the bookmobile keys," the text read. "Three of my coworkers saw them the day before and day of the bishop's death. I trust them. Those keys weren't used."

I frowned. Another dead end.

After I slipped my cell phone into the back pocket of my jeans, Oliver sighed at his food bowl. I kept an extra food bowl and some dog food in the shop for such an occasion. I filled his food bowl and dish of water from the sink in the bathroom. "There you go, Ollie."

He took a mouthful of kibble and carried it over to his cushion. It was breakfast in bed, Frenchie style. I carried his meal over to him and set it by his bed.

He gave me a goofy dog smile, and I wondered which one of us was the one who was trained.

My stomach rumbled, as I hadn't had breakfast either. Miller's Amish Bakery was open. Rachel would give me that blueberry muffin, no questions asked. I certainly didn't want to tell her about the conversation I had just had with head township trustee Caroline Cramer. It would only make her worry.

My phone rang again. I glanced at the screen, and Mitchell's face came up. He was smiling and the sun was on his hair, making the silver flecks in his hair sparkle. I had taken it a few weeks earlier at the dog park we visited often with Oliver and Tux, Mitchell's

Boston terrier. It was a rare moment when Mitchell didn't have a care in the world.

The phone's cheerful ring, which sounds like an electronic mamba, was insistent. I picked this ringtone for the sheriff because Mitchell thought it was ridiculous, and I liked the face he made any time he heard it. His reaction was much more enjoyable than the sound itself, which I had to admit was pretty annoying, especially in the morning. If it had not been for the coffee that Sarah had given me in her kitchen, I might have chucked the phone across the shop.

"Hey, stranger," I said.

He laughed. "Sorry I haven't called you back by now. It was a long night."

"Oh?" I asked, wondering whether it had something to do with the bishop's murder.

"Car accident—a bad one outside of Charm."

"Oh, no. I'm sorry. Is everyone all right?"

"They're all alive." He left it at that, and I didn't press. I knew that, as sheriff of Holmes County, Mitchell had much more to deal with than Bartholomew's murder, and my heart hurt for all the pain and suffering he witnessed on a daily basis. The fact that he was still a loving father to Zander and put up with me said a lot about him. I couldn't do anything that would jeopardize that, not even to protect a friend.

"So what's up?" he asked. "I assume you have been nosing around on the Beiler case."

"Who told you that?" I joked.

"I know you."

He did.

"I've found out a couple of interesting things." I told

him about my conversations with Amber and Bunny yesterday, and with the intoxicated Levi and with Gil Kauffman just that morning.

Mitchell was silent the entire time. "You *have* been busy. One of my deputies or I will talk to each of them."

"Be careful," I warned. "When you are at Bunny's, you might be greeted at the front door with a shotgun."

"What?" He yelped.

I explained, and then I added, "Amber from the library just texted me that she doesn't think the bookmobile keys were taken from the library. No one on staff noticed them missing."

"That fits with what we have learned. Both sets of keys at the library were dusted for prints. All the prints belong to library workers."

"Like Bunny," I said.

He sighed, and I suspected that he was questioning his taste in girlfriends. "Anything else?" he asked.

"Nothing concrete."

"Anything not concrete?" He sounded suspicious. Mitchell could tell I was holding something back.

I leaned on the counter. "I ran into Nahum Shetler yesterday. It shook me up a little."

"Oh," Mitchell said. "He didn't bother you, did he? What did he do?"

I shook my head even though he couldn't see me. "No, he didn't bother me."

"If he does, let me know right away. The guy is a nut."

"I will. There's—"

He interrupted me. "Angie, I have to go, okay?"

"Okay," I said, not able to keep the disappointment out of my voice.

Mitchell didn't catch my mood. He was too distracted by whatever was happening on his end of the line. "Call you later. Love you." He hung up.

Great. I didn't even get to tell him about Nahum seeing Austina, and then he hit me with the "Love you" thing again. Did he have any idea what he was doing to my nerves?

Chapter Twenty-nine

I was preparing to open the shop for the day when there was a knock on the front door. I looked up and saw Anna peering into the store with her hand shading her eyes.

Oliver hopped out of his bed and hurried to the door. I had to gently nudge him away with my foot to unlock it.

"Anna, what are you doing here?" I asked as I opened the door.

"Hello to you too, Angie." She bustled into the shop with her ever-present quilting basket in her hand.

I chuckled. "Not that I'm not happy to see you. I thought you would still be at Sarah's for a little while."

"I was there for a *gut* piece. Sarah was understandably shaken up by her drunken brother-in-law appearing on her doorstep. She was fine and talking a mile a minute by the time I left."

"I'm glad."

"I dropped in because I thought you might need help minding the store today with Mattie tied up in the factory opening."

"I was planning to go back and forth as I had the time. Technically, I'm still in charge of the book sale." I grimaced.

She shook her head and removed her black bonnet, exposing her gray hair pulled back into a tight bun and her small white prayer cap. "That will never do. You need to be down there at the scene of the crime."

"But don't you want to go?" I asked.

"I'll drop in at some point, but I will be much more comfortable right here." She hung her bonnet and cape on the hooks on the wall, leaving no room for debate.

"If you are sure," I said. "I am eager to see what's going on down there. Who knows what my mother and Willow cooked up." I gave a mock shiver.

"Then go." She adjusted her glasses on her nose. "Jonah is already at the farmers' market. This works fine for me. I can help customers, and when no one is here, I can sit in the rocker and quilt. What better advertisement can you have for the shop than an old Amish woman quilting in the window?"

I grinned. "I can't think of any, and for the record, you are not old."

She snorted and set her quilting basket beside my aunt's rocking chair and sat. "There's one more thing before you go."

"What's that?" I asked as I removed my jacket from the peg. I had had the good sense to wear the flannel-lined one that day. It was a wardrobe addition I had purchased since moving to Ohio. There wasn't much need for flannel anything in Dallas.

"We need to have a quilting circle meeting. Today. This afternoon. We need to go over the case. I think we each know something that will help the culprit become more clear to us, or at least point us in the right direction."

I shrugged. "Might as well have another meeting this afternoon."

"Another one?" Anna asked.

I gave her a brief version of my conversation with Caroline Cramer.

Anna rested her hands on her wide hips. "If Caroline knows what's *gut* for her, she will leave Rachel and Aaron alone. That woman is absolutely infuriating. I thought it was awful when Farley Jung was head trustee, but she's so much worse. The only thing that woman sees is her rules."

I silently agreed. "What about Sarah? Will she be able to come to the quilting circle meeting? She said Jeremiah was away on a job."

"We can go to her."

I slipped into my coat and grabbed Oliver's leash. I shoved it into my jacket pocket. He could walk unleashed to the Millers' factory, but it was good to have the lead with me in case I needed it. "If you're sure . . ."

She shooed me with her hands. "Go, go—clear this up before Rachel and Aaron hear about what that awful woman has planned."

I didn't argue with her anymore and opened the front door. Oliver ran out of the shop ahead of me.

As Oliver and I strolled up the street, I waved to my shop neighbors and the tourists I saw. It was a quarter until ten, and the tour buses were just starting to roll into town. The tourist season picked up like this in early October as brochures and Web sites advertised trips to Amish Country to see the gorgeous fall foliage. And it was gorgeous. The sky was high with only a few cirrus clouds suspended in the blue. There was a faint smell of burning leaves that gave the air a campfire quality I never smelled in Dallas. The leaf burning was most likely happening on an Amish farm close to Sugartree Street. A jarring thought hit me as I passed the woodworkers' shop, where Old Ben, an eighty-something Amish carpenter, sat on a three-legged stool, whittling a chunk of wood the size of Oliver's head. *Murder happens here*, I thought. If it happens here, it could truly happen anywhere.

I removed my cell phone from my pocket and tried Mitchell's number. It went directly to voice mail. I asked him to call me and told him it was about the Beiler case. I was starting to get desperate to tell him what Nahum had revealed to me the day before. I should have told him the moment Nahum left me there on the sidewalk.

For half a second, I wondered whether Rachel's wayward father could be the killer. He certainly was crazy enough and I had seen him angry enough to kill a person before. However, other than being crazy, I couldn't think of a motive. He had no attachment to Bartholomew Beiler's district as far as I knew.

I moved on to other suspects: Phoebe, the teacher with the secret reading habit; Gil Kauffman, the bishop's protégé, who would no longer be marrying Faith. I needed to talk to Faith about him, but how would I find her? I seriously doubted that she would be coming to the grand opening of the factory, the scene of her father's death.

Then there was Bunny Gallagher. Could she have killed the bishop to exact revenge on Austina? She was just crazy enough to do it, and she was still my front-runner, although Gil was a close second.

And then there was Austina.

When I reached Miller's Amish Pie Factory, I was overwhelmed by at least a dozen buggies and twice as many cars that filled their side parking lot. There were so many cars that an Amish teenager was directing them to park on the grass behind the parking lot. Half the paved area was filled with farm stands for the farmers' market, not to mention the large white book sale tent.

My mother stood in front of the book sale tent wearing a pink apron over her designer wool coat. I recognized the apron from her volunteer days at the children's hospital in Dallas. She gestured with her hands as she directed a volunteer where to put a box of books. The flaps of the book sale tent were tied back, revealing three rows of cafeteria-length tables full to bursting with books. All the books' spines were orderly and upright, with spines up to the tent's ceiling. I couldn't help but smile. My mother must have been in charge of the book organization. Had it been Willow, she would have thrown the books, still in the boxes, on the table and made the customers root through them.

"Please," my mother was saying to the volunteer when I was within earshot. "Please keep the children's and adult books separated."

The older man nodded, chastised, and carried his box of books away.

"Angie!" Someone called my name.

I turned to see Rachel standing at the back entrance of the pie factory, grinning from ear to ear. I went over to her.

She clasped her hands together. "Can you believe how many people are here? Aaron is already giving his second tour of the factory for the day, and we had to ask some guests to wait for the next one. I can't believe this many people came out."

I grinned back. "I haven't seen a crowd like this since the Nissleys closed their auction yard."

"I know," she said, her eyes shining. "Maybe this farmers' market idea will fill in the gap the loss of the Nissleys' business left behind."

I gave Rachel a hug. "Congratulations. This is a big day for you and Aaron."

Her cheeks turned pink.

Rachel's happiness was only more ammunition to make sure Caroline didn't ruin this moment for Rachel and her husband. I was going to give her more congratulations when something rammed into my side, and I went flying onto the blacktop.

Chapter Thirty

"Ow," I moaned, opening my eyes. Above me I found Rachel, Oliver, Jonah, and Petunia, the culprit, staring at me.

"You know," Jonah said, "I think Petunia really likes you, Angie. She gives you more head butts than anyone else."

"What a compliment." I held out my hand and Jonah grabbed it, pulling me to my feet. The first thing I checked was whether my cowboy boots were scuffed. They were fine, which was good news for Petunia; it meant she would live to see another day.

"Are you hurt?" Rachel asked.

I glanced around and found both Amish and English staring at me openmouthed. "Both my dignity and my hip are bruised." I brushed gravel from my jeans and jacket. At least I wasn't as wrecked as the time Petunia knocked me over into dirt. I supposed that was an improvement of sorts.

Rachel folded her arms across her chest. "Jonah, you should not have brought Petunia with you."

Jonah rubbed the back of his neck. "I couldn't leave

her at home. Miriam threatened to throw her into the
stewpot if I did."

Petunia *baa*-ed. She didn't like the sound of that. Oliver stepped closer to his goat friend as if to protect her.

"Besides," Jonah said, "Petunia is the mascot for my
business."

"Mascot?" I arched an eyebrow.

He reached into his coat and pulled out a card. It
was handwritten in block letters: "Graber Lawn Service. Eco-friendly. We do it all." There was a small
drawing of Petunia in the corner. I had to admit it was
a good likeness.

"I made the cards up myself," Jonah said, puffing
out his chest.

"Who knew you were such an artist," I said, handing him back the card. "But I still don't understand
what Petunia has to do with the lawn service."

Jonah stuck the card back into his pocket. "I read in
the *Budget* about this Amish man in Indiana who made
a business out of taking his goats to clear farmland for
other farmers, both English and Amish. I thought it
was a great service I could offer here in Holmes County.
I have Petunia now, but I thought I could take her on
small jobs. If it goes well, I can buy more goats."

I bit back a warning about another business venture.
I knew he must have already heard it from Miriam ten-
fold.

Rachel dropped her arms. "Well, keep an eye on
her."

I patted Petunia on the head. "I had better go check
in on the book sale and my mom."

Rachel smiled. "Your mother has been here since

eight this morning, barking orders at the volunteers."
She lowered her voice. "I had no idea she was so
bossy."

"You haven't seen the half of it." I waved to them
and headed to the book sale tent.

After giving Petunia a head butt of his own—albeit
a much gentler one than I received—Oliver trotted after me.

Mom smiled at me as I approached. "What do you
think?"

"I'm impressed," I said honestly.

"Good, and I'm glad you're here early. I have work
for you to do." She walked back into the tent on her
impractical heels as if expecting me to follow. "The
children's books are a complete mess. I don't know
how the volunteers expect anyone to find anything."

I caught up with her. "I'm happy to do it, but I need
to talk to Willow first. It's trustee business."

"Oh," Mom said with a frown. "I think she is on the
other side of the tent. Last time I saw her, she was setting up the cash register."

I thanked my mother and walked around the corner
of the tent. To my amazement, there was already a line
of book lovers. Amber Rustle was at the cash register,
doing a brisk business. She waved. "Hi, Angie."

"This is amazing," I said.

She beamed. "We're pretty happy with the turnout.
This is even better than when we hold the book sale at
the main library."

"And people are already buying books."

She handed the man in front of her a receipt. "The
book dealers always come to the book sale first," Am-

ber said. "They're looking for something that they can sell for a higher price at their stores or online. You will be able to pick them out." She pointed to a man running a handheld scanner over the spine of each book that he picked up. "They all have a scanner like that, which tells them what each book is worth."

"A high-tech Amish book sale. Who knew?"

She laughed and said to the customer, "That will be thirty-fifty."

The book buyer had four huge crates of books. I wondered whether all of those would make him a profit.

"I'm looking for Willow. Have you seen her?" I asked.

She shook her head. "Not since we opened."

That was strange. Typically, Willow was in the middle of things.

"If you see her, will you tell her that I was looking for her?"

"No problem," Amber said, and helped the next customer.

Before I headed back to Mom and the children's books, I decided to take a loop through the farmers' market to try to find Willow. Normally I wouldn't have been concerned, but there had already been one murder related to the library book sale . . .

"Would you like to try the honey, miss?" An Amish man held out a wooden tongue depressor to me.

I took it. "Sure." Maybe the sugar would clear my head.

"Choose any flavor you like. We have clover honey, wildflower honey, buckwheat honey—all from Amish farms right here in Holmes County. Just one dip per flavor."

I dipped my depressor into the jar of wildflower honey. It was some of the sweetest I ever tasted. My father would love it, and I could imagine him eating it straight from the jar. I still had the depressor in my mouth when I reached into my bag to take out my wallet. As I did so, something hit me on the back, and the depressor hit the back of my mouth, making me gag. I couldn't believe I was under Petunia attack again.

I spat the depressor out onto the pavement. I bent over coughing and sputtering.

Someone was rubbing my back. When I finally straightened up, I saw that it was Willow.

The Amish man at the honey stand stared at me openmouthed.

Willow rubbed my back some more. "I'm so sorry to sneak up on you like that, Angie. Amber told me that you were looking for me. What are you doing standing around with a tongue depressor in your mouth? You could have choked to death."

Oliver placed his white forepaws on my legs and whimpered.

I rubbed his black ear. "I'm okay, Ollie," I said hoarsely.

I was beginning to wonder whether I should have stayed back at the shop. I had been attacked twice since I came to the pie factory grand opening, and once had been a near-death experience. Who knew that an Amish farmers' market could be so dangerous?

"Angie, you need to be more careful," Willow went on.

I rubbed my throat and opened my wallet.

The Amish man held out the jar of wildflower honey. "Here, take it. No charge." I tried to insist on paying, but he shook his head. "*Nee*. It is free for you."

As we walked away, Willow said, "He's probably worried that you will sue him for nearly killing you with that dangerous honey." She reached into her tote bag and pulled out an unopened bottle of water. "Here, have a drink of this—it will make you feel better. And you might want to have some tea with honey too. I could make you some tea. I have a small tea stand beside the book sale." She grinned, pointing at the honey jar in my hand. "And you have plenty of honey."

I gave her a sidelong glance. "Where have you been?" I asked in an accusing tone. Most likely, my question would have been nicer if she hadn't almost caused me to choke to death.

Willow didn't seem to mind my sharpness. "I have a surprise that will make you feel better."

"A surprise?" I asked warily. I wasn't sure I could take any more surprises. "What is it?"

"I may have found your killer."

I stared at her. "My killer?"

She nodded happily. "I found the one who killed the bishop."

"Who? Where is he?"

She clasped her hands together and her gauzy blouse blew in the breeze. "In the woods. I have him tied up in the trees."

I blinked at her.

Chapter Thirty-one

"Wh-what?" I stammered.

Willow took my hand. "Let me show you."

Willow led me away from the pie factory and the farmers' market and into the woods. As soon as we crossed the tree line, I could hear faint swearing. She really did have someone tied up among the trees.

She dropped my hand and increased her pace. "It's not far."

I followed her as she wove in and out of trees. Who knew that Willow felt so at home in the forest?

She pointed in front of her. I came around a tree trunk and saw Nahum Shetler lying on the forest floor, holding on to his thigh. A wire snare was around his leg just above the ankle.

He glared at me. "Cut me out of this thing. My knife is in my pack over there." With a knobby finger, he pointed at a gray knapsack just out of reach of his left hand.

I flapped my mouth open and closed. "Nahum?"

"I said, cut me out!" he yelled.

I turned to Willow. "Willow, you caught him with a snare?"

Willow twirled the purple crystal hanging from her neck. "Technically, he caught himself. I saw someone moving through the trees while I was talking to Amber at the cash register, so I did what you would do, Angie—I followed him."

I touched my forehead. I could feel a migraine coming on, right between the eyes.

"Cut me out!" Nahum bellowed again.

Willow shook her finger at him. "You be quiet, so that I can finish my story."

He growled in return. The man sounded like a rabid bobcat. Not that I had ever heard one in person, but Oliver, Dodger, and I watched a lot of Animal Planet.

"So I followed him and saw him playing on the ground with something. I yelled at him, and he jumped three feet in the air. When he landed, he screamed." Willow folded her arms across her chest. "Caught in his own trap. Serves him right for trying to catch poor defenseless bunny rabbits."

Nahum's lip curled back into a snarl. "That purple-haired witch spooked me and I got caught in my own rabbit snare." He held on to his leg.

The snare explained what Nahum had been doing in the woods outside the bookmobile the night that Bartholomew was murdered. It also explained why he would have been in a position to see Austina coming and going from the bookmobile so late. He was likely out there to check his traps, but I had to be sure.

"Were you out here the night before the bishop's body was discovered to check these snares?" I asked.

"I already told you that I was, and I saw who killed the bishop."

I found Willow watching me. "You mean someone other than you did it? Angie, do you know who?"

"Of course she does. I told her yesterday." He turned his gaze on me. "I suppose you haven't told your sheriff about what I saw yet, have you?"

I glared back. "Why haven't you? You're the one who claims to have seen something."

His smile broadened. "I have nothing to gain from it. I don't do anything that doesn't work to my advantage."

"What an Amish way to live," I snapped.

He jerked up, but the snare held him back. "Don't you tell me what an Amish way to live is—you know nothing of my culture."

"I know Amish aren't supposed to be selfish like you. How could you set a snare so close to the pie factory?" I asked, becoming angry. "Your grandchildren play in these woods."

He flinched but said, "I will set a snare anywhere I well please."

I glared at him. I couldn't remember the last time I had been so furious. One of Rachel's children could have been seriously hurt or even maimed by one of Nahum's snares. Mentally, I took back every thought I had ever had about believing that Rachel should reestablish her relationship with her father. A man who would put her children at risk like this didn't deserve to know her.

Willow touched my arm. "Should we call the police?"

I looked back through the trees at the pie factory. I didn't want to make a scene and ruin the Millers' grand opening. A slight form moved through the trees.

I hurried over to her to stop her, but I was too slow.

"Angie, is everything al—" Rachel stopped midsentence when she saw her father lying on the ground with wire snared around his leg.

"Cut me out of here," Nahum said to Rachel.

"He said there are wire cutters in his pack," Willow said.

Without saying a word, Rachel knelt beside Nahum's knapsack. After rooting through it, she came up with the cutters and clipped the wire, holding Nahum in place.

He winced as the pressure released from his leg.

Rachel stood.

Nahum had trouble getting to his feet. I rushed forward to help him. At first, he pushed me away, but when he realized that he couldn't stand on his own, he let me. When he was upright, I stepped back.

Rachel still had the wire cutters in her hands, and Nahum snatched them from her, nearly cutting her with the razor-sharp tip. "Give those to me."

"Are you all right?" Rachel managed to ask.

"*Nee.*" He pointed at Willow and me. "These are the ones you call your friends, ones who would let an old man writhe on the forest floor like that?"

"I—I—" Rachel stammered.

Rachel couldn't finish her sentence because Nahum spun around and hobbled away. He had a slight limp.

"You should see a doctor," I called after him.

He said nothing and kept going.

After he disappeared deeper into the trees, Rachel looked to me. "Why didn't you cut him out?"

"I—I was questioning him." My brow knit together.

Tears welled in Rachel's eyes. "Angie, how could you do that when he was in pain?"

I bit my lip. "I know. I wasn't thinking. I was so angry about the snares. I'm sorry."

She lowered her eyes so that we no longer made eye contact. "I have to return to the factory."

"Rachel!" I called after her, but she kept walking.

I felt an ache in my chest. Nahum had been in the wrong, but I had been too.

Willow picked up what was left of the snare from the forest floor. "I'm going to report this to the police. There is no trapping this close to town. The sheriff can give him a citation."

A lot of good that would do, I thought. Nahum would just ignore it.

"Don't worry about Rachel," Willow said. "She was only surprised by seeing her father like that. When was the last time that she spoke to him?"

"I'm not sure if she ever has before today." I stared in the direction Rachel had gone.

"Oh." She smiled. "Well, now they broke the ice."

Leave it to Willow to put a positive spin on this.

She started toward the parking lot.

I stopped her. "Willow, Caroline has called an emergency trustees' meeting for today."

She grimaced at me over her shoulder. "Why?"

"She wasn't too happy that you authorized the farmers' market." I stepped over a tree branch and followed her out of the woods.

Willow snorted. "She always gets bent out of shape over something."

I had to agree with her. "In any case, she's demanded that we vote on the farmers' market today."

Willow twirled her crystal as we came into the clearing beside the parking lot. "Where and when?"

I stepped over a fallen log. "My shop at high noon."

"Seems appropriate," Willow said.

Chapter Thirty-two

I left Willow at the edge of the woods and went in search of Rachel. It was midmorning now, and the farmers' market was packed even though it had had only word-of-mouth advertising and little preparation. English tourists and Rolling Brook townspeople milled around the half dozen farm stands and wandered in and out of the pie factory. I spotted Jonah and Petunia talking to a pastor from a local church. I knew he was pitching his goat lawn service. Oliver stood beside him and wagged his stubby tail at me. I made the motion for him to stay and headed to the factory's back door. Oliver would be fine with Petunia at his side. If anyone tried to bother him, she would go all ninja goat on him.

It was just as busy inside the pie factory as it was outside. Clumps of tourists waited for the tour of the factory floor, and others stood in line to purchase pies. I was happy to see my favorite, the pumpkin fluff, was a popular item. Through the glass observation windows, which peered down onto the pie-making operation, I could see Aaron leading a tour of a half dozen English tourists. They all wore hairnets. Aaron even wore one over his Amish hat. There was no sign of Rachel.

I left the observation room and went down a narrow hallway. The walls were white and the floor was tiled. At the end of the hallways there were two metal doors that led to the factory floor. Before that door there was a half-open door to my right. Whimpers came from that room.

"You need to get a handle on yourself," an angry male voice said.

There were only tears in response.

"Do you have any idea how your behavior will seem?" the man asked.

Again no answer, only sniffles.

Thinking it was maybe Rachel crying over Nahum, I pushed open the door, which opened into a large storage room holding huge containers of flour, sugar, spices, and every dry ingredient that a baker would need to make every pie he could imagine.

Phillip and Phoebe Truber stood in the middle of the room facing each other. Phoebe leaned on a crate that had FLOUR stenciled on the side of it. Tears streamed down her face. Phillip scowled at his sister with his arms folded across his chest. They both turned and stared at me standing in the doorway.

"Oh, I'm sorry," I muttered. "I was looking for Rachel."

Phillip's jaw twitched. "She is not here."

"I can see that. Do you know where she is?"

He glared at me. *"Nee."*

I hesitated in the doorway. "Phoebe, are you all right?"

She covered her face and brushed past me and into the hallway. She was already in the observation room by the time I turned around.

I turned back to Phillip. "What's wrong with your sister?"

"That is none of your business." Phillip stepped into my face. "The Millers may not mind it, but do not get involved in my family's affairs." He left the room.

Was that a threat?

I stood in the middle of the storage room, considering what I had just seen.

"Angie, what are you doing in here?" someone asked.

Realizing I was gripping the jar of honey the Amish farmer had given me, I dropped it into my bag. I spun around to find Mattie in the doorway with a hairnet over her chestnut hair and prayer cap.

"I was looking for Rachel and lost my way." I stepped out of the storage room and shut the door behind me. "The strangest thing just happened." I went on to tell her about the argument I witnessed between the Truber siblings.

Mattie shrugged. "Phillip is just tense because it's the grand opening."

I didn't think she was right. There was more to it than that. "Do you know where Rachel is?"

She nodded. "She started a tour of the factory floor."

"Oh," I said, disappointed. Rachel would be caught up in the tour for at least a half hour, and by that time I would need to leave for the trustees' meeting at my shop.

Mattie cocked her head. "Why are you looking for her?"

"I need to talk to her," I said evasively.

Mattie frowned, and I knew she didn't believe me. I was relieved when she didn't press the issue. I followed Mattie out into the hall. "I should head out to the book sale, but I have one more question."

Mattie waited.

"Mattie, do you know where I can find Faith Beiler?"

Mattie was quiet for a moment. "I guess your best shot is her family's farm."

I sighed. I had a feeling that the Beiler family wasn't going to let me anywhere near their farm, especially when news got around the district about Jonah's and my visit to the Kauffman farm.

Mattie snapped her fingers. "Wait."

"What?" I asked.

"I remembered something," she said excitedly. "Faith works at a candy shop in Charm. She might be there. I remember seeing her there when I was out for a buggy ride a little while ago."

I arched an eyebrow. "On a buggy ride by yourself?"

Despite the unbecoming hairnet, Mattie blushed prettily.

"Mattie Miller, were you on a date?"

Her face deepened to a darker shade of red. "The Amish don't date."

"Courting then? Is someone courting you?" I was eager for all the details. If Sarah had been here, she would have wanted to know even more. Mattie had not had much luck in the love department. Her last beau had turned out to be a jerk. That was my word, not Mattie's. I had called him other names too, but they didn't bear repeating. "Who is it?"

Mattie fiddled with the edge of her apron. "I'd rather not say."

I opened my mouth to question her more, but she shook her head. "Angie, please."

I sighed. "I'll let it go for now."

She gave me a small smile. "*Danki.*"

"Do you think Faith will be at the candy shop when her father was murdered only two days ago?"

She nodded. "Her district is very strict about work. I wouldn't be surprised if all of the bishop's children are already back at work."

It was the best chance I had to talk to the bishop's daughter. "Where is it?"

Mattie rattled off the directions.

Taking a piece of paper and pen from my bag, I jotted them down.

"I had better head back onto the factory floor." Mattie sighed. "I've been splattered with blueberry filling twice today. Working here today reminds me why I enjoy my job at the quilt shop so much."

I smiled. "I'm glad to hear it. I would hate to lose you to the factory."

Her face lit up. "There's not a chance of that happening."

Mattie and I parted ways and went opposite directions down the hallway. In the observation room, I peered through the window onto the factory floor. Finally, I spotted Rachel speaking to a group of tourists. She smiled prettily at them as she spoke. She appeared fine, but I knew she wasn't fine, and I was partly to blame for that.

Sighing, I went back outside to the book sale.

Outside, I headed straight for the task my mother had assigned me earlier, organizing the children's books. Oliver left his goat companion to join me. He whimpered at me. He could always sense when I was upset. I had disappointed Rachel.

I tried to forget about it for the moment and focus on the task at hand. Oliver curled up under the children's book table as I set the books spine up on the very last table in the tent. As I worked, I discovered dozens of books I thought Zander would like. By the time I finished the table, I had a stack of books for Z that was over a foot high.

"Angie." Amber joined me at the children's book table. "Don't you have a trustees' meeting?"

My shoulders sagged. My subconscious must have repressed the meeting. "Yes," I said, falling just short of a whine. I picked up the stack of books and frowned when I saw the long line at the cash register. It wrapped halfway around the tent. "Can you hold these for me until I get back?"

She shook her head. "I think a twenty will cover all of those. Pay me now and we will call it even."

"Done," I said, reaching into my wallet. After giving her the money, I said, "I had better find Willow."

"She already left." Amber dropped the twenty-dollar bill into the cash box on her table and snapped it closed. "She said she had to prep for battle."

Great.

Chapter Thirty-three

By the time I reached my own quilt shop, all of the other township trustees were gathered there. Caroline Cramer stood by the display window with her arms folded, tapping her foot. Her silky hair was pulled back into an elaborate twist. Jason Rustle and Farley Jung sat in folding chairs on one half of a small circle, and Willow sat on the other side, looking cool and collected and much more at ease than Caroline.

Oliver took one look at them and headed for his dog bed. I wished that I could do the same.

Farley Jung gave me a slow smile as I hung my coat on the peg. From the looks of it, he had slicked back his hair with a generous helping of gel. I turned toward the wall so that he would not see the disgusted face I made.

Jason Rustle pulled back the sleeve of his business suit and glared at his watch. "I only have forty minutes left on my lunch break, so let's get started."

Caroline joined the circle, sitting next to Jason, which left me with the only empty seat next to Farley. Terrific.

Caroline removed a file from her briefcase. "Hopefully this won't take more than forty minutes, but we have a lot to get to."

Jason scowled at Caroline and glanced at his watch again. "I'm leaving in thirty-seven minutes whether this is over or not. Some of us have to work for a living. I'm sorry if that is inconvenient for your schedule."

Caroline glared at him. "You should have more concern for the township."

"Thirty-six minutes," Jason said.

Caroline gritted her teeth so hard I was surprised she didn't crack her jaw. "I call this meeting to order."

Farley raised a finger at her. "Now, Caroline, there is no need to call the meeting to order since this is not an open session in front of the township."

She gave him a withering glance. As the former head trustee, Farley was sort of a backseat driver at trustees' meetings. It was one of the few things that I liked about him.

"Thank you, Farley," Caroline said, but her tone had no gratitude in it. "As this is a closed meeting, Anna, I'm going to have to ask you to leave."

Anna, quilting in the rocker by the window, froze. "Excuse me?"

"I'm sorry, but we will have to ask you to leave."

Anna looked to me.

"I don't think we have to worry about Anna saying anything about the meeting."

"Rules are rules," Caroline said.

"Thirty-one minutes," Jason barked.

Anna gathered up her quilting supplies and stood. "I will be across the street at the bakery. You can find me there when you're done, Angie."

"Thank you." I sighed.

She nodded.

After the shop door closed behind Anna, Caroline said, "I have called this meeting because of the unauthorized farmers' market, which is happening at the end of this street at this very moment."

Willow straightened in her seat. "Who said it was unauthorized? I told the Millers that it was fine."

Caroline sniffed. "This is not a dictatorship, Willow. You cannot make unilateral decisions. We need to vote on such things."

"All right then. Whoever is in favor of the farmers' market, raise your hand." Willow lifted her hand into the air.

Willow, Jason, and I threw our hands up as well. After a moment's hesitation, Farley's hand joined ours.

Caroline glared at us. "Don't any of you care about the disregard that Willow gave the rules of the township?"

"Caroline," Jason said, "the farmers' market is a great success. It's on private property too. There is no reason we should even be disputing it."

"B-but—" she stammered.

Willow stood. "I, for one, am glad we had this meeting. It will be nice to go back to the Millers and tell them that the farmers' market can be a regular event." She tapped her finger to her cheek. "In fact, I'm seeing possibilities for expansion. I'll go talk to them now while I'm thinking about it." She stood up and headed for the door.

Caroline jumped to her feet. "Wait! This meeting isn't over."

Jason stood and put on his coat. "As far as I'm concerned it is. I have to get back to the office."

"I haven't adjourned the meeting," Caroline complained.

"Actually, Caroline," Farley said from his seat, "it's not necessary for you to adjourn since this is not an official trustees' meeting in front of the entire township."

"You be quiet!" the head trustee snapped.

I stood, wondering how to break up the fight, when my cell phone rang. I really needed to change my ringtone. I set the phone to my ear. "Hello?"

"Angie, I need to talk to you," Austina said. Her voice was hoarse, as if she had been crying for half the night.

I watched as Caroline and Jason argued in front of my display window. I would be lucky if the two of them didn't come to blows. At the very least, their behavior was bound to chase away customers. "Do you want me to come to your house?" I asked Austina. Leaving Running Stitch would give me an excuse to kick the trustees out of the shop and force them to deal with their differences somewhere else.

"No, I need to get out of this house." Her voice sounded a bit stronger, as if she was forcing herself to be firm. "I've locked myself in my home for the last two days. It's time I faced the world. I have learned that hiding from it does not make me look any less guilty."

"We can meet at the Double Dime Diner." I looked at the clock on the wall behind the cash register. "It's almost one now. I could be there within the hour."

"That sounds like a good idea."

"Great. Just let me finish up with a few things here." Those few things were four irate township trustees.

Willow squared off in front of Caroline. "You aren't being reasonable."

"Reasonable? I'm trying to follow the rules and regulations this township set up."

"We are the trustees," Willow scoffed. "We can change those."

"Not without a unanimous vote," Caroline countered.

"Angie?" Austina asked in my ear. "Is everything all right? I can hear arguing."

"Everything's fine," I told the librarian. "I'll see you at the Double Dime later." Before she could ask any more questions, I hung up.

Jason had slipped out of the shop during my conversation with Austina. Caroline and Willow were still arguing, and Farley seemed to be enjoying the show.

"I hate to break this up," I said, hating nothing of the kind. "But I'm going to have to ask you to leave because I have to run an important errand."

Caroline turned from Willow and gaped at me. "Is this some sort of mutiny?"

Farley stood. "Caroline, don't be so dramatic. Why don't you and I go walk down to the farmers' market? Perhaps we can find some other township violations."

She scowled. "Very well." She pointed at Willow. "I won't forget your cavalier behavior, Willow."

After the trustees left, I went across the street and told Anna my plans.

"*Gut*," she said. "Austina needs a friend right now. We are having the quilting circle meeting at Sarah's house this evening. I will tell the others where you are, and if you're not back in time, I will close up the shop for the night."

I thanked her and left.

By the time I reached the diner, I could already see Austina sitting at one of the tables by the window. I waved to her as Oliver and I walked to the diner's front door.

Linda, the head and only waitress, patted her bee-hive hair. It had so much hair spray in it, I suspected nothing less than an erupting volcano would make it move. She and Farley should compare notes on their hairstyling products. "There's my friend," Linda crowed as we entered the store.

She wasn't talking to me but to Oliver. On the day they met, the two bonded over their mutual love of bacon.

"I was hoping you would come in this week," she said to me after cooing over my Frenchie. "I have a nice slab of bacon just for you." She turned around and yelled into the pass-through to the kitchen. "Whip up that special bacon I bought for Oliver."

The cook, who rarely ventured out into the dining area, grumbled.

Linda wagged her finger at the hole in the wall. "You get it done. Poor Oliver is completely famished." She turned her critical gaze on me. "Have you been feeding him?"

"Yes." I gave her a look.

Oliver whimpered, contradicting my statement.

Linda squatted down to be at eye level with my dog. "You poor, deprived creature. Bacon will make it better." She stood up and her knees cracked. "While I'm tending to Oliver, why don't you take a seat at your regular table?"

"I'm here to have lunch with Austina," I said.

Linda tucked her pencil behind her ear. "Ahh," she said knowingly. "She said that she was meeting someone here. I should have known it was you."

"Bacon's up!" the cook called, and Oliver did a happy dance.

I sighed. "Don't give him more than two pieces. I don't want him getting sick."

"I wouldn't dream of it," Linda said, but I thought I saw her crossing her fingers behind her back. There was no point in fighting it. It was two against one. Or three against one if I counted the cook.

Austina waved to me as I walked over to the table.

"You go sit down," Linda said. "Oliver and I will be just fine."

"That's what I'm afraid of," I said before heading to the booth.

The sound of Linda's throaty laugh followed me all the way to where Austina was sitting.

I took the booth seat across from Austina. There were bags under her eyes and deep lines etched around her mouth I had never noticed before. She looked positively awful.

"Thanks for meeting me here, Angie." Her voice cracked. "I don't think I could stand one more day cooped up inside of my house. I know people out here are talking about me." She straightened her shoulders and flattened her hand on the tabletop between us. "But I won't cower at home any longer. It's time to face this head-on."

"That's the spirit," I said. "You wanted to talk to me about something."

Austina's shoulders drooped. "Let's order first. I think it will be easier to talk about with food in front of us."

Linda was at our table within seconds. I didn't even have a chance to look at the menu, but it didn't matter. I already knew what I was having. Linda pointed her pencil at me. "Chicken and dumpling soup."

"How do you know?"

"Because your cute little nose is red from being out in the cold. Looks to me that you've been outside for a long while, and you always order soup when you're cold."

I handed her my menu. "You got me."

Linda tapped her pencil against her cheek and stared at Austina.

Austina opened her mouth as if to order.

"Nope," Linda said. "Give me a second."

Austina snapped her mouth shut.

"Looks to me that you need a decent meal. I see how your cheeks are all sunken in. What have you been eating lately?"

"Lots of canned soup," Austina said, wincing as if in fear of Linda's judgment.

Linda wrinkled her nose. "Soup should not come from a can. What you need is roast beef with two sides—green beans and mashed potatoes and gravy." She wrote this on her order pad. "And hot rolls. You need hot rolls after what you've been through." Linda nodded to herself. "I'll bring out water and hot tea for you both." She marched away.

"Wow," Austina said. "She knew exactly what I wanted. It'll be nice to have a real meal after living on peanut butter and canned soup for the last few days."

Linda was back a second later and placed a steaming teapot, a little basket with tea bags, two white mugs, and two waters on our table.

I selected one of the tea bags. "How's Oliver? Recovered from his lack of bacon?"

Linda smiled. "He's making up for lost time." She moved on to the next table.

I poured hot water into my mug and dunked a tea bag into it. I offered some to Austina.

She shook her head. "The water is fine for now." She took a big gulp from the glass.

"What did you want to tell me?" I asked.

"I've asked you to help me, and I haven't been completely honest with you." She stared into her water glass.

"You mean you didn't tell me that you went to the bookmobile the night before the bishop's body was found." I spooned sugar into my tea and waited.

Her glass stopped halfway to her mouth. "How did you know that?"

"A reliable witness saw you and told me," I said. That was sort of true. Nahum wasn't reliable per se, but I couldn't think of why he would have lied about it. He had nothing to gain, other than perhaps upsetting me. In any case, her reaction confirmed that Nahum was telling the truth. "Why were you there?"

She sipped her water and set it back onto the table. "I was there to leave the key."

That explained why there was no forced entry at the crime scene.

"And then I left," she added.

"Why were you leaving the key? Who was it for?"

She swallowed. "I was helping someone."

I sat back in my seat and folded my arms on the tabletop. "By leaving the key? How?"

She wrapped both hands around her water glass as if to brace herself as she told the story. "You have to remember, this was before the bishop died, and I was still determined to provide the readers in his districts the books they wanted to read. I realize now how foolish I had been. I felt I was in the right, so I didn't care. I felt I was justified in leaving the key, so that the person could access the bookmobile."

I frowned. "You weren't going to be there when they were in the bookmobile? I can't see the library being happy with that."

She plucked an unopened tea bag from the basket and fidgeted with it. "The library didn't know."

"Who is it?" I asked. "Who wanted to get into the bookmobile at such an early hour?"

She lowered her voice. "I don't want to get anyone in trouble."

I leaned across the table. "Do you understand you might end up going to prison?"

She nodded.

"Who wanted access to the bookmobile? I want the names." My eyes bore into her. I was shooting for Mitchell's deadly cop stare.

Austina bent the corners of the tea bag. "There's only one name."

"Here you go." Linda set an enormous bowl of chicken and dumpling soup in front of me. It was so large I thought it might double as a mixing bowl. In front of Linda, she set a full roast beef dinner. Looking at Austina's plate, I was starting to question my meal choice. "Eat up before it gets cold," Linda ordered, and went to the next table.

I blew on my soup. It would take some time to cool off. "Name, Austina." I picked up my soup spoon.

She set the unopened tea bag aside and poked at her green beans with her fork. "Faith Beiler."

The spoon landed in my bowl with a splat, sending hot soup all over my paper place mat. I grabbed napkins from the dispenser to wipe it up. "The bishop's daughter?"

Chapter Thirty-four

"Shhh," Austina hissed, looking around the room, but the only other customers were three old men in the back drinking coffee and arguing over the highlights of Millersburg High School's football season.

Still, I lowered my voice. "The bishop's daughter wanted to get into the bookmobile when you weren't there?"

She nodded. "She had been to the bookmobile before, but it was months ago, before her father started cracking down on all the young women from his district who were reading. I don't believe he knew his daughter also checked books out from the library. Faith wanted to keep it that way."

I dipped my spoon into my soup and stirred. "So she asked you to leave the keys where?"

"I set them on top of the bookmobile's rear right tire."

"When did she ask you to do this?" I stirred some more.

Her face turned red. "She didn't ask me in person. At the end of the day after I had already parked the bookmobile behind the factory and had gone home, I found a note asking me to leave the key for her outside the bookmobile, so that she could get in and read."

"You were willing to leave the keys near the book-mobile because of a note?" It sounded even more ridiculous when I said it aloud.

Austina blushed. "I know it was stupid, and I almost didn't do it. I thought about it all night. Finally—I guess it was a little after eleven—I decided to take the key over."

I set my spoon on the side of the bowl. The soup was still very hot. "In the middle of the night?"

She gazed out the window. "I couldn't sleep because I was so furious with the bishop that I wasn't thinking clearly. I was trying to prove my point that his church members would defy him if he took away their right to read. I was especially happy it was his daughter who wanted inside the bookmobile." She pushed away her plate. "I realize now how irresponsible I was."

"Austina, this is important. Since the bookmobile was unlocked, that explains how the bishop got in there." I sipped my tea.

She nodded.

"Do you know why he was there? Do you think he followed his daughter there?"

"Maybe, but I don't know for certain."

I heard the door of the diner open, but I was too distracted by Austina's story to give it much attention.

Austina stared over my shoulder with her mouth hanging open.

Oliver barked a sharp greeting from his spot by the breakfast counter, and I turned to see Mitchell and

Deputy Anderson walking toward us. Mitchell frowned at me.

Oliver seemed to sense that the sheriff was on the job, because he backpedaled behind the revolving pie case.

Mitchell wouldn't look at me. "Austina, why don't you come outside with Deputy Anderson and me?"

I tossed my napkin on the table. "What's going on?"

Austina's face was drawn. "It's okay, Angie." She pushed herself out of the booth. "I've been expecting this."

Deputy Anderson started to remove his handcuffs from his belt.

The sheriff put a hand on the deputy's wrist and whispered, "Outside."

My heart started to beat faster. Mitchell was going to arrest Austina.

She gave me a small smile. "I'll be all right. Thank you for trying to help me."

"B-but—" I stammered.

Mitchell met my gaze with his startling blue-green eyes. "Angie, don't cause a scene."

I gritted my teeth and watched the two police officers march Austina out of the diner. I waited approximately three seconds before I ran after them.

I rushed out onto the sidewalk. Mitchell and Deputy Anderson took Austina to the corner, where a police cruiser waited. Deputy Anderson slapped handcuffs on her wrists and recited her rights.

I ran over to them. "Wait!"

Deputy Anderson opened the back cruiser door and

placed a hand on Austina's head as she ducked into the car.

"Austina!" I cried.

Mitchell ignored me. "Anderson, take Ms. Shaker to the station."

The young deputy nodded and walked around the car.

"Austina?" I shouted and tapped on her window.

She wouldn't look at me. Her head was bent down and focused on her handcuffed hands.

Mitchell gently grabbed my forearm. "Please step back from the vehicle."

I jerked my arm away. "How can you arrest her?"

"Please, Angie," Mitchell said in a low voice. "People are watching."

I looked up the street back at the Double Dime Diner and saw it was true. Linda, the cook, and the three old men stood on the sidewalk watching our exchange. I wasn't helping Austina this way. I stepped away from the car.

"Thank you," Mitchell breathed in my ear.

Deputy Anderson started the cruiser and was about to pull away when Austina beat on her window. Mitchell signaled Deputy Anderson to lower the window. "Yes, Ms. Shaker."

"I need to tell Angie something." She was breathless.

"I don't think you should be talking to Ms. Braddock about your situation," Mitchell said.

Ms. Braddock? That's what I was to him now?

"It's not about my situation." Tears streamed down her face. "It's about my mother."

Mitchell nodded, and I stepped up to the side of the

car. Mitchell made no move to step away. Our arms brushed each other as I leaned in to hear what Austina had to say.

"Can you tell my mother what has happened? I don't want her to hear about it from anyone else." She wiped at the tears on her cheek with her bound hands. "I know it won't be long before the news reaches those working at the nursing home. I don't want Mom to be taken off guard."

"Of course," I said.

Her tears came faster, and she leaned back in her seat. "Thank you."

Mitchell tapped the top of the cruiser, telling Deputy Anderson that it was all right to drive. The cruiser silently pulled away from the curb.

I watched until the taillights disappeared around the corner. Then I turned to Mitchell. "What's going on? Do you have enough evidence to arrest Austina?"

He frowned. "You know I wouldn't have arrested her otherwise."

"What is it?" I demanded.

His eyes narrowed. "Angie, this is police business."

"I know that, but you can't possibly think that she killed Bartholomew over library books." I threw my hands in the air. "That's the most ridiculous motive I've ever heard!"

"She mostly likely will be charged with manslaughter. That's the prosecutor's decision."

"Well, if it's only manslaughter, then I guess it's okay." I folded my arms. "What about Bunny Gallagher? What about Gil Kauffman? Are you arresting them too?"

"Angie," he said, and somehow broke my name into five syllables.

I met his gaze.

"Please." He stared at me with those swoon-worthy eyes, but now they didn't hold their usual charm over me. "I know Austina is your friend, but it doesn't change the facts. I have to do my job."

"I know, but—"

"It's awful to see when an *Englischer* is arrested," a gravelly voice behind me said.

I spun around and found Nahum Shetler standing behind us with his hands in the pockets of his black wool coat. His Rip Van Winkle beard had a leaf sticking to it. He didn't seem to notice.

"I can't understand why you are surprised." Nahum pointed at me. "Didn't I tell you yesterday I saw the librarian leaving the bookmobile late at night just before Bartholomew died? I thought when I mentioned it to your sheriff, you would have already told him. Imagine my surprise when I found out he had never heard a word of it."

"Is this true?" Mitchell's eyes were like laser beams. "Is this true?" he repeated his question, this time much more slowly.

"Yes, but—"

He clenched his jaw. "How can there possibly be a but?"

"I tried to tell you."

"You tried, but you didn't." Mitchell's voice was clipped. "You would have made a point to tell me if you really wanted to. I know you, Angie. You're the most persistent person I have ever met."

I didn't think he meant that as a compliment. At least not right then. My cheeks grew hot. "I'm sorry. I wanted to talk to Austina first."

He scowled. "To tip her off?"

"No—I wanted to hear her side, and before I even asked her about it, she told me that she was there to leave the key so the bishop's daughter had access to the bookmobile."

"You have been busy," Mitchell said darkly. He took a step toward me and my breath caught. "It is not your job to hear anyone's side. Go back to the shop and make a quilt." He spun around and marched to his SUV.

I stood on the sidewalk with Nahum Shetler, of all people, in disbelief.

Nahum tsked. "Lovers' spat?"

"Be quiet," I snapped, and I stomped away.

"What, no good-bye?" he called after me.

I glanced over my shoulder. "Good-bye, Nahum."

The sound of his laughter followed me down the sidewalk.

Chapter Thirty-five

When I returned to the Double Dime Diner to collect Oliver, Linda insisted on packing my soup in a to-go container. "Let's roll, Ollie."

He accepted one last piece of bacon from Linda and followed me out of the diner.

We drove to the Heavenly Gardens nursing home, which was on top of a hill overlooking downtown Millersburg, after a quick stop at a grocery store to buy flowers. From the parking lot, I could see the courthouse, the Double Dime Diner, and even Out of Time, Jessica's antiques shop.

I pressed the buzzer to be let inside. I held Oliver's leash in one hand and a bouquet of flowers in the other.

I stopped at the receptionist's desk and asked for Lorna Shaker's room.

A pleasant woman smiled at me. "Room 104." She peered over the desk at Oliver. "Is that a therapy dog?"

I looked down at Oliver. "He provides me therapy every day."

She smiled. "He seems well behaved. I'll pretend I didn't see him."

I thanked her and walked by red-beaked finches twittering in a floor-to-ceiling enclosure. Oliver quivered beside me.

"They're behind glass, Ollie," I whispered. "They can't get you."

He didn't stop shaking until we were around the corner in another hallway, and even then he looked over his shoulder every few steps.

The door to room 104 was open. Austina's mother's name was on the door.

Lorna Shaker sat up in a plastic-covered recliner. The quilt my quilting circle had made her covered her legs. The television, set to a morning talk show, was turned up to the sound barrier.

I knocked on the doorframe. "Mrs. Shaker?" I had to shout to be heard over the blaring screen.

She turned her head toward me with sharp eyes. "Who are you?"

I opened my mouth to answer.

She picked up her remote and pointed it at the television. "I can't hear a word you're saying. Let me turn this off."

The room was suddenly silent. The only noise was the sound coming from the hallway. A light beeping of medical equipment and two aides chatting about their plans for the weekend. My ears rang.

"Who did you say you were?" she asked.

I stepped into the room and closed the door halfway to lessen the sound of the chatter going on in the hall. "I'm Angie Braddock, " I said, and set the flowers on a dresser.

"Oh." She clapped her hands when Oliver peeked out around my legs. "You brought a therapy dog. He's a beauty. French bulldog, am I right? I always had boxers. I'm a sucker for that pushed-in face. Can you bring him closer?"

I pulled a chair across the room and sat on it near her left hand. I patted my lap and Oliver jumped into it.

"Can I pet him?" Austina's mother asked.

I nodded.

She fondled Oliver's ears. "Oh, he feels just like my old Bruno. Bruno was always my favorite. I know you're not supposed to have favorites, but sometimes you connect with an animal on a spiritual level. You know what I mean?"

I stroked Oliver's back. I did know.

"How long has he been a therapy dog?" She scratched Oliver under the chin. "I've seen most of them in the county in the time I've lived here, but never a black-and-white Frenchie."

I rested my hand on Oliver's back. "He's not actually a therapy dog. At least, he's not certified."

"Oh?" Lorna asked but continued to pet Oliver. She couldn't keep her hands off him. "Then what are you doing here?"

"I'm Austina's friend. She asked me to come." I scooted my chair a little bit closer so that she wouldn't have to reach so far to pet Oliver.

She looked at the flowers on the dresser. "Aren't those pretty?" Lorna placed a gnarled hand to her chest. I suspected her knuckles were bent and swollen from rheumatism. "I think I know the name Angie, but I can't place where from. If Austina was here, she'd be able to remind me. She has a very good memory."

"I own the quilt shop. My quilt circle made the quilt on your lap," I said.

She rested her hands on the quilt top. "Oh, yes, that's right. It's lovely, so lovely." She ran her hands over the fine stitching. "I've never seen one so lovely."

Tears sprang to my eyes. It was the best compliment one of my quilting circle's quilts had ever received.

"It's an Ohio Star, isn't it?" she asked.

I nodded.

She seemed pleased that she remembered the pattern's name. "I dabbled in quilting when I was younger. It was a lifetime ago now. I wasn't very good at it. I always envied the quilts the Amish ladies made. I never seemed to have the patience that came to them so naturally."

I understood that completely. I never seemed to have the patience my Amish friends had either. "This one is Amish made. It's from my Amish quilt shop in Rolling Brook called Running Stitch."

"I think I've been in the store, but it's been many, many years. The woman who worked there was always so pleasant. She had a kind face. Sometimes you just know you are talking to a good person from their face. That woman had one of those faces."

I felt a pang of grief in my chest as she described my aunt perfectly. "That was my aunt Eleanor. She passed away over a year ago and left the shop to me."

"Seems like yesterday that I was in there." She touched her chin thoughtfully. "Time begins to run together when you're my age."

I chuckled. "When you're my age too."

She smiled. "I'm glad Austina asked you to come. My Austina is a good girl. I always knew she would be a librarian. You never see that girl without a book. She used to even sneak and read them at church when she thought I didn't notice. I did. I just never said anything. I thought God couldn't say anything bad about reading since the most we know about him comes from the Bible, and that's a book too."

I bit the inside of my cheek. "There's another reason she asked me to come. She wants me to tell you something."

"It is about the bishop dying in her bookmobile. It was highly inconvenient of him to do that, if you ask me. I'd even say it was downright disrespectful of all those lovely books."

It was inconvenient for Bartholomew too, considering he was the one who was dead.

"I spoke to Austina on the telephone yesterday and told her not to worry so much about it. The police would sort it out."

I wondered whether I should tell her about Austina's arrest. Austina wanted me to, so I took a deep breath. "The police arrested Austina."

A hand flew to her forehead. "Oh my, oh my—are you sure? How could the police believe my little girl did anything wrong? She always was a passionate child, especially about her books, but she would never hurt anyone."

"I know that," I said.

She blinked at me through tears. "You do?"

I nodded. "And the sheriff will too."

Weakly, she squeezed my hand. "Good. Thank you. People need to know. If I were able, I would be out there fighting for my girl." Tears were in her eyes. "But I cannot. This body won't let me. I need people like you to do it for me."

I felt a lump in my throat. "I will do my best."

"Good. Good. That's all I ask for." She patted my knee.

Oliver and I sat a little while until Lorna dozed off, holding a corner of the quilt in her hand. Before we left, I squeezed her hand one more time, more determined than ever to find the real killer so that Austina could be free and see her mother again. The best way I could do that would be to track down Faith Beiler and question her about the bookmobile key.

I drove into Charm, a quaint Holmes County town that reminded me of Rolling Brook. The biggest business there was a German restaurant that sold fondue and soft pretzels the size of Oliver. Oliver stuck his head out the window when I drove past the restaurant and its cuckoo clock with wooden characters dressed in lederhosen striking the hour. Outside the restaurant, a Swartzentruber Amish family sold handmade baskets and cornhusk dolls to tourists who were staring up at the clock.

"You won't find a clock like that in Rolling Brook," I told him. "Caroline Cramer would lose her mind over it."

Oliver looked over his shoulder at me.

I followed the directions to the candy shop. It was in the center of town, so I parked on the side street, and Oliver and I walked to the storefront. What Mattie had forgotten to tell me was the name of the sweet shop. A hand-painted sign announced it as YODER'S SWEETS.

Oliver looked up to me and whimpered, and not for the first time I wondered whether he could read.

"Just because it has the name Yoder doesn't mean the owner or anyone in the shop is related to Martha," I told him.

He pressed against my leg. I tried not to take his comforting as a bad sign. Yoder was like the surname Smith in Holmes County. Just because the candy shop was owned by some guy who had the same last name as Martha didn't mean they were related.

There was a small breezeway at the shop's entrance. I knelt and tied Oliver's leash to a gumball machine there. "You are going to have to stay out here, buddy."

He sighed and then crawled behind the gumball machine and lay down. I wished that I had thought to leave Oliver in the car. I hated him being alone in a strange place for even a moment.

"I won't be long," I promised him.

I pushed on the second set of glass doors and went into Yoder's Sweets. The smell of chocolate and strawberries hit me as soon as I stepped inside the shop. Another smell floated on the air. It might have been butterscotch. Whatever it was, the combination made my stomach rumble, especially after my lunch being interrupted by Austina's arrest. There was an island in the middle of the room filled with glass candy jars, containing everything from peppermints to gummy bears, from licorice to Pixy Stix. My teeth ached just looking at it all, but that didn't mean I didn't want a handful of each.

I picked up a shopping basket in a ruse I was there to spend money. It was late afternoon, maybe a half hour before closing time, and I was the only customer in the store. An Amish girl worked behind the counter, dipping pretzel sticks into molten chocolate and then setting them on wax paper to dry.

Was that Faith? I wished I had asked Mattie what the Amish girl looked like before I left the quilt shop.

"Can I help you?" another young girl asked me. Her name tag read, FAITH. Bingo.

I dropped a bag of buckeyes into my basket. They were Mitchell's favorite. Maybe he would consider them a peace offering.

I smiled at the girl. "Actually, yes. Are you Faith Beiler?"

Her face paled almost to the color of her white-blond hair. "Who are you?"

"I'm Angie Braddock." I held out my hand for her to shake.

She didn't take it.

I let my hand fall to my side. "I'm so very sorry about your father."

"Do I know you?" She took a step back.

"No, but we have some friends in common. Austina Shaker . . ." I trailed off.

"She is not my friend." She pointed at the buckeyes in my basket. "If that's all you are buying, maybe you should pay and leave."

"Austina told me that you asked her to leave the keys to the bookmobile out, so that you could get the books without your father knowing."

"Just take the candy and go. You don't even have to pay for it. It is a gift."

"You did ask her to leave the key, didn't you?" I asked.

She wouldn't look at me. "I am going to have to ask you to leave. If you don't leave, I will find the owner, and he will make you leave."

I lowered my voice. "Faith, if you don't talk to me, you will have to talk to the police. They know you were involved in the murder."

Her eyes grew wide. "I wasn't." Tears welled in her eyes.

"Why did you want inside the bookmobile?" I shifted my shopping basket from one hand to the other. "Was it to get books?"

"Nee," she said, barely above a whisper. "I did not want inside of the bookmobile. My father did. He made me write that note to the librarian so that he could go inside."

My eyes widened. "Why?"

She touched the glass jar of peppermints, straightening it by a fraction of an inch. "He said that he was going to stop the bookmobile from coming to our district once and for all."

"What was he planning to do? How was he going to stop her?"

"I—I don't know." She moved another jar.

"Did you tell Levi about the note?"

She closed her eyes. *"Nee."*

"Why not?" I asked.

"I don't want him to know what I did—that I was more responsible for my father's death than he even knows." A tear rolled down her cheek.

"How are you more responsible?" I asked.

"I was selfish. My father said if I wrote that note to the librarian for him, he would allow me to marry Levi. I agreed. I didn't know how Gil would react."

"You think Gil killed your father?"

"I don't know. Maybe." She wiped a tear from her flawless cheek. "All I know is my father would still be alive if I hadn't written that note." She took a breath. "I love Levi—I do—but I can't marry him. There has to be some sort of repercussion for what I did."

"I don't think—"

"I think it's time for you to leave," she said, again barely more than a whisper. "Or I will find the owner."

I followed her to the cash register and placed the basket with my buckeyes on the counter.

"That will be five-sixty." She was in a rush to get me out the door.

I opened my bag and removed my wallet.

She silently held her hand out for the money.

I handed her a ten. "The police have arrested Austina for your father's murder."

She dropped the bill on the counter and picked it up again with clumsy fingers. "Why would they do that?"

"Because a witness saw Austina at the bookmobile hours before you father was killed. She was leaving the key there"—I paused—"for you, or so she thought."

Her hands shook as she punched in the amount into the cash register. "All this time, I thought it was Gil. Maybe I was wrong?"

"I still don't believe she killed him," I said. "Are you sure that your father was going to the bookmobile alone that night? Could anyone else have gone with him? Was he meeting anyone there? Gil, maybe?"

"I don't know. He told me nothing." She dropped my candies into a plastic shopping bag and slid it across the counter to me.

A round woman came from the back room. "Faith, is everything all right? Ginny said that she heard arguing."

That was a bit of an exaggeration. I suspected Ginny was the girl dipping pretzels in chocolate.

Faith looked at her hands. "Everything is fine."

I picked up my shopping bag from the counter. "We were just discussing quilts."

Faith stared at the counter.

"Oh?" the older woman asked, studying me. "My cousin owns a quilt shop in Rolling Brook, Authentic Amish Quilts. Do you know it?"

I suppressed a groan but forced a smile onto my face. "Yes, I know it. I own Running Stitch. It's right next to Martha's shop."

His eyes narrowed. "Are you the *Englischer* who stole the other quilt shop from my cousin?"

"Stole it?" I yelped. "Is that what Martha is telling people?"

"It is what she told me. She said that Eleanor Lapp planned to give her the quilt shop when she died because she took such *gut* care of her, but you swooped in and talked Eleanor into leaving it to you."

I gritted my teeth. Nothing could be further from the truth. I had been as shocked as Martha when my aunt left me the shop. "That's not true."

Faith looked from the Amish woman to me and back again. "I think you should leave."

I marched out of the candy shop with my head held high.

Chapter Thirty-six

I left the small town of Charm feeling more confused about the case than ever. I hoped that the ladies from my quilting circle could shed light on something that I had missed. Instead of going back to Running Stitch, I went straight to the Lehams' farm. Anna would have closed the shop for the day by now.

I turned on the Lehams' road, where neighbors were miles apart. To my right, the sun was setting over the pumpkin patch. Two figures stood in the patch. I recognized Levi's stocky form. The second person was a woman in Amish dress. In the lengthening shadows I couldn't make out her features.

I drove farther up the road and pulled into a dirt driveway that gave trucks and buggies access to the fields.

Oliver cocked his head at me.

"I need to know who Levi is with in the pumpkin patch. It can't be Faith. There is no way she could have beat me here."

I debated leaving Oliver in the car, but I hesitated too long with the door open. My determined Frenchie hopped out and trotted toward the field. I grabbed my cell phone from the dash and locked my bag in the car. "Oliver, come back here!" I hissed.

He looked over his shoulder with his tongue hanging out, but kept going.

When Sarah said that she and Jeremiah had a bumper crop of pumpkins, she hadn't been lying. There were so many pumpkins that it was a miracle I could walk through the field without breaking an ankle. The pumpkins came in every shape and size. Oliver wove in and out of them, disappearing behind the largest ones.

"Oliver," I hissed again.

He ignored me and kept going. I debated running and tackling him, but didn't think that was worth a broken leg. We were almost to the place where I had seen Levi and the Amish woman, but by now no one was there.

I glanced around the pumpkin patch. The setting sun painted purple, grays, and pinks on the clouds overhead. The temperature dropped with each inch the sun fell. Levi and his lady friend were gone. There was nowhere to hide unless they'd dove between the rows of pumpkins, and that was hard to imagine.

"Ollie," I said, no longer bothering to whisper.

Oliver was two rows of pumpkins away digging a hole. I stepped over a large pumpkin with my right foot while the toe of my other boot got caught in a neighboring one. I pitched forward and landed in a muddy row between the pumpkins. Groaning, I rolled onto my side. I just lay there for a moment.

Oliver whimpered and licked my cheek. "I'm all right, Ollie. At least almost breaking my ankle gets your attention," I told him.

"Who's there?" a voice called.

Maybe we weren't alone after all. I rolled onto my stomach and peeked over a pumpkin.

The sun was almost gone now, and a yellow light bobbed through the field.

I grabbed Oliver and forced him to lie down next to me. "Shh," I whispered.

He buried his face under my arm.

The voice called a second time. This time in Pennsylvania Dutch.

As the shadow moved closer, I was wondering what I should do. Oliver shook next to me and snuggled up so close he was practically on top of me.

The glow of the lantern disappeared. Oliver and I lay there for a little while longer. Could whoever was in the field have left? Was it Levi, or someone else? By now, the ladies of the quilting circle would start to wonder what had happened to me.

I peeked over the pumpkin again, but by this time it was so dark I could only make out rough shapes, and nothing in the field moved. Then I heard something.

"I told you someone was listening." It was a woman's voice.

"There is no one here," a man said. "I looked."

"I should go home," the woman said.

An owl hooted somewhere in the trees that blocked the view of the pumpkin patch from the warm light of the Leham farmhouse. Oliver shivered.

"*Nee*," the man said. "I need to talk to you. You are the only friend I have in the district."

"My *bruder* would not like that I'm here." The woman's voice quavered.

"Don't worry about him."

"That is easy for you to say."

Something crawled up the back of my neck. I squelched a squeal as I knocked it away.

"Did you hear that?" Levi asked.

"I told you someone was here."

I couldn't identify the woman's hoarse whisper. It might have been Faith, but I still believed that it would have been impossible for her to beat me there.

Then my cell phone rang. I frantically reached into my pocket to try to stop it, but the damage was done.

The lantern blinked on and the light was directed at my eyes. I held up my hand to block the light, and Oliver wedged himself between two large pumpkins.

The phone continued to ring.

Levi glared down at me. "Are you going to answer that?" he asked, just as the call went to voice mail.

I scrambled to my feet, still shielding my eyes. "Can you lower your light?"

Levi lowered the lantern a fraction of an inch. As he did, I could make out the woman's face. It was Phoebe Truber, the redheaded schoolteacher. I blinked at her as my suspicions rose. "What are the two of you doing here? Together?"

"This is my family's land," Levi said.

I brushed dirt from my jacket, a futile gesture as I was covered head to foot in mud. I knew Oliver probably was too. "Why are you out here, Phoebe?"

"Levi asked me to come." Her teeth chattered.

"I needed to talk to her." Levi shone the light in my eyes again.

I raised my hand over my face. "Do you have to keep doing that?"

"You deserve worse for spying on us." He lowered the light.

I scooped up Oliver and held him to my chest. "I think we should all go to your brother's house and talk this over."

Phoebe looked to Levi. "I should go home."

"*Nee*. You are my friend. You should come too."

Phoebe chewed on her lip but didn't argue.

He sighed. "All right. *Ya*, let's go to my *bruder*'s house."

Silently, we walked through the woods to the Leham home. All the while I wondered what Levi and Phoebe were going to reveal. Was it a secret romance? Phoebe was easily ten years Levi's senior, but that didn't mean it was impossible. But he had been so broken up about Faith calling off their wedding.

Breaking through the trees, I recognized the Millers' and the Grabers' buggies parked in the driveway. Heavy black horse blankets protected both horses from the cold. Mattie stood on the front porch holding the lantern and hurried down the steps toward us. If she was surprised to see Levi and Phoebe with me, she didn't say anything. "Angie, Rachel and I saw your car and wondered what became of you."

"Rachel came?" I said.

Mattie's brow furrowed. "*Ya*, of course she came. She always comes to quilting circle meetings."

"Right." I realized that Mattie still didn't know about the incident in the woods with Nahum.

She held the lantern higher and inspected me. "What happened to you? You're covered in mud."

"Pumpkins," I said.

She shook her head. "Everyone is inside." She looked

to Levi and Phoebe. "Sarah and Anna made plenty of food. You two should come inside and eat. You look cold." Dozens of unasked questions played across Mattie's face.

Phoebe shook her head, but Levi said, "That would be nice."

"Angie," Sarah said. "There you are. We were all getting worried when we saw your car but not you." She blinked when she saw Levi and Phoebe standing behind me. "I see you're not alone."

I stepped into the house and set Oliver on the floor. He headed for the warmth of the potbelly stove. "I met up with Levi and Phoebe in the pumpkin patch," I said, as if it was the most natural thing in the world. "I told them that they should come inside for a chat."

"Oh, *ya*, please come inside." She looked to her brother-in-law. "It's *gut* to see you are feeling better."

In the warm lantern light of the Lehams' home, it was easy to see that Levi's eyes looked better after that morning's incident. They were bloodshot, but alert.

She nodded at Phoebe. "It is nice to see you."

Anna and Rachel were in the living room. Both of them were piecing quilt toppers on their laps and froze midstitch when they recognized our visitors.

"Please sit," Sarah said. "I will go make coffee for everyone. Mattie, will you help me?"

Nervously, Phoebe perched on the only open seat on the couch between Rachel and Anna.

Levi sat on the hearth.

I excused myself to go to the bathroom to wash what mud I could from my hands and coat. The coat might be a lost cause. Luckily, most of the mud was on my upper half. My boots would be okay with a little boot polish. When I returned to the living room, Anna set her work aside and rooted through her basket. She came up with several pieces of cloth, a needle, and a spool of white thread. Anna handed Phoebe cut pieces of cloth. "We are having a quilting circle meeting tonight, and if you are going to join us, you have to quilt. You can sew, can't you?"

Phoebe nodded and seemed to be happy to have something to occupy her hands.

"How are the children at your school, Phoebe?" Rachel asked in her gentle voice.

"I don't know." She concentrated on her work. "We have not had school the last two days. I hope they will return on Monday. Without the bishop, many families in the district are confused about what to do. He was a big part of our everyday lives. Levi is not the only one in the district who has shared his concerns with me. Many in the district have come to me for comfort." She dropped her gaze to the needle and thread in her lap.

Sarah stepped into the living room with her eyebrows raised. "Levi asked to talk to you?"

"Phoebe is like an older sister to me," Levi said. "I asked to talk to her because of what happened with Faith. She knows what I'm going through." He stared at the floor and his face turned red.

Phoebe smiled at him and seemed more relaxed now that she was quilting. "Faith is confused like so many in our district after the bishop's death. I told Levi not to worry. She still loves him. She needs time."

"I saw Faith today," I said, sitting on a kitchen chair, which Mattie had quietly brought into the room.

Levi's head snapped up.

I met his gaze. "I think Phoebe is right."

"If that is true, Levi, you need to talk to her," Rachel said.

He shook his head. "She was so certain we shouldn't marry."

"She wasn't as certain when I spoke to her," I said.

He jumped to his feet. "I'll go talk to her now."

"Levi," Sarah said, setting the coffee tray in the middle of an oak end table. "It's late, and the Beiler family is in mourning. Wait until tomorrow."

He sat back down and dropped his head into his hands.

"Bruder," Sarah said. "Why don't you sleep here tonight, and then you can go see Faith when you are refreshed in the morning? It will only scare her and upset her family if you go over at this hour."

"Ya," Anna agreed. "And in the morning your eyes will have cleared of any trace of drinking." She gave him her best disapproving look.

He removed his black felt hat and held it lightly. "I suppose you're right. Earlier, Phoebe told me the same." He looked at each woman in the room. "I never expected to have this conversation with all of you."

"Ah," Anna said. "We are *gut* shoulders to cry on."

He laughed lightly. "I will go upstairs and see what the children are doing." He looked at Phoebe. *"Danki."*

I couldn't help but wonder whether he was thanking her for more than meeting him in the pumpkin patch.

Levi went up the stairs with heavy steps.

Chapter Thirty-seven

After Levi was out of sight, Sarah asked, "Would you like to stay for dinner, Phoebe? We have plenty."

"*Nee*, I should be getting home. My family will worry."

"How are you getting home?" Rachel asked.

"I will walk. It is how I got here."

I stood up. "Don't be silly," I said. "I'll drive you."

"I don't mind walking." She tied the ribbons of her bonnet. "It is not far."

"So it will not be far for me to take you."

"That is a very *gut* idea, Angie," Anna said.

Phoebe tried to argue more, but it was the five members of my quilting circle against one. She didn't stand a chance.

I touched Rachel's arm. "Before I leave, can I talk to you?"

She frowned but nodded.

I felt the other ladies from the quilting circle watching us as we went into the kitchen. I half expected Sarah to follow us, but no one did.

Rachel stirred the stew on the stovetop. "If you take Phoebe home, you will miss dinner."

"It's all right. I'm not hungry," I said.

She turned and arched an eyebrow at me.

I smiled. "I'm not *that* hungry." I paused. "Rachel, I'm sorry about today—about what happened to Nahum."

She concentrated on the pot. "You should not have left him there with his leg caught like that."

"I know. I was so taken aback. Willow and I were there only a couple of minutes before you appeared."

She picked up a dishtowel from the counter and folded it. It was impossible for an Amish woman to stand still in a kitchen. "I asked you not to talk to him about me."

"I know, and at that time I wasn't. I was as surprised as you were when Willow led me to him in the woods. I was questioning him about Austina."

"But you have spoken to him about me before," she said.

I bit the inside of my cheek. "Yes."

She placed the dishtowel on the counter and sighed. "I know that you mean well, but I have asked you not to talk to him because I'm not ready to speak to my father myself. When I am, you will know. I'm asking you to be patient."

"I'm not the most patient person in the world."

The corner of her mouth turned up into a small smile. "I have noticed."

I gave a sigh of relief at her smile. "Okay, we have a deal. No more Nahum talk."

She laughed. "*Gut.*"

Not long after that, Phoebe, Oliver, and I left the Lehams' farm. In my car, as Phoebe buckled her seat belt, she said, "I live on Hock Trail."

"So you live near your school. That is nice."

She nodded and stared out the window.

"It was nice of you to talk to Levi." I watched her out the corner of my eye.

She didn't look at me. "I know how he felt. I lost someone I was going to marry once. I don't want that to happen to my friend."

"What happened?" I asked.

"He was from a different district," she said softly.

"Who was it?" I couldn't help asking the question.

"It does not matter. It was a long time ago."

"I was engaged to be married once. Not to the sheriff," I said quickly. "To someone else back in Texas, so I sort of understand what you've gone through."

She shook her head. "No, you can't. You can make your own decisions." She cleared her throat. "It was for the best. Had I married, I would no longer be teaching, and I love my children so much."

She didn't say another word after that. I suspected that she was sorry she'd said anything at all to me about him. Even when we drove by her school, she said nothing.

A mile south of the school, my headlights hit a white mailbox. "That is my driveway. I will get out here."

I shifted the car into park.

"*Danki*—thank you for the ride. I am home much quicker than I would have been had I walked." She got out of the car.

As I backed up, my headlights caught sight of Phoebe's brother, Phillip, standing in the driveway. He glared at me through the windshield.

I shook off the creeping feeling that Phillip gave me

and stopped at the end of Hock Trail to check my phone to see whose call had given away my hiding spot in the pumpkin patch. It was the sheriff.

Taking a deep breath, I called Mitchell back. I was ready for the lecture about keeping information from him and meddling in a police investigation.

"Thank goodness it's you," Mitchell said, honestly relieved.

That was a much friendlier greeting than I had expected after our argument outside the diner.

"Angie, I'm in a bit of a bind," he said.

"What's wrong?" I sat up straight.

"I'm supposed to have Zander tonight, but I have to work late. I suppose you can guess why."

Because he arrested Austina. I knew he must be questioning her. I knew from experience that police questioning, especially when it came to murder, could take hours. I bit my lip. "I can."

"Z is at Hillary's right now."

"He can't stay there?" I asked.

"She has a date."

"Oh!" I said. "Oh."

"Yes," Mitchell agreed. "And I told her I don't want her to cancel."

Neither did I. Hillary dating might mean that she was finally over Mitchell, or at least trying to be. I would take whatever I could get in that direction.

"Could you pick him up and stay with him until I can leave the station?" Mitchell asked in a rush.

I blew out a breath. Since he asked me to watch Z, I knew he couldn't be that mad at me. "Sure, I can pick him up. Do you want me to take him to my house or yours?"

"Mine," he said, sounding relieved. "Would that be all right?"

"No problem." I had a key he'd given me several weeks earlier. "How late will you be?"

He sighed. "I don't know."

"Don't worry. Zander and I will be fine. I'll feed him junk food, and we will stay up late."

He didn't even react to my joke. "Great. I'll let Hillary know." He paused. "And, Angie, we need to talk about today. Not now, but later."

"I know." That was not a conversation I was looking forward to.

"See you tonight."

"Tonight." All the warm fuzzies I had gotten over being asked to watch Zander dissolved with his promise of a talk.

Hillary Mitchell, Mitchell's ex-wife and my sort of friend, lived in Millersburg in a large two-story home. I knew from Zander it was the house that Hillary and Mitchell had shared before the divorce. I tried not to think about that as I turned into the driveway. What woman wanted to visit the home her boyfriend had shared with another woman?

I rang the doorbell, and Hillary answered. Her long black hair cascaded over her shoulders, and her makeup was expertly applied. She wore a navy cocktail dress that fit her perfectly. Not for the first time, I was struck by how stunning Mitchell's ex-wife was. I felt like a frump in comparison, wearing my cowboy boots, jeans, and a cotton-blend sweater, not to mention the traces of dirt on my clothes from my spill in the pumpkin patch.

"Come on in." She held the door open wide.

I stepped over the threshold. It was the first time I had ever entered Zander's other home. The decor was a nice blend of modern and traditional, a lot like Hillary herself. I could see her touch everywhere. I wondered whether it had looked the same when Mitchell lived there, but I pushed those thoughts away.

"Thanks for coming on such short notice. I should have known that James would be called into work and had a backup sitter lined up. It's always the same."

Automatically, I came to Mitchell's defense. "There is a murder investigation going on."

"Zander, hurry up," Hillary shouted over her shoulder. Then, turning back to me, she said, "If it wasn't a murder, it would be something else."

I bit back a smart retort.

There was a muffled response from the next room over the drone of the television. Something might have been exploding. Explosions were Z's favorite.

"I don't mind at all. Mitchell said you have a date." I tried to keep my tone conversational.

She groaned. "I should have canceled it. Dating is such a waste of time."

"It doesn't have to be. Dating can be good." I hoped I gave her an encouraging smile.

"We'll see." She picked up a small black-beaded purse from the side table by the door. It was so small I didn't even know why she bothered with it. "One of my coworkers set me up with her brother. He's taking me to a winery for a tasting and dinner. It may turn out to be a complete disaster."

"But there will be wine," I said, keeping it positive.

"True, so it won't be a complete loss."

Zander bounced into the living room with an over-sized backpack on his back.

"Did you pack your homework?" his mother asked.

He rolled his eyes. "Mom, it's Friday. No one does homework on Friday." He promptly dropped his back-pack on the floor as if it weighed a thousand pounds.

Hillary shook her head. "The eye rolling thing is new," she said to me. "It drives me nuts. I have no idea how I'm going to survive his teenage years, and if he's anything like his father, he will be a handful."

"Wait. The sheriff was a handful when he was grow-ing up?" This was news. I had always thought Mitchell had permanently been on the straight and narrow. I'd yet to see the man so much as jaywalk, and he was the sheriff. It wasn't as if someone was going to arrest him for crossing the street in the wrong place.

"The stories I could tell . . . ," Hillary said ominously.

I would have asked for more details if Zander hadn't been standing there.

"We should do coffee sometime, Angie. Just you and me, and I can tell you all about James's wild past."

I smiled. I knew Mitchell wouldn't like that. He was leery that Hillary and I were even on speaking terms. Maybe it was because she could clue me into his mis-spent youth.

She opened and closed her clutch. "If anything hap-pens, you have my cell number. You just call me. I might want an excuse to escape my date anyway."

I smiled. "Don't worry. We'll be fine."

She gave Zander a hug. "Be good."

He rolled his eyes again. I could see why this might

become a problem. I hoped he hadn't picked up the eye rolling from me, but I was afraid he might have.

Hillary and I said good-bye, and I tousled Zander's hair on the way to the car. "What kind of junk food do you want for dinner, kid?"

"Pizza."

"Toppings?"

"Extra cheese and pepperoni."

"Ahh, a boy after my own heart."

Fifteen minutes later, Zander and I were waiting at the pizza place to pick up our order, which also included a side of buffalo wings, garlic bread, and a salad. I consoled myself that I had included a salad. Sure, the salad was half mozzarella cheese, but it still counted. Amish Country wasn't known for its pizza, but there was a pretty good mom-and-pop place in Millersburg.

Zander fed Oliver pieces of mozzarella from the salad while we waited for the pizza.

My cell phone rang. I was beginning to wonder when I had become so popular. I knew it couldn't be Mitchell. I had texted him right after picking Zander up, and he said he thought he would be home at eleven if he was lucky and that he couldn't talk.

"We need an emergency meeting for the book sale tonight," Willow said in my ear.

When had a library book sale equated to a state of emergency?

"We need you to come back to town." Willow sounded winded, as if she had just sprinted down Sugartree Street.

I glanced over at Zander, who had stuffed his cheek

full of cheese until he looked like a chipmunk. "I'm with Zander. Mitchell had to work late."

"Drop him off with his mother," Willow said dismissively.

"She had a date."

"Oh," Willow said. That derailed her for just a moment. "Then bring him with you."

Mitchell would love that.

"Angie, we need you." She paused. "The bookmobile is back."

That grabbed my attention, as she knew it would. "What? Why?"

"See you in ten minutes at my shop, and we will explain." She ended the call.

I hung up and sighed. "Can I have another cheese pizza to go?" I asked the teen at the counter.

Chapter Thirty-eight

I'd been hoping Willow was pulling some sort of cruel joke, but, alas, the giant silver-and-green behemoth was indeed parked in the middle of Sugartree Street, right in front of the Dutchman's Tea Shop. I parked behind the bookmobile and unloaded two dogs and a child.

After collecting the pizzas, Zander had insisted we stop at Mitchell's house to pick up Tux. He said it wasn't fair that Tux had been home alone all day. So I went into the tea shop with two dogs and a nine-year-old. Yeah, this wasn't a recipe for disaster.

Willow threw open the door to the tea shop.

Holding the pizzas, I said, "I thought you were joking about the bookmobile."

"Why would I joke about that? Come in, come in. Your parents are already inside."

Terrific.

Willow ushered Oliver, Tux, Zander, and me inside.

"Be careful," I said to Zander, including the dogs in my statement. "Try not to break anything."

There were only two customers in the tea shop sitting at separate tables working on laptop computers. The Dutchman's Tea Shop did most of its business with the breakfast and lunch crowd. Most people left Sugartree Street when the other shops on the road closed at four. Willow stayed opened until seven because she lived above the tea shop in a small apartment on the second floor, and since she had such a short commute, it made sense to stay open and make a little more money.

My mother and father sat at a table by the front window. There was a pot of tea in between them. I set the pizzas on a neighboring table.

"Kara, can you get some plates and napkins?" Willow asked her server.

The girl nodded and headed back to the kitchen, then reappeared within seconds with paper plates and napkins. She probably took one look at Zander and realized Willow's fine china wasn't going to work.

Zander settled into his seat. I knew from experience that we had about ten minutes before he got bored with eating and started exploring the shop. There were far too many things in Willow's shop for him to break, so I couldn't allow that to happen.

"Angela," Mom said, "why do you have dirt on your clothes?"

I handed Zander a paper napkin. "Pumpkins."

"Pumpkins can be dangerous," Dad said.

"So what's the emergency?" I asked. "I mean, other than the bookmobile being back. And why is it here?" I put two pieces of pepperoni pizza on a plate for Zander before taking two for myself. I suspected I was going to need a third.

My mother raised her eyebrow at my dinner.

Dad stood and moved over to Zander's table. "Since you have official book sale business, the guys will sit over here with the pizza. Right, Z-man?"

Zander high-fived my dad. "Right."

I couldn't help but smile at how well they got along. It was a good sign if we ever became a real family.

My mother dragged me from my happy thoughts back to reality. "The sheriff's department was done processing the bookmobile and released it back to the library." She shot Willow a look. "Willow insisted that the bookmobile be brought back here and parked in the middle of the farmers' market."

Willow put a piece of cheese pizza on her plate and sat at our table. "But Aaron Miller doesn't want me to park it at the factory. When the library brought it into the township, he blocked his drive so it couldn't get onto his property. So then they brought it back here and parked it."

"Why didn't they take it back to the library? That's where it should go." I stared out the window at the huge vehicle, half illuminated by a lamppost.

Willow raised her chin. "I told them not to. We need it here to advertise the book sale."

Mom pursed her lips. I was willing to bet she was beginning to regret drafting Willow into the book sale planning. Had she asked me, I could have told her that it would come to something like this.

Out of the corner of my eye, I saw Dad trying very hard not to look our way. Smart man.

"So it's sitting here." I pointed my thumb at the window.

"Yep," Willow said around a piece of cheese pizza.

Thankfully, my mother chose to ignore Willow's poor etiquette.

"Why am I here exactly?" I asked. "Other than to tell you that having the bookmobile parked in the middle of Sugartree Street is a terrible idea?"

"It's not a terrible idea." Willow pouted just a little.

I was actually starting to lose my appetite. "Some of the Amish might find it offensive because Bartholomew died in there."

"That's ridiculous," Willow said. "The people in Beiler's Amish district don't come to the book sale. Think of how many tourists the bookmobile will attract when they're driving down the street." She fished into her pants pocket and came up with a set of keys. She slapped them on the table.

"What are those?" I asked, even though I knew.

"Keys to the bookmobile. I think you should keep them." She slid the bookmobile keys across the table to me.

I slid them back. "I don't want those. I have nothing to do with this."

Willow left the keys on the table. "Why not? The bookmobile parked in front of my tea shop will be great publicity for the library. They could use some good press right now."

I shook my head. "Leaving the bookmobile in the middle of Sugartree Street will not get the library good press. In fact, the opposite will be true."

Willow took a bite of pizza as if she hadn't heard.

An hour later, the pizza was all gone, thanks mostly to my dad and Zander. Willow and I were still at a stalemate over the bookmobile. Zander and the two dogs had fallen asleep in the tea shop's window seat.

"It's late," I said after throwing away the pizza boxes. "I need to take Zander home."

"Angie's right," my dad said, speaking up suddenly. "I'm almost as tired as those three." He pointed at the sleeping dogs and boy. "Let's go home, Daphne."

"Angie," Willow said, "I'm not giving up on this."

I sighed. "I wouldn't expect you to." I gathered up the boy and dogs and headed for the door.

At the sheriff's house, I unlocked the front door. Oliver and Tux ran inside and curled up in Tux's dog bed. Zander wobbled next to me, half asleep. Finally, I gave up making him walk, and I carried him to his bedroom at the end of the hallway.

In his room, I dodged cars and action figures on the way to his bed. I laid him on it, removed his shoes, and covered him with the quilt that my quilting circle had made for his birthday. It was unique as far as Amish quilts went. It was a nine-block, with a different superhero in each block, from Batman to Thor. While making the quilt, I had to explain to my quilting circle who most of the characters were.

"Night," I whispered. I kissed Zander's forehead and smiled. He would have never stood for the kiss had he been awake.

Half asleep myself, I stumbled back to the living room. Tux and Oliver were sound asleep. I kicked off my cowboy boots and lay on the couch just to rest my eyes.

The next thing I knew, I felt something touch my forehead. I blinked my eyes open and found Mitchell's blue-green eyes staring bemused into my blurry ones. "What time is it?" I mumbled.

He was sitting on the edge of the couch, and he tucked a curl behind my ear. "Two in the morning."

I blinked. "And you are just getting home?"

"I've been here a little bit. Not long."

I stretched an arm over my head. "Doing what?"

"I've been watching you sleep."

"Creepy," I muttered, but a smile took the bite out of my words.

"It was a very Sleeping Beauty moment. I wanted to kiss you awake, but I was afraid you might wake up and punch me." He grinned.

I snorted, and Mitchell smiled. He nodded at the huge stack of picture books and the buckeyes on his coffee table. "What are those for?"

I rubbed my eyes. "The buckeyes are a peace offering for you, and the books are for Z. I thought Zander and I could read them together. I might have gotten carried away. I bought them at the book sale today. There are even more in my car, because I thought it would be good to keep some at my house for when he comes over." I rolled onto my side and looked at him. "I was thinking of turning the spare room into a hangout for him. Not a bedroom. He already has two of those, but a place he can call his own at my house."

There were tears in Mitchell's eyes. In the time that I had known him, I had never seen him cry.

I sat up alarmed. "What's wrong? I—I won't, if you don't want me to. You and Hillary have a right to decide who spends time with Zander and what he does.

I don't want to presume he will stay at my house. It was just an idea for a night like tonight."

Mitchell took my face in both of his hands. "You want to spend time with my son."

I swallowed, searching his eyes. "Yes, but if you don't want that, it's fine—"

He stopped my babbling with a kiss that made my toes curl.

When he pulled away, I blinked. "What was that for?"

"For wanting to spend time with my son, for caring about him when I'm not around." He continued to hold on to my face. "I didn't know I would find anyone who would do that."

I blinked away my own tears and fixed his already straight collar. "He's a great kid, and I care about him. I care about you both."

"I more than care," he said. "I love you."

"Not 'Love you,'" I whispered to myself. "No question."

"What?" he asked.

"Me too," I said against his lips.

Chapter Thirty-nine

The next morning, I fell off Mitchell's couch and groaned. Oliver and Tux took turns licking my face.

"Morning, sunshine," Mitchell said, looking bright-eyed and bushy-tailed. I hated him for it.

After Mitchell woke me up at two in the morning, he insisted that I spend the night. I agreed but insisted that I sleep on his couch even though he'd offered me his bed and volunteered for the sofa. No way was I sleeping in Mitchell's king-sized bed. In a lot of ways, I was as old-fashioned as my Amish friends.

Now lying on the floor covered in doggy slobber, I sort of wished I had taken him up on his offer. I pushed the dogs away and sat up. "What time is it?"

"Eight," he said.

I groaned.

I could hear the television droning in the den. "Zander is already up."

Mitchell smiled. "Oh, yes, for a couple of hours now."

"So you are both morning people," I mumbled.

His grin widened. "Definitely."

I rubbed my eyes. "At least I know what I'm getting myself into." I sat back on the couch.

"I'm going to take Zander with me to the station today. His mom will pick him up later this morning there."

I nodded, still half asleep. "I'd better get home. Who knows what havoc Dodger has wreaked alone in the house all night, and it's the book sale again today." I slapped my forehead. "The bookmobile!"

"What about it?" Mitchell asked.

"The bookmobile is parked in the middle of Sugartree Street." I groaned.

"Why?" Mitchell asked, genuinely confused.

"Willow," I said. "When it was released from your department, she convinced the library to let her park it there to get more attention for the book sale."

He shook his head. "It will certainly do that."

"I have to get it out of there somehow before it offends every Amish person in the county." I scrambled back onto the couch.

"Speaking of the bookmobile, we need to talk," he said, sounding much less like a boyfriend and more like a cop.

I grimaced. "About Austina."

He nodded. "Yes."

"Before you say anything, let me say, you're right. I should have told you right away when Nahum told me what he saw. Don't forget the buckeyes. The buckeyes were a peace offering." I pointed to the open bag on the coffee table. Quite a few were missing. Chocolate and peanut butter, the breakfast of champions and rural county sheriffs everywhere.

"I didn't forget the buckeyes," he said. "But yes, you should have told me right away."

"And I shouldn't have talked to Austina about it first before I talked to you."

"Also true," he agreed.

"Does it help that I'm sorry—really sorry?" I gave him my most dazzling smile. A trick I had learned from my child beauty pageant days.

The right side of his face tilted up in a smile. "A little. The buckeyes helped too."

"Because I am, and I don't want my curiosity to ruin what we have."

"Neither do I."

"Since you're being so agreeable," I said, knowing that I was pushing my luck, "I just have to say I don't believe that Austina was the one who murdered the bishop. His death has put her bookmobile and career at risk."

"Neither do I," he repeated.

I opened my mouth to argue my point further. "Wait—what?"

He leaned back in the armchair across from me. "I don't think she killed the bishop. After hours of questioning her last night, I'm even more convinced."

I blinked at him. "Then why did you arrest her?"

"I had to. It's my job to report the evidence I have to the prosecutor. He felt there was enough there to bring Austina in. It was his call."

I sat back in the couch, placated. "Does that mean you will let her out?"

"I'm working on it. It would be a lot easier if I could find the real criminal. Right now, the prosecutor wants someone behind bars, and that someone is Austina. He wants to show the Amish that we are doing something about the bishop's death and that we care."

I pushed my hair out of my eyes. "I still can't believe Nahum told you about seeing Austina. He's usually not that cooperative with the police." I held up my hand when Mitchell frowned. "I'm not saying he shouldn't have told you. I'm surprised he did so voluntarily." Mentally, I added, *I wished he hadn't.*

"He didn't," Mitchell said. "At least not directly."

"What does that mean?" I frowned.

He sighed. "Remember when I left your parents' house during dinner a few nights ago?"

I nodded. "You had trouble with kids using Amish mailboxes as batting practice."

"Right. Well, we caught the kids, and to lessen the trouble they were in they told us about some illegal poaching with snares they knew about in the woods near Sugartree Street. They saw Nahum setting snares late one night when they were out joyriding."

It was starting to make sense. "And when you spoke to Nahum about it, he told you about Austina to get some of the heat off of him for the illegal poaching."

Mitchell nodded.

"So it was each crook trying to save his own hide."

Mitchell smiled at my use of the word "crook." "Yes."

"That's a pretty sad commentary on society."

"No honor among thieves," Mitchell quoted. "Many times we have a break in a case because we catch someone else doing a lesser crime who wants to save him- or herself." The sheriff chuckled. "I can practically see the wheels turning in your head trying to figure this out. I'm starting to realize I can't stop you from meddling." He stood up and walked over to me.

I looked up at him. "You can't. I need to protect my friends. I can't stop myself."

"That's both endearing and frustrating. Somehow, I will learn to live with it." He leaned forward and kissed me.

"Gross!" Zander yelled, but Mitchell and I ignored him.

After I left the sheriff's house, Oliver and I made a quick stop at home, so I could shower and change and check on Dodger.

Dodger was waiting for us when I unlocked the front door. The moment we stepped inside, he arched his back and hissed. As I suspected, he was not pleased by our impromptu sleepover at the sheriff's house.

I closed the front door and dropped my bag on the floor.

Oliver bowed into downward dog, groveling and begging forgiveness from his feline bestie.

Dodger sniffed and turned his tail, giving both Oliver and me an unpleasant view of his back end. Oliver whined.

"I'll let you two work it out," I said as I headed for the stairs.

An hour later, Dodger had deigned to allow Oliver to sit next to him on the living room couch. I hated to break up the duo again, but it was time Oliver and I left for the book sale and dealt with Willow and the bookmobile.

I hoped that the bookmobile would be gone when I turned onto Sugartree Street twenty minutes later. No such luck. The silver-and-green monster sat in the middle of the street in front of the tea shop, backing up

traffic for two blocks. Apparently, the stalemate between the Millers and Willow continued.

Cars and buggies crawled down the street toward
the pie factory as the massive bookmobile forced traffic
down to one lane. I turned left into the community lot
in front of the Amish mercantile and parked.

Oliver and I walked the half block to Running Stitch.
Mattie stood outside of the shop. "If that bookmobile
doesn't move, we aren't going to have a single customer today. It's going to ruin the farmers' market and
the factory's grand opening too."

I sighed. "I'll talk to Willow."

I picked up Oliver and crossed the street, avoiding
both angry English and Amish drivers as I went.

Willow stood in front of her tea shop with her hands
on her hips, staring at the bookmobile. She glanced
over at me. "Good. You're here."

I set Oliver on the sidewalk. "What are you going to
do about the bookmobile? It's hurting business."

Willow ran her hand through her purple hair.
"Maybe you were right. You should move it."

"Me?" I pointed a thumb at myself. "I don't know
how to drive that thing. It's a tank."

Willow frowned. "Do you want me to do it?"

"No!" I yelped. Knowing my luck, Willow would
drive the monster vehicle right through the front window of Running Stitch.

"Okay, then," she pulled the keys out of her jeans
pocket. "It's all yours."

"You're nuts. I can't drive it. The biggest thing I have
ever driven was my friend's mom's station wagon when

I was sixteen. Trust me, it didn't go well for the station wagon or for me."

Willow dangled the keys in front of me. "You don't have to drive it far. Move it to the end of the street and pull it off the road. Someone from the library can come later to collect it." She ran a hand over her now dark purple spiky hair. "I think you may have been right about this bookmobile. I have noticed the Amish heading to the farmers' market have been avoiding it."

"I'm right for once," I said. "What a miracle."

She shook the keys at me. "Don't get cheeky. Move the bookmobile."

I stuck my hands on my hips. "Call someone from the library and tell them to collect it now."

"I already did that. It's Saturday, and there are only two people there. They can't leave." She shrugged.

I wasn't giving up that easily. "Then call someone else. Call the director at home. I thought you had connections."

Willow shook her head. "Tried that too. She's in Cincinnati for the weekend."

Well, that sounded a little too convenient. I wondered whether the library director made those travel plans after Willow had talked her into lending her the bookmobile. Willow dropped the keys into my hand before I could stop her. "You'll be fine. I'll direct traffic so you can get out." She disappeared around the bookmobile and into the street.

"Willow!" I shouted.

She ignored me.

Oliver and I shared a look. I climbed up the single

step to the bookmobile and opened the side door. All the lights were on. Immediately, my eyes went to the spot in the aisle where Bartholomew Beiler's body had lain. The carpet in that area had been cut out, revealing the metal floor below. I supposed that was better than seeing the bloodstains.

I turned to the cockpit and slipped into the driver's seat. There were so many levers and buttons, I wondered whether the astronauts drove bookmobiles for practice. It was much closer to a space shuttle than to any car I had ever been in. I put the key in the ignition and turned over the engine.

Behind me, Oliver barked.

"Ollie, I'm trying to figure out how to drive this spaceship." I flicked on a switch and the windshield wipers ran back and forth over the windshield.

Oliver barked more insistently.

I looked over my shoulder. "What is it?"

He was staring at the back of the bookmobile between two bookshelves. He looked at me and at the bookshelves and back again.

I sighed and got out of my seat. "What is it? A spider?"

I left the keys in the ignition and hurried to the back of the bookmobile. There I found Phoebe Truber tucked in between the shelving.

I knelt in front of her. "Phoebe?"

Her hair had fallen from her prayer cap. Tears streamed down her face, and she held her knees to her chest. "I did it. I can't keep it secret anymore. I killed the bishop."

"What? How?"

"I was there when he died." Her entire body shook.

"Wait." I held her hand. It was as cold as ice. "Back up. Tell me from the beginning."

"I can't." She squeezed her eyes shut.

An idea struck me. "Tell me like it's a story in one of your books."

She brushed a tear from her cheek. "My books are what caused this."

"Please, Phoebe. What were you doing on the book-mobile that night?"

"Phillip was working late at the pie factory. He had told my sister-in-law that he wanted to perfect his recipe for the pumpkin fluff pie. There was something not right. My brother is a perfectionist when it comes to baking—when it comes to most things—and he was so happy about the new job for the Millers. I hadn't seen him that happy in a very long time. My sister-in-law sent me into town to bring him dinner because he was gone so long."

"When was this?" I asked.

"Very late," she said. "A little after midnight."

So she had been there just after Austina had dropped off the key for the bishop, albeit unknowingly. "Then what happened?"

She squeezed her eyes closed. "I gave my brother the meal. I didn't stay long. When I was leaving, I noticed the bookmobile was in the parking lot. I went over to it and tried the door. I don't know why I did that. I was just curious, I suppose. The door was unlocked, so I went inside. The bishop was there with a canister of gasoline." She opened her eyes. "I think he was going to burn the bookmobile down."

The sheriff had been wrong. The gasoline had not been on the bookmobile to cover up the murder. Bartholomew had taken it there himself to set the bookmobile on fire. That's how he was going to ruin Austina, as he'd promised his daughter.

"I surprised him. He dropped the canister and hit his head on the bookshelf."

"What part of his head?" I asked.

She touched her forehead. It was the place where I had seen the wound on Bartholomew the morning I had found Austina with the body.

"I—I stood there staring at him bleeding. I didn't know what to do. Then Phillip came. My *bruder* must have wondered why my buggy was still in the parking lot and came out to investigate. He saw me with the bishop. He told me that he was dead." She took a shuddered breath. "He said he would take care of it and made me promise not to tell anyone what had happened. I tried. I tried to keep it a secret." Her voice dropped to a whisper. "But I can't anymore."

Something was wrong about her account. "The bishop only hit his head once on the front of his head?"

"*Ya.*" She nodded.

My forehead wrinkled. There had been two wounds on the bishop's head. The sheriff had been very clear on the point. The first wound matched up to the one Phoebe described, but it had not been the one that killed him. The one that killed him had been the one on the back of his head. That meant someone finished the job after Phoebe left, and there had been only one other conscious person inside the bookmobile. Her brother.

The side door of the bookmobile opened. I looked back to the door, expecting to see Willow. Instead I saw Phoebe's brother, Phillip, standing in the aisle holding a gun.

Chapter Forty

M y first thought was Oliver. I didn't see him, and I
prayed that he had found someplace to hide.
"Phillip, what are you doing?" I jumped to my feet.

"Shut up," he said.

Phoebe struggled to her feet. "I told her the truth. I
told her that I killed the bishop." She lowered her
eyes. "I am sorry, *bruder*. I could not keep the secret
any longer."

"Don't say anymore," her brother snapped.

"Don't worry," Phoebe said. "I will take all the blame.
I will tell the police you had nothing to do with it."

Phillip gripped the gun in his hand. "Don't tell them
anything."

"That's because *he's* the one who killed the bishop,"
I said.

"*Nee*, I am." Phoebe shook her head. "I have just told
you."

"I know you believe that you murdered the bishop,
Phoebe." I kept my eyes on Phillip as I spoke. "But he
didn't die from hitting his head on the bookshelf. He
died from a second blow to the back of his head, one

your brother gave him after you left. Right, Phillip? What did you use, Phillip? A rock you found in the woods? What did you do with it after you killed the bishop?"

He leveled the gun at my head and walked toward me. "Phoebe, come here."

Shaking, his sister stepped around me.

He handed her a roll of duct tape. "Tape up her hands."

"*Bruder?*" Phoebe whispered.

His lip curled into a sneer. "Do it."

I backed away. "No way."

He moved the gun to his sister's head. "If you don't let her tie your hands, I start shooting, beginning with my own sister."

I held out my hands.

He shook his head. "Behind her back."

"I'm sorry," Phoebe said as she walked around me.

I glared at him. "Did you hate Bartholomew Beiler so much that you saw an opportunity to get rid of him and took it?"

"*Ya*, I hated him," he snapped. "Everyone in the district hated him. He was a terrible man. I refused to believe *Gott* chose him as our bishop, but he and I were fine until recently. He left me alone, and I returned the favor. Then he threatened to shun me."

Phoebe's hands shook as she wrapped the tape around my wrists. I held my wrists apart, hoping that would make the tape looser. "Why would he shun you?"

"He said that *Gott* told him it was wrong for me to work for the Millers because they were pagan New Order Amish. He said that I had to leave my job or he would shun me and the entire family." He shuddered.

Phoebe gasped.

"Now tape her to the bookcase," Phillip ordered Phoebe.

Phoebe placed a hand on my shoulder, moving me close to the bookcase and did as he asked.

"What are you going to do now?" I asked.

"Leave. I don't have any other choice, but I will get rid of you first." He looked around the bookmobile.

"Where's that dog that's always with you?" Phillip asked.

I shivered. "He's at home." I prayed Oliver had found the perfect hiding space.

He squinted at me. "You have a very nice home. I was impressed with the backyard when I was there."

I felt sick to my stomach. "You've been watching my house?"

He smiled. "I know your reputation in this county for meddling in Amish business. I had to make sure that you weren't meddling in mine. Imagine my disappointment when I discovered that you were."

Now I knew without a doubt that Phillip had been the Peeping Tom watching my house.

He pointed the gun at my chest again. "I hoped that you would give up, but you just kept turning up. When I saw you at the pie tasting, I knew it would come to this eventually. We would have been fine if you had just let it be. No one misses Bishop Beiler."

"What about his daughter Faith?" I asked. "And the rest of his family?"

He moved the gun slightly. "They are better off now

that he's gone. Like the rest of us, they can make up their own minds now without the bishop looking over their shoulders."

I swallowed. "You can't just drive away with me in the bookmobile. Willow is outside the bus. She won't let you do it."

He laughed. "She's too busy talking to tourists to notice what is going on, and she happens to be terrible at directing traffic. She didn't even notice when I climbed onto the bus." He turned, headed to the front of the bookmobile, and climbed into the driver's seat. Before I knew what was happening, the bookmobile started to move.

Through the walls of the bookmobile I could hear horns honking as we pulled away from the curb. I couldn't let Phillip take me somewhere to kill me. I knew that Phoebe wasn't safe either.

I gave Phoebe a pleading look. "Untie me," I hissed.

"I am sorry. I can't." She closed her eyes and shook her head like a toddler refusing to eat her carrots. "He is my *bruder*. I must do what he tells me to."

"Not when it's wrong," I whispered. "He's not a good man. He was willing to let you believe you killed someone so he could get away with the crime. If he loved you, he wouldn't have done that."

"He didn't have a choice. He would have been shunned." She opened her eyes wide. "It would have ruined him and the entire family."

"Killing someone is better than being shunned?" I wanted to smack her upside her head, and I just might have if my hands hadn't been taped to the bookshelf behind my back.

"Is everything all right, Phoebe? Is she tied up?" Phillip glared at us over his shoulder.

"Ya, bruder," she called to him. She stood on shaky legs.

The bookmobile shook, and paperbacks went flying from their shelves. A huge history book fell to the floor next to me. I toppled over onto my side. I flopped like a beached fish, but at least toppling over broke me free from being taped to the bookshelves. Phoebe sat back down beside me with her eyes squeezed shut.

"When did you learn to drive? *Rumspringa?*" I shouted at Phillip.

"Be quiet," Phillip ordered.

I had to reach Oliver so that we could escape before we left Sugartree Street. Just beyond the factory, there would be enough open land to run at Phillip to make him stop the bookmobile without crashing into any storefronts or pedestrians.

"Phoebe," I whispered. "You have to untie me."

I had use of my feet, but I would much rather face off with Phillip with all four of my limbs in working order.

She squeezed her eyes shut and tears leaked out. "I don't know what to do." She added something in Pennsylvania Dutch that I didn't understand.

I scooted closer to her. "Untie me."

"Nee," she whispered. "It will make him angry."

"Who cares!" I hissed. "He's already angry. Do you think everything will go back to normal for you after he kills me? You will be a witness. Phillip will go to prison when he's caught—and trust me, Sheriff Mitchell will catch him—and you will go too for being an accomplice."

"I'm not an accomplice," she whispered.

"You tied me up, so that makes you one."

She mumbled in her language again.

We were running out of time. When Phillip hit the open road, he would pick up speed, and it would be too late to escape. "Just untie me already," I said.

She took her gaze off the back of Phillip's head for a split second. Her eyes were the size of Ping-Pong balls.

"Phoebe, please. I'll tell him that I untied myself," I said.

She scooted over to me, staring forward the entire time on the lookout for any reaction from her brother. "The tape is too tight," she said. "It's hurting my fingers."

"Think how it feels for me. Now do it!" My voice was sharp, but the circumstances called for it.

The tape loosened. I could rotate my wrists. Soon I didn't feel the tape at all. My hands ached with the sudden rush of blood to my fingertips. My right wrist throbbed almost as badly as the knot on my forehead. "I'm going to make him stop the bookmobile. When he stops, you need to run out. Don't stop—just go. Find someone to call for help."

"What about you?" she whispered.

"I will get out too, but don't wait for me." I mentally added, *I hope.*

She nodded.

I struggled to my feet, clasping my hands behind me as if they were still tied together. It was no easy task with the bookmobile lurching back and forth.

"Sit back down," Phillip ordered.

I grabbed a hardback book, an encyclopedia of food,

off the shelf. It wasn't much of a weapon, but it was the biggest one in reach.

"Sit back down!" Phillip cried again.

I glared at him. "Make me."

Phillip's back stiffened.

I stumbled toward the front of the bookmobile.

"Sit down!" he ordered.

The bookmobile began to slow. He was going to stop it. This would be my one and maybe only chance to escape. As soon as the bookmobile came to a stop, I waved at Phoebe and pointed at the door. She took a second to collect herself, but then ran to the front, passing me as she went.

Suddenly, Phillip screamed as the bookmobile pitched to the side, rolling onto uneven ground. I fell forward, dropping the book as I tumbled to the floor. I grunted as my arm connected with hard metal. My right elbow would have a nice bruise from the tumble, but at least I had managed not to hit my head.

I was about to struggle to my feet when there was a horrible crunching sound. The vehicle shuddered. Books flew off the shelves, and I curled into a ball on my side, protecting my head with my arms. Paperbacks bounced off my back.

The bookmobile came to a stop. We'd crashed into something hard. Maybe a tree.

I uncurled my body, pushing away the books that had landed on me during the crash. I stumbled to my feet. Phoebe was on the floor just a foot from the door. She groaned but sat up.

Phillip's shouts pulled my attention away from his sister.

"Get it off of me. It's biting my ankle!" Phillip screamed.

There was thrashing at the front of the bookmobile, and I heard a dog yelp.

Oliver!

I scooped up the encyclopedia and charged, knocking Phillip on the back of the head with it.

Phillip grunted and his hand flew to the back of his head. I could see Oliver at Phillip's feet. He let go of Phillip's ankle and wriggled out from under the dashboard.

"Oliver," I said encouragingly. He slipped through the break between the two front seats, but it was tight and he got stuck.

Phillip moaned. "You hit me." He sounded almost offended by it. The man had his sister tie me up, kidnapped me with the intention of killing me, and he's offended that I hit him on the back of the head with a book. I resisted the urge to give him another whack with the hardback.

Behind me, Phoebe did as instructed and ran out of the bookmobile. Oliver wriggled in the tight spot between the seats, but couldn't seem to escape. He whimpered. I dropped the book and crouched by his head. I wrapped my hands around his broad chest and yanked. He didn't budge, but after two more strong yanks, Oliver flew out of the spot. I landed on my back with the Frenchie on my chest. There was no time to celebrate. We still had to get out of the bookmobile. I scrambled to my feet and was about to scoop up Oliver when I spotted Phillip's gun on the floor under the passenger seat. I snatched it from the floor and picked up Oliver.

Phillip unbuckled his seat belt and started to stand.

I took that as my cue to get out of there. I threw open the door and jumped out. I landed on the grass near a cluster of trees. It took me a second to realize that we were at the edge of the woods behind the pie factory. That gave me an idea. I slipped into the trees just as Phillip jumped out of the bookmobile. Blood ran down his face.

I fled into the woods, holding Oliver like a football under my arm and Phillip's gun in the other. I concentrated on keeping my fingers as far away from the trigger as possible. Shooting someone was not part of my plan.

I knew exactly where I was going. I didn't run too fast, because I wanted Phillip to be able to track me, and his footsteps were unsure since he was still recovering from the crash. From the blood on his face, I wondered whether he'd hit his head on the steering wheel.

Running through the trees, I went directly to the place where Nahum had set his rabbit snares. I could see the glisten of wire. It was something I wouldn't have noticed if I didn't know it was there.

I stopped and stood on the other side of the snare. Phillip ran at me with murder in his eyes. I jumped back, and his foot landed right where I needed it to. The snare sprung, and Phillip fell to the forest floor, screaming.

I hobbled to a stump a few yards away. Oliver lay on my lap.

"I'll kill you," Phillip yelled at me.

I frowned at him. Between the dog bite, head injury, and now Nahum's snare, I was betting Phillip was hurting pretty bad. Sadly, I didn't have much sympathy for him since he had attacked me.

I set Phillip's gun in the grass, happy to be rid of it, and pulled my cell phone out of my pocket to call the sheriff.

"Where are you?" Mitchell demanded. His voice was strained.

"I have a reason for you to release Austina," I told him over the phone. "Can you meet me in the woods behind the pie factory?"

Before the call ended, I could already hear the sirens over Phillip's curses. Phoebe stepped out of the trees and stared at her brother.

I jumped to my feet, still holding Oliver. "Phoebe, are you all right?"

"This all happened because I read books?" she asked me with tears in her eyes.

Before I could answer, Mitchell, Anderson, and what looked like the rest of the sheriff's department arrived. Mitchell took one look at me and gave a huge sigh of relief. He was relieved now. He'd be angry and frustrated later, but since he loved me, I knew he'd get over it.

And that brought a smile to my face.

Epilogue

Two weeks later, I watched as Phoebe Truber waved to her last student as he walked home from Hock Trail School. The wipers on Mitchell's department SUV worked overtime, wicking away water as a cold fall rain steadily came down.

After the boy was out of sight, I said, "I should go in before she heads home too."

Mitchell reached across the console and squeezed my hand. "Are you sure you don't want me to come in with you?"

I smiled. "Thanks for the offer, but I think Phoebe has had enough dealings with the police to last her a lifetime. I know she must have seen your car out here and it probably made her nervous."

He squeezed my hand one more time and let it go.

I leaned over and kissed his cheek. "I am glad that you came with me, though."

He grinned. "Me too. I'll wait right here for you."

Oliver and I exited my car. I reached into the back-seat and grabbed the crate I needed to deliver. I waved to Mitchell, and my Frenchie and I dashed through the rain for the school's front door. I pushed open the door with my foot.

Phoebe was erasing the chalkboard and didn't turn around when I came inside. Her hand shook as she held the eraser, making a wavy pattern on the board. "What are the police doing here? Is it about Phillip?"

I wiped rainwater from my eyes. "The sheriff drove me to see you, but he's not here on official business, no. I came to see if you were all right. I hadn't heard from you."

Oliver shook water off his fur.

She continued to erase and didn't turn around. "I am fine. Thank you for stopping by."

"I brought you something too," I said, setting the crate of books on one of the children's desks in the front row. "I thought it might help keep your mind off things."

She set her eraser in the chalkboard well but still did not turn around. "I'm not sure what can help me now. My brother is in prison for murdering my district's bishop. I'm living alone on my family's farm, not sure how to take care of it. Everyone in the community avoids me."

My heart broke for her. "The community just needs time, and you have friends. Levi and Faith are speaking to you, aren't they?"

She nodded. "I'm glad they are getting married after all. They are happy together."

"And you're still the only teacher in your district. That's a good sign. It means the district still trusts you, no matter what your brother may have done."

She turned and saw, behind me, the paperback novels she'd tried to burn in the stove the day after her brother had killed the bishop.

"You kept them," she whispered.

"They're yours," I said. "I thought they would be a good distraction from your troubles."

She picked up a novel at the top of the pile and flipped lovingly through its pages. "I'm not sure I should have them after what happened. This all started because of books."

"No, Phoebe, it started because of the fear of the ideas in the books." I paused. "Maybe it's time that you decide for yourself if you believe those ideas."

"Maybe," she whispered. She held one of the novels to her chest. "*Danki*. I think I need to decide what I believe about a lot of things."

I smiled. "If you ever need to talk, look me up. I know I'm not Amish, but I am a good listener. No judgment, I promise."

"*Danki*," she repeated.

"I had better let you close up the schoolhouse for the day," I said.

She nodded, and Oliver and I quietly left the schoolhouse. I took one last look at her as I shut the door and saw she had sunk into one of the desks, already reading one of the paperbacks.

During the short time that Oliver and I had been inside the schoolhouse, the rain had ceased. It was still damp and cold, though. Mitchell stood outside his car talking on his cell phone. When he saw me, he ended the call. Oliver trotted toward him, and the sheriff bent over and patted Oliver's head.

I nodded to the phone in his hand. "You get a call-out?"

He shook his head. "That was Anderson. He was just giving me an update on Phillip Truber. Phillip has another court date next week, and I have to be there to represent the police." His hand tightened around his phone. "He's facing charges for murder, attempted murder, kidnapping, and lying to police." His jaw tightened when he mentioned the charges concerning me.

I placed my hand on the sheriff's arm. "Stand down, Officer. I'm fine."

He took a deep breath. "But you might not have been. I still don't know why you didn't call me right away instead of leading Phillip on a chase through the woods. Anything could have happened. He had a gun . . ."

"He didn't by the time we were in the woods. I had it."

He gave me a look as if that was just a small technicality. "It was a risk. There was a one-in-a-million-chance he would step into the snare like he did."

"But he did," I said.

Mitchell sighed in defeat. "Zander asked me this morning if it was true you chased a man through the woods into a bear trap. That's the story he heard at school."

My mouth twitched. "What did you tell him?"

"That you got yourself into a difficult predicament, but, by luck, got out of it."

I frowned.

Mitchell studied me. "What's wrong? Why no wise-cracking remark?"

I sighed. "Thinking of Nahum's snare makes me think of Nahum, the man who is Rachel's father. I wish that Rachel would talk to her father—really talk to him—even if she only speaks to him one time. I think she needs some closure over her childhood."

"What does Rachel want?" he asked.

"She asked me to leave it alone for now." My shoulders drooped.

He grinned. "And that's killing you because you are a fixer. You like to fix things even if it's not your job."

"Well, yeah," I said. True enough.

"Give Rachel time. I think she will eventually be able to deal with her father, and when she is, she will come to you for help."

I met his gaze. "You think so?"

He nodded. "I've accepted the fact that the Amish come to you with their problems, and there is nothing I can do to stop you from helping them." He wrapped me in a hug. "I just hope in the future those problems don't involve murder and kidnapping."

"They don't always," I said, looking up at him.

He snorted.

I grinned back, and the rain picked up again. Oliver whimpered at our feet. He was ready to head back to Running Stitch, to see how Dodger was terrorizing Mattie, and to curl up in his dog bed for a late-afternoon snooze. Returning to the quilt shop sounded like a good idea to me too. "Okay, Ollie," I said. "Let's go home."

Mitchell grinned. "Good idea, and on the ride home you can explain something to me."

"What's that?" I asked suspiciously.

"Why your mother called me this morning and asked if I thought yellow was a good color for a baby's room." His aquamarine eyes twinkled.

I gulped. "Oh, you know my mom. She's always redecorating."

As the three of us walked back to Mitchell's car, I frowned—though it wasn't over my mother's uncanny ability to embarrass me. My thoughts were still on my best friend. I hoped the sheriff was right, and that Rachel would ask me for help when she needed it.

Amish Quilted Pumpkin

by Angela Braddock, Owner of Running Stitch

When I think about fall, I think about pumpkins and autumn crafts. Running Stitch has you covered on both counts. Stop by our quilt shop in beautiful Rolling Brook, and we can get your started on the your next project. If you are like me and are thinking pumpkins, we have the perfect quilted-pumpkin project just for you. You can make one for all your friends. They make wonderful autumn decorations and gifts.

Supplies

fabric
scissors
thread
needle
dowel rod cut into two-inch pieces
polyester stuffing

wide green ribbon
thin green ribbon
glue gun

Step One

Choose a quilting pattern and create one twelve-by-twelve-inch quilting square. You can always adjust the size to make the pumpkin you are creating larger or smaller.

Step Two

Take polyester stuffing and form a ball to place inside of the completed quilt block. Wrap the block around the ball and stitch closed.

Step Three

Now you should have a pumpkin. Pull thread from the top of the pumpkin to the bottom, tight to create a rib in the side of the pumpkin. Repeat four more times.

Step Four

Glue the dowel rod onto the top of the pumpkin to become the stem.

Step Five

Cut leaves out of the wide green ribbon and sew to the top of the pumpkin. Using your scissors, curl several pieces of thin green ribbon to make vines. Sew the end of the vines to the top of the pumpkin. You're done!

Read on sneak peek of

CRIME AND POETRY

a Magical Bookshop Mystery
written by Isabella Alan
writing as Amanda Flower.
Coming from Obsidian in April 2016.

"Grandma! Grandma Daisy!" I called as soon as I was inside Charming Books. There were books everywhere—on the crowded shelves, the end tables, the sales counter, and the floor. Everywhere. But there was no sign of my ailing grandmother.

Browsing customers in brightly colored T-shirts and shorts stared at me openmouthed. I knew I must have looked a fright. I had driven from Chicago to Cascade Springs, New York, the small town nestled on the banks of the Niagara River just minutes from world-famous Niagara Falls. I made the drive in seven hours, stopping only twice for gas and potty breaks. My fingernails were bitten to the quick, dark circles hovered beneath my bloodshot blue eyes, and my wavy strawberry blond hair was in a knot on top of my head. Last time I had caught sight of it in the rearview mirror, it had resembled a pom-pom that had been caught in a dryer's lint trap. I stopped looking in the rearview mirror after that.

A crow gripping a perch in the shop's large bay window cawed.

I jumped, and my hands flew to my chest. I had thought the crow was stuffed.

The bird glared at me with his beady black eyes. He certainly wasn't stuffed. "Grandma Daisy!" he mimicked me. "Grandma!"

I sidestepped away from the black bird. I thought parrots were the only birds that could talk. The crow was the only one who spoke. None of the customers made a peep. A few slipped out the front door behind me. "Escape from the crazy lady" was written all over their faces. I couldn't say I blamed them.

A slim woman stepped out from between packed bookshelves. She wore jeans, a hot pink T-shirt with the bookshop's logo on it, and, despite the summer's heat, a long silken scarf. Silk scarves were Grandma Daisy's signature. I could count on one hand the number of times I had seen her without one intricately tied around her neck. Today's scarf was white with silver dollar–sized ladybugs marching across it. Her straight silver hair was cut in a sleek bob that fell to her chin. Cat's-eye-shaped glasses perched on her nose. She was a woman in her seventies, but clearly someone who took care of herself. Clearly someone who was not dying.

My mouth fell open, and I knew I must look a lot like those tourists I'd frightened. "Grandma!" The word came out of my mouth somewhere between a curse and a prayer.

"Violet, my girl." She haphazardly dropped the pile of books she had in her arms onto one of the two matching couches in the middle of the room at the base of the birch tree, which seemed to grow out of the floor. "You came!"

I stepped back. "Of course I came. You were *dying*."

More customers skirted for the door. They knew what was good for them. I wouldn't have hung around either. The only one who seemed to be enjoying the show was the crow. He was no longer in the front window, but on the end table to my right. Great. A crow was loose in my grandmother's bookshop. I wished I could say this surprised me, but it didn't.

Grandma Daisy chuckled. "Oh, that."

"'Oh, that'? That's all you can say?" I screeched. "Do you have any idea what you've put me through? I left school. I left my job. I left *everything* to be with you at your deathbed."

Grandma had the decency to wince.

"Look at you. You look like you are ready to run a marathon. When I spoke to you on the phone last night, you were coughing and gasping. You sounded like you were at death's door."

Grandma Daisy faked a cough. "Like this?" Her face morphed into pathetic. "Oh, Violet, I need you. Please come." Fake cough. Fake cough. "The doctor said I don't have much more time."

Heat surged up from the base of my neck to the top of my head. I couldn't remember the last time I had been this angry. Oh, yeah, I did: It was the first time I left Cascade Springs twelve years ago. I had promised myself I would never come back that day, and look where I was: back in Cascade Springs tricked by my very own grandmother.

"You were dying," the crow said.

"Quiet, Faulkner," Grandma Daisy ordered.

The large black bird sidestepped across the tabletop.

It seemed that the crow was a new addition to the shop. It'd been twelve years, but I would have remembered Faulkner. I wondered why Grandma Daisy had never mentioned the bird. I would have thought a talking pet crow would have made a great conversation piece.

Grandma Daisy searched my face. "I may have fibbed a bit. Can you forgive me?" she asked, giving me her elfish smile. It wasn't going to work, not this time.

I spun around, ignored Faulkner, who was spouting "You were dying!" over and over again, and stomped out of the shop.

Behind me the screen door smacked against the doorframe. I stumbled across the front porch and gripped the whitewashed wooden railing. Charming Books, "where the perfect book picks you," sat in the center of River Road in the middle of Old Town Cascade Springs, a historic part of the village that was on the National Historic Landmarks list. Every house and small business on the street was more adorable than the last, but none was as stunning as Charming Books, a periwinkle Queen Anne Victorian with gingerbread to spare and a wraparound porch that was twice the size of my studio apartment back in Chicago.

The tiny front yard was full to bursting with blooming roses and, of course, daisies—Grandma's personal favorite. On the brick road in front of me, gas lampposts lined the street on either side, and prancing horses and white carriages waited on the curbs, ready to take tourists for a spin around the village and along the famous riverwalk at a moment's notice. The horses' manes were elaborately braided with satiny ribbons, and their drivers wore red coats with tails and top hats.

It was charming. It was perfect. It was the last place on planet Earth I wanted to be.

I had half a mind to jump in my car and head west for Chicago, never looking back. I couldn't do that. My shoulders slumped. I was so incredibly tired. Coffee wouldn't be any help. Coffee had lost its ability to keep me alert my third year of grad school. And as much as she vexed me, I couldn't leave Grandma Daisy, without saying good-bye. For better or worse, she was all the family I had left in the world. And then, there was the whole pom pom-hair situation, which could only be tolerated for so long. I'd need a hairbrush and maybe a blowtorch to get that under control.

The screen door to the Queen Anne creaked open. I didn't have to turn around to know it was my grandmother. The scent of lavender talcum powder that always surrounded her floated on the breeze. "Violet, I know it wasn't right for me to lie to you."

I folded my arms, refusing to look at her. I knew it was childish, but I was going on two hours of sleep and tons of betrayal. Being a grown-up wasn't on the top of my priority list.

She placed her hand on my shoulder. "It was wrong of me. Very wrong, but it was the only way I could convince you to come back here."

She was probably right in that assumption, but I wasn't going to make it easy for her. "So you pretended to be dying?"

She let out a breath. "What I said about needing you to come back was true. I do need you here. I want you to stay."

She had to be kidding. She knew what had happened to me in this town. She knew why I had left the day after I graduated high school. She knew better than anyone. "Well, that's too bad," I said. "I'm not staying."

"Can't you stay a little while? For me?"

I felt a pang in my heart. I didn't want to leave Grandma Daisy, and despite the whole lying thing, it was wonderful to see her, but I couldn't stay. It was too hard. "I'll wait until tomorrow, but I'll leave in the morning."

Of course that last statement came to be known as "famous last words."